Trust No One

ANTHONY MOSAWI

PENGUIN BOOKS

PENGUIN BOOKS

UK | USA | Canada | Ireland | Australia
India | New Zealand | South Africa

Penguin Books is part of the Penguin Random House group of companies
whose addresses can be found at global.penguinrandomhouse.com.

First published 2018
001

Copyright © Anthony Mosawi, 2018

The moral right of the author has been asserted

Set in 12.5/14.75 pt Garamond MT Std
Typeset by Jouve (UK), Milton Keynes

Printed and bound in Great Britain by Clays Ltd, Elcograf S.p.A.

A CIP catalogue record for this book is available from the British Library

PAPERBACK ISBN: 978–0–718–18638–8
OM PAPERBACK ISBN: 978–0–718–18641–8

www.greenpenguin.co.uk

For my family

Prologue

One week ago

Despite his best efforts, fear consumed Myers as he eased the black Mercedes into the alleyway behind the large redbrick building. Dry-mouthed, heart-palpitating, sphincter-tightening fear.

It had been nine minutes since his last visual of the target. Entering through the front door.

Nine minutes. It was too long. The order should have been given by now. What were they waiting for?

Four other units had pulled into place two minutes after Myers' arrival, sliding along the sides of the pavement slowly, like sharks circulating near a coastal shelf. Sniper teams were on adjoining roofs in four minutes. High above them, two surveillance helicopters equipped with thermal-imaging devices hovered above the cloud layer, unseen and unheard.

Orpheus.

Even thinking the name caused Myers' arms to gooseflesh.

Orpheus: the great white whale of UK military intelligence. The most wanted name on their list.

He was still in school the last time F Squad thought they had cornered Orpheus. Back then, a team had followed the fugitive to a different building, hundreds of miles away. A different agent had sat in a car just like this one, planning an assault just like this. Life comes full circle.

They were woefully unprepared that day. Twelve men were not enough. One died, his body torn to shreds in a frenzied attack. The leader, Bonner, escaped with only a scar across his throat that still throbs on rainy days.

Now it was Daniel Spokes leading, sitting in one of the helicopters high above, and Myers in charge of the ground operation.

Twenty years later: they would not make the same mistakes.

Every precaution had been taken. Nothing had been assumed. Could Orpheus have penetrated GCHQ or MI5? Chinese walls separated the attack plans, giving each unit only their own in-the-trenches orders. Water supplies had been shut off, and armed amphibian teams crouched in each underground access tunnel. Could Orpheus have accomplices that could come to his aid? That was easy. No. Orpheus always worked alone.

This was the largest coordinated operation in UK military intelligence history. By the end of today, Orpheus would be their captive. Or dead.

The road ended here, in a building that housed what Orpheus had been seeking for a lifetime.

Orpheus walked up the stairs to the main records room, fingertips trailing along the banister.

The entire building seemed to throb through the

polished wood, from the basement to the rafters, like an organic entity constructed of brick and glass rather than bone and living tissue. Orpheus could feel the totality of it, from the flickering blue cyclopoid eye of the pilot light peering out from the basement boiler to the buzzing of the pillarbox-red Coke machine on the second floor, to the smell of mouldy stacks of paper in the upper-floor offices and the silent tread of mice feet in the attic.

Fingertips left the polished wood, breaking the connection, and pushed on the crenellated glass doors, which swung open noisily.

The space was empty. No worker at the enquiry desk. No stacker to push the squeaky trolley around. No vagrant at the corner table, napping on newspapers.

Empty.

As if Orpheus had slept through the apocalypse.

Although Orpheus was anything but alone.

The scopes of the snipers felt like voyeurs' eyes scanning the interior through high windows. Orpheus sensed men in thick rubber suits staring up at the underside of drain covers under the two bathrooms, waiting for their quarry to drop through. High above, the public records office appeared as a magnified cross-section on helicopters' thermal tracking devices, its walls and roof transparent through X-ray, a single red heat trace throbbing like a character in a videogame.

Orpheus ignored them, keeping focus on the prize. It was in this building. The search was almost over.

Orpheus walked up to the card cataloguing cabinet

that ran along the side wall and followed the alphabetized system – *Aa, Ab, Ac* – until finding the reference and pulling out the index card drawer, which overextended, like a long wooden tongue.

The secure line buzzed on Myers' phone, sending it skittering across the dashboard.

He swiped it up immediately and answered the call.

It was Spokes: the operation was a go.

Myers took a swig from his bottle of water; his mouth was desert-dry and he couldn't risk signalling fear to the others. He then dialled the secure broadcast line to the assembled teams.

'All units proceed. Orpheus is to be taken alive if possible.'

The antique typewriter font on the index card guided Orpheus to the towering stacks of paper files in the recessed rear of the room.

Stack C.

Row 4.

Motion sensor lights *plinged* on above.

Shelf 3.

There.

A stack of papers lay in a hammock created by the hanging file, damp from decades of sitting in the dark, kept company by a handful of woodlice that scrambled across the wedge as it was lifted out.

The certificate was in the middle of the sheaf, recognizable from the stamp of the hospital.

Orpheus hesitated, hands suspended, savouring the moment, then peeled back one side and read the block of double-spaced typewriting and the handwritten ink signature beneath.

A deep breath, and then a sigh of dismay.

It was not the end of the journey.

But finally, there was a name.

A chill suddenly ran down Orpheus' spine, and palms pressed to the table.

They were moving outside, assembling, preparing their assault. Car doors swinging open, boots stepping out, snipers' fingers hooking around triggers.

Orpheus wasn't concerned, the escape route would be revealed.

Deep breath. Discern their strategy.

First, containment. Exits were being sealed off with foot soldier and sniper teams. Aerial support formed a second line of cover. Next, they would storm the building. Aiming to corner and then capture. But where would they enter first?

And then a spider-sense fired deep in Orpheus' head, the high alert of imminent death. Their whole strategy had been a ploy to distract, to draw attention away from the true attack. An elaborate trap. Capture was never their intention.

Orpheus looked up at the high-vaulted ceiling. In the split second before it exploded, Orpheus noticed for the first time the mural that had been staring benignly down. A loving artist's tribute to the most famous fresco in history. Adam anchored to the earth, reaching for his divine creator. Two worlds separated from each other, fingertip-close and yet forever apart.

And then everything was consumed in the detonation and flashfire.

Having fired its payload of four Hellfire missiles, the Predator drone banked, tracing a wide parabola back towards its secret base in Scotland.

At an altitude of ten miles, the detonation flashed white across its black-and-white video monitors, taking out the entire building with what would later be described to the press as a controlled explosion conducted during a terror operation by police.

When the fire subsided, Myers approached the smoking ruin of the building. A crater had been carved out, an angry black hole in the ground, the contents of the registry office melted and compacted into it.

Orpheus was gone.

PART ONE

1993

I

'I hope you've got a stronger stomach.'

The police sergeant's voice was brittle as he stood in the teeming rain at the entrance of the house. His hulking form almost blocked out the doorframe.

The fact that he had come personally was an indication to Claire that the crime was a serious one. As the only social services officer working on the local police force, she attended each incident, and this was only the second time she had ever seen him.

Claire stared at the house for a moment, trying to dampen the fear in her gut. This happened each time: each drab façade hid chambers of cruelty and neglect. She never knew what horrors lay in wait for her.

The rain lashed at her, falling in liquid columns from the eaves of the house. She knew the sergeant was trying to get under her skin. He was referring to the first time they had met, when four young kids had been found in a crack house. Two were still alive among the debris of the spare room, while their junkie parents lay in a torpor next door. When she'd seen the infants' state, she'd rushed outside and vomited in the garden.

Claire acknowledged him with a grim nod. He barely moved to make way for her. It took a moment for her eyes to adjust when she stepped inside. She was used to slovenly accommodations – they went hand in hand with neglect – and this was no different. The carpet was covered with ramshackle stacks of old newspapers and dirty crockery.

Sitting on the only piece of furniture in the room was a haggard woman, her greasy hair falling limply around the sides of her face. The ravages of drugs made it difficult to gauge her age. She could be late twenties or early fifties. She looked up at Claire with dead eyes that followed her as Claire stepped carefully through the room.

Claire reminded herself that she had a job to do. A Polaroid photograph lay on the couch. Claire picked it up, keeping her eyes on the woman to see if she would react. She didn't.

The picture looked like it had been taken without the subject's knowledge. He was well dressed – suit and tie – in his mid-twenties; the bottom part of his body obscured by the fence he was next to. It took Claire a few seconds to recognize the surroundings: it was the front of the house in which she was standing.

She turned over the photograph, and found writing scrawled across the back.

DO NOT TRUST THIS MAN.

Claire was pondering this so intently that she didn't hear the sergeant approach her from behind.

'Up there.'

His voice was loud enough to make her flinch. She turned to see him thrusting his chin towards the stairs.

There were two more officers upstairs. Claire could

see that the situation was bad. They appeared shell-shocked, their features drained of the usual professional courtesy. A lanky officer standing nearest to her pointed to the door next to him.

Claire took the pair of white latex gloves that he extended to her, pulled them on with a practised snap and walked on to the cracked tiles of the bathroom.

'We found the girl in there. They used the bath. Trapped her inside it.'

'Where's the child?'

'Dried her off. She's next door.'

Claire began taking photos with her camera phone. The horror was palpable in the room, rolling off the dingy walls.

'That's the mother downstairs?'

The officer shook his head.

'No. Some junkie.'

She moved closer to the white enamel tub. It was three inches full of filthy water and a layer of scum that floated in swirling continents on the surface. Lying on the edge of the bath were four scraps of torn paper. One word was written on each scrap, but Claire couldn't combine them in any way that made any sense for the situation. Next to the scraps was a necklace. Claire already knew the locket and chain were cheap. If they had been worth anything, the junkie downstairs would have pocketed it.

'That covered it when we arrived.'

He pointed to a long slab of corkboard that lay at an angle on top of the bath, like a displaced coffin lid.

She shuddered for a second as she imagined the young girl shivering in the darkness, buried alive.

'Kid had these. Could have electrocuted herself. Suppose the minder thought she was doing her a favour.'

He held up a Sony cassette Walkman and a pair of bedraggled headphones.

When she entered the bedroom, the girl's face was averted, her little form hunched over the side of the bed, head buried in her hands.

Claire inched forward.

'I'm from the social services. We're here to help you.'

The little girl did not move. Claire moved closer, lowering herself to perch on the end of the filthy bed. She could now see the girl's mouth through the webbed space between her knitted fingers. It moved constantly, mouthing silent words.

She reached out and put a tentative hand on the girl's back, letting it rest there, allowing her to feel the connection.

'It's not what you think.'

Claire and the officer turned around to find the dead-eyed woman standing in the door. Her voice was smoky and harsh, slicing through the silence in the room.

'Get her out of here.'

The officer grabbed the woman by the arm and twisted it behind her back.

'Out! Now!'

'No, listen! This was a job. The mother. She paid me!'

He herded her down the stairs as the burly sergeant walked in the bedroom door.

'Just spoke to the foster home,' he said, breathing deeply from his climb up the stairs. 'They've got an arrival date for her in a week's time.'

'Who checked her in?'

'Someone calling herself the mother, but later the ID turned out to be stolen. Find out what the girl is saying?'

She shook her head.

He took a long look around him, at the room, the corridor and the bathroom.

'Just when you think you've seen the worst . . .' he said, before heading down the stairs again.

Claire placed the Polaroid of the man she'd found downstairs into a clear plastic bag. She lowered the necklace in as well. As she held it by the chain, she took a longer look at the locket. It had a small circular design, bright turquoise-blue with a dark-blue dot inside it.

When Claire walked down the stairs, the sergeant and two policemen were standing in the middle of the room, handcuffing the junkie's hands behind her back.

'Janey Small, I am arresting you for child abduction, assault . . .'

'It wasn't abduction.'

The sergeant stopped and looked at Claire.

'What?'

'The woman was right,' continued Claire. 'The girl wasn't snatched. This was a job, for the mother.'

'What are you talking about?'

'The colour in the water upstairs, that's not dirt, it's dye,' she said.

'Stick to the social work.'

'And it wasn't being used as a bathtub; it's a sensory deprivation chamber. They used them in the Cold War to brainwash people.'

The sergeant's face darkened, and he took a step closer to Claire.

'Get out. Now.'

Claire saw him notice what she was carrying in her left hand – the bedraggled Walkman. He reached out and swiped it from her.

'That's evidence.'

'Listen to it.'

'Why?'

She looked at him directly in the eye.

'Listen to what is playing.'

The sergeant paused but could not lose face in front of her. He pulled one damp headphone to his ear.

A woman's voice was speaking, warm and kind, intoning the same sentences in an endless loop. Claire spoke to him slowly, as if English was not his first language.

'Someone paid that junkie. The girl's hair has been dyed. New identity made. An alternative history brainwashed into her . . .'

The sergeant stared at her, a look of hesitation on his face for the first time.

'Why?'

'I would have thought that's obvious. The mother

14

didn't just want to get rid of her own daughter. She wanted to make sure her daughter never found out who she really was.'

'And what about the photo?' asked the sergeant.

Claire pursed her lips. She had been mulling over how the man in the Polaroid fitted into this enigma.

'Best guess . . . maybe the father of the girl . . . and the reason why the mother is running away . . .'

She was also thinking of the words on the four scraps of paper, still lying upstairs on the bathtub: PHOEBE. A. WIFE. RESTS.

It sounded like the obituary on a failed marriage, written by a disintegrating mind. Claire would have continued her train of thought, but the sergeant held up a hand for her to stop and looked over her shoulder.

Claire turned to see the little girl coming down the stairs, her eyes downcast. Her mouth never stopped moving as she breathed out indistinct words. As she walked past them, the social services officer knelt down and held her in her arms.

Claire could feel the girl's warm breath near her ear as her voice became clear.

'My name is Sara Eden . . . I was born in Scotland in 1983 . . . My mother died at birth . . . My father was a tourist . . .'

2

Weeks later

Sara stands at the very edge of the gardens. Her lip is split and her knees torn to shreds. Blood slides down her shinbone. Her back presses up against the chain-link fence that separates the home from the road as hot tears run down her cheeks. The shame of the attack separates her mentally as well as physically from the other children. She can see them now. After delivering their beating, the group has moved to play on the lawn directly in front of the large bay windows of the main office.

She can see the prize for which they are competing. A silhouette, mostly claimed by the shadows in the room, sits in front of the matron's desk. A would-be parent. The matron turns to the window and points to certain children with her finger, her mouth moving soundlessly. The children, for their part, cavort on the grass in a transparent attempt to show themselves to their best advantage.

Sara is not the shortest of the kids. Nor the weakest physically. But she is unlike them in many ways, and in this home of rejected children, any difference is a reason for the others to unite against a common prey.

16

The matron points to Sara, gives a minute shake of her head, and her mouth never stops moving.

Sara knows what she is saying, even from here, through double-glazed windows and across over a hundred feet of worn garden. The matron is recounting the erratic behaviour, about how Sara sometimes screams out loud, at the top of her voice, when she is alone. The matron will then go on to describe the amnesia that blocks out any memories from before a month ago. She will talk about the abandonment and the fruitless efforts to find her parents. Soon she will hand him a paper that describes the blood tests on Sara that failed to find matching samples at any blood banks or hospitals in the country, and how untraceable parents means there is no way to identify any genetic health issues that might have been handed down. And without a full medical history, she is especially vulnerable. She is, in short, damaged goods: the runt of the litter. Picked on by others.

Sara has sat on the top step of the central stairway and heard the matron deliver this speech in her study multiple times. It is Sara's history and the only one she knows. The parents always disengage at this point.

But not this time.

This time the silhouette stands and approaches the window, materializing into the form of a man who stares at Sara in an unabashed way. He shows the matron a sheet of paper and then returns his gaze, looking over the heads of the prancing children to the forlorn figure at the edge of the property.

The shrieks coming from outside increase in volume when the matron appears at the door to the garden. She leads the man towards the children as the tiny forms beam up at the adults. One by one their smiles falter and disappear as the adults march past them, heading for the large oak tree at the back. By the time they are halfway to Sara, the other kids have fallen completely quiet and stand as still as statues, watching the procession move away.

The matron stands in front of Sara, exuding a waft of antiseptic in her direction.

'Sara,' says the matron, 'this is Mr Dobbs. Do you remember him?'

'Hi Sara, it's me, Lionel,' he says with a smile.

Sara can see him clearly now for the first time. He is taller than the matron by a few inches but has a burly physique, which gives him the impression of seeming much larger. He has round, cherubic cheeks and soft, brown eyes. He crouches down next to Sara so his face is at her level.

It has been a long time since she's seen a face that friendly, and for the first time, a memory stirs for her. That face. It is not the first time she has seen that face. She racks her brain, but her memory dead-ends on her arrival at the home. Before then, there is simply a mist of nothingness.

'I think so,' she replies to the matron.

'Don't worry, your memory will come back. I promise you,' says Lionel.

The matron clears her throat. She has folded her arms and is looking with concern at Sara.

'Sara, Mr Dobbs has papers for you, but the final decision to release you to him is mine. I would like some proof you know him.'

She looks at Sara expectantly.

Sara stares at Lionel, waiting for some other piece to fall into place. But nothing comes. She takes a step towards him, hoping some miracle will supply the proof that will allow him to take her away.

'Let's see,' says Lionel, 'maybe I can help. Sara loves reading adventure books, her favourite colour is green, and she's a whizz at hide-and-seek.'

At one level, it is like Lionel is describing someone else, a stranger, and yet on another level, the mention of these things seems to resonate with her. An image pops into her mind – her fingers pulling back a tree branch as she runs deeper into a wood, weaving among the trees as she looks behind her. Is it a memory or a scene from a television show she has watched at the home? She is not sure, but her heart begins to beat faster.

'I want to go with Lionel, Matron,' says Sara.

The matron seems nonplussed.

'I need something I can verify.'

Lionel stands up from his crouch and nods in agreement.

'Fair enough. How about if I told you Sara has a birthmark on her upper right arm in the shape of an infinity sign?'

The matron considers them both for a second before nodding.

'Good,' he says, as if the matter is settled. 'Let's take you home, Sara.'

Sara follows them as they walk back to the home. She does her best to ignore the incomprehensible whispers that murmur at the edges of her consciousness. The sounds are muffled, like they are coming from the other side of a locked door. She never understands anything that is said, but, at times, the voices have such violence and urgency that they terrify her, and screaming out loud is the only way to drown them out.

The matron sends her upstairs to pack. She has the clothes she has been given by the home, a few books, her toothbrush and nothing more. After all is packed, she looks around to check she is alone, then reaches under her mattress to pull out the plastic bag that contains the two things she has from before the time when things went blank.

She first pulls out the locket and lays it with care on the bed. Then she removes the worn Polaroid picture.

She stares at the man in the photo: the man she should not trust. After poring over it, she knows. It is not Lionel. She is sure of it. But she knew this already. She can trust Lionel. The words of her imaginary companion can't be heard, but she knows what it is saying. It wants her to go with Lionel Dobbs.

He is waiting for her in front of the home, standing by a black Mercedes car. The rear passenger side door is open, and Sara sees a young woman sitting in the back seat. She is pretty, with short dark hair.

Once they are on the road, Sara looks over and asks

the question she has been mulling over since she first saw the woman.

'Are you my mother?'

The woman does not reply, and Lionel twists in his seat.

'No, this is Penny. She's going to help you, Sara. Help you get your memory back.'

'Do you know my mother?' Sara asks Lionel.

'Probably better than anyone else in the world,' he replies. He turns back to look at the road and presses a button on the compact disc player. The car fills with classical music.

Sara looks out of the window and takes a deep breath.

Her first questions have gone unanswered, and she desperately needs someone to tell her what is happening. She turns back to the two adults in the car and tries again, with the question that dominates the waking hours of each of her days.

'Have I always had these voices in my head?'

The music must be too loud, as neither of them respond.

The house is set back from the main road and other houses and is surrounded by woods. It feels like a remote destination, and Sara's eyes take in the exterior of the house, hoping for some memory to surface. But it is alien to her. All of the curtains are closed, and she can't see inside.

The car crunches into the gravel drive, and Lionel

parks it in front of the garage. Penny gets out and motions for Sara to follow her. As they walk to the front door, Sara reaches up and takes her hand. It's an instinctive act, and she's pleased when Penny doesn't pull away. To Sara's surprise, Penny's hand feels cold, rubbery and smooth, like the dolls in the play room of the home she has come from. Sara doesn't mind, she squeezes tightly and doesn't want to ever let go. Some-one has found her, someone who knew her from before, and soon she will be reunited with her parents.

It is dusk, and a dog bounces in from the street and sits in the driveway, watching them, its tail wagging fre-netically. He looks so friendly Sara wants to pet him and stops, but Penny tugs her towards the house.

As they enter, Sara looks around, craning for a view of each room. But it is not what she expects. No memor-ies come back. Indeed, the house does not feel like a home at all. There is no furniture in any of the rooms, and what she thought were curtains are in fact wooden boards that cover the windows. A hallway mirror is the only evidence of habitation she can see.

They take her to the kitchen, which has been stripped down so only the sink remains. A single chair sits in the middle of the floor, and she is placed on to it. Lionel stands in front of her. She sees that his hands have a dull sheen and as she stares at them, she realizes they are covered with some form of thin membrane that is catching the light. She looks back at Penny, who is crouching down in the corner of the room, where a host of metal parts lie on the floor. Penny's hands have the same reflective cast, and it is then that Sara realizes they have both been wearing tight, see-through plastic gloves the whole time.

'Sara,' says Lionel, his voice soft, 'we're going to help you remember. I know this looks scary, but believe me this is the best way to do it.'

The dog begins barking outside. Lionel looks around, distracted for the first time, waiting for the yapping to end. But it is persistent. Penny shakes her head.

'I'm going to need total quiet.'

Lionel leaves the kitchen. He takes care to close the door, but the catch is loose, and it swings back a couple of inches. Sara can see him, in the reflection of the hall-way mirror, as he opens the front door.

The dog bounds over, its tail wagging back and forth, and lifts itself up on hind legs and offers its front paws playfully as Lionel crouches down and holds out his hand and tickles its ears.

Sara hopes the dog can stay. She's never had a pet, not that she can recall anyway. The animal has lifted its head and is lapping its tongue on Lionel's face. Looking at Lionel play with the dog makes her feel less apprehensive about the strange house and the equipment Penny is assembling.

Lionel's hands drop to rub the fur on the animal's front legs. The dog cocks its head to the side and wags its tail furiously, excited to find a play partner. Sara then watches as Lionel's hands grip the front paws like a double handshake and abruptly yank the front legs apart, as easily as he might snap a turkey bone, his strength profound and unexpected. The animal's spine cracks instantly, the dog dead before it hits the ground.

Sara's scream is cut short by Penny's gloved hand, which clamps over her mouth.

She can hear Lionel mutter as he walks back to the kitchen.

'Fucking dogs.'

He sees Sara's reaction when he walks in through the door. His face falls, and his earnest expression returns. 'I'm sorry, Sara. I didn't want you to see that. That dog was threatening what we were doing. I can't let anything get in our way.'

Sara has stopped struggling and sits motionless on the edge of the chair. The tap drips insidiously into the sink, the *plink plink plink* is mutating, shifting into something else, a thumping sound, like a demented monster banging on a basement door. There is a whisper too, but what it is saying, if anything, makes no sense to her.

And with it, the same image returns to her mind, her fingers resting against a canopy of leaves, pressing them down, and slipping in between the trees.

'I need to go to the toilet,' says Sara.

Dobbs looks at her for a long moment, as if sensing something between them has been lost. Finally, he purses his lips, as if this could not be helped, then nods to Penny.

'Take her upstairs.'

*

'Don't lock the door,' is all Penny says as Sara steps into the bathroom. Her voice is cold and robotic, and Sara nods in agreement as she shuts the door behind her.

The moment the door closes, Sara crams her fists in her ears. The entire house seems to have animated and is babbling at full volume now, and her heart is beating so loudly it seems ready to burst from her chest.

She walks as far as she can from the door. She wants to run. As far as she can away from this place. As much as she wants to remember, she knows it is not safe.

Sara climbs on to the cistern and opens the window. It is a ten-foot drop on to the paving stones below.

'I'm giving you one more minute,' says Penny from the other side of the door.

Sara looks around and notices how thick the hedge is that runs flush to the side of the garden fence.

By the time the doorknob begins to turn, she is standing on the outside window ledge. She pushes hard and launches herself at the shrubbery.

Seconds later, she is running down the alleyway by the side of the house, her arms and legs still stinging from scratches.

She runs along the gravel driveway and into the field opposite. Her legs pump like they have never before. Each time she feels herself tire, she digs deeper and squeezes more energy from her reserves. She does not stop running. Even though her lungs feel like they could burst and her throat is burning with acid.

She doesn't look back until she reaches the tree line.

Her hands reach out to pull the branches aside, and she realizes with shock she has seen this moment before. The leaves, the sapling branches bending under the pressure of her fingers, it was not a memory. It is this moment.

3

Sara crouches low, the toes of her bare feet pressing into the dirt. It is cold outside, and her skin goose-bumps as she watches the flashlight beams bounce up and down as they approach her.

She is hiding in a thicket of trees on common land in front of the house. Lionel and Penny are less than a hundred yards away from her now, and she can hear his voice cutting through the darkness.

'You were meant to check every window. You know the dangers. Seeing me could have triggered a memory. It could all come back at any time. Even without your machine.'

He is talking to Penny. His tone is both calm and threatening, and he walks slowly, as if he knows Sara has nowhere to go.

'I thought you meant the windows on the ground floor,' replies Penny. Sara can hear the stress in her voice.

'Losing her is not an option. Not after losing the mother. Wait here. You might scare her off,' says Dobbs.

The second flashlight stops, its beam directed down, lighting up Penny's trouser legs.

The mention of her mother trips something deep inside Sara, disconnecting what had been a reflex reach for abstract parents. An orphan's desire to be reclaimed.

Now something more tangible tugs at her. Her mother. That is who she craves. 'Mother' is still just a word, the image it conjures just a hollow in space in her mind's eye, but Sara's yearning is now visceral, urgent. She needs to reunite with her mother like a beached, dying fish needs to return to the sea.

Dobbs is getting closer to Sara now. The trees are too thinly leaved to protect her from the light if he shines it directly at her. He is less than ten feet away, and she can hear his breathing.

'I know you're here, Sara.'

The flashlight trains on the thicket ten feet to the left of Sara, the spotlight washing the darkness from the space and illuminating it with a ghostly glow. The beam then swings to the right, lighting up the area just next to her. The next move of the flashlight will expose her.

'There's nowhere for you to go. So, there's no point in running. I know you are scared. But I promise you I am not going to hurt you. I wish you remembered me. You would know I could never do that. What we're doing here . . . it's to help you.'

'I want to see my mother,' shouts Sara.

It's too dark for her to see Lionel's reaction, but she can hear the injured tone that creeps into his voice.

'I don't know what, if anything, you remember about your mother, Sara. It was always me that kept you safe.'

'My mother!' shouts Sara, so loudly her throat becomes momentarily hoarse.

'OK,' replies Dobbs. 'If you come back now, I'll take you to your mother.'

Sara holds her breath. And then the thicket plunges back into darkness as he switches the flashlight off.

She hears the sound of his shoes brushing against the wet grass, retreating. Penny switches off her light as well, and soon they are nothing more than two silhouettes.

Sara waits for several minutes, not daring to move. Waiting to see if it is a trap. She is dressed only in a thin t-shirt and trousers. It's too cold to stay and too cold to run. Besides, she has no idea where she is. And she has nowhere to go.

Around her, the night begins to animate. A branch cracks, and in the distance an owl hoots. The sounds feel ancient, as if the night is formally reclaiming its territory.

Lionel and Penny are not coming back.

A sense of emptiness washes over her, and she feels defeated. Lionel is right: there is nowhere else she can go.

She touches her locket and pats her trouser pocket where the photograph is folded. The things that her mother left her are still with her. The thought of her mother makes her think about Lionel's promise. Her desire to see her mother is so primal it is overpowering.

Sara stares at the house while trying to control the shivering, her small form pulsing with what feels like periodic electric shocks.

The house stares back at her, the windows in the white frame upstairs resembling closed eyelids, ready to pop open if disturbed, the open front door, a gaping mouth.

*

Minutes later, she is tiptoeing along the alleyway to the window of the room from which she jumped. The top of it is ajar. Not by much, just a few millimetres.

She is not going to walk through that open front door. She is fearful of what might be lying in wait just past the ink-black threshold.

There is a trowel lying discarded by the garden fence, and she picks it up. A drainpipe running down the side of the house serves as a useful prop to help her clamber back up to the window ledge. She slips the tip of the trowel into the gap in the window, jemmies it open and climbs inside.

Sara puts her hand on the bathroom door handle and tips it downwards, slowly enough to avoid a click when the catch gives out. The door releases, and Sara pushes it open in a long arc.

The corridor is silent, and she steps out, allowing her eyes to adjust to the darkness. For the first time, she wishes the voices would appear. It would be nice not to feel alone. But it is quiet, and she stands barefoot on the carpet, alone in the stillness.

The kitchen is downstairs and on her left, and she creeps towards it. The door is half closed, obscuring the room within. She pushes it open, with infinite care.

She sees him the moment she sets foot inside.

He sits on the kitchen chair. There is no sign of Penny.

'Where's my mother?'

'You tell me, Sara.'

Sara looks at him in confusion.

'What do you mean?'

30

Lionel folds his arms. He is not speaking to her like a child any more.

'You're the only one who knows.'

Sara shakes her head.

'I don't remember anything.'

A noise in the corner causes her to turn. Penny is standing there. She has finished whatever she was assembling and stands aside for Sara to get a better look. It is an inclined chair, its armrests crisscrossed with restraints. A spherical cage the size of a football is fixed to the top.

Penny opens a small compact and pulls out a syringe.

'This won't hurt. Pull up your sleeve.'

Sara eyes Penny as the young woman approaches her.

She can feel her heart rate spiking, and around her the air seems to warp, making her feel light-headed. Her blood thrums in her ears, and she feels as if she is about to pass out.

'Be careful,' says Lionel, his voice suddenly sharp. 'You're exposed.'

Penny looks down, seeing that Sara is in reach of her face and neck, which are uncovered. She flinches in fear, taking her eyes off Sara for a crucial second, moving backwards with a faltering step.

A blurred hand swipes the syringe from Penny and drives it downwards. The movements are so fast that Penny does not react until the plunger has sunk down and delivered its payload into her leg.

Penny gasps and looks in shock at Sara. Her eyes then roll up into her head, and she falls like a sack to the ground.

Lionel rushes towards Sara, his hands outstretched. But he never reaches her. Instead, he drops to the ground, screaming in pain. She doesn't realize what she has done until she sees he is clutching his thigh, where the trowel she was holding is buried into the flesh.

He stares at her, his eyes widening in fear. He scrambles backwards on two arms and one leg, like an injured crab, leaving greasy smears of blood on the floor behind him, until he is pressed into the corner of the kitchen. He clamps down his eyes in fear and waits. Then . . . nothing.

When he finally opens his eyes, the kitchen is empty. The sounds of small footsteps can be heard crunching on the gravel outside.

4

Three weeks later

Baz stood inside the concrete skate-park on the south side of the River Thames next to Waterloo Bridge. Outside, sleeting rain lashed a sea of umbrellas bobbing along the Embankment. The weather had turned the skate-park into a temporary shelter for the homeless, displacing them from the various pavements and benches that dotted the South Bank.

The atmosphere in the concrete park was fetid, with steam rising from the sleeping figures crowded into each other. There was a sense of menace too, the inevitable by-product of too many homeless gathered into one place. Each had their worldly possessions on them, and in confined spaces like this, the weakest became vulnerable to the powerful and unscrupulous.

Standing on the periphery of the group, he was aware of the tension in the space but didn't care. Most of those here knew he'd been a trained soldier, and those that didn't couldn't miss his size. Nor the constant tics and twitches that racked his body. Everyone gave him a wide berth.

His focus now was on the rumbling of his belly, and he cast a professional eye over the commuters and tourists that rushed along the Embankment. He was not by nature a violent man, so feeding himself through brute force wasn't an option. Nor was begging. He had seen one of the older homeless men take out a sign that morning with the words, 'I AM TOO ASHAMED TO LOOK AT YOU' and take up a position on the Embankment, kneeling, his eyes cast down on the ground. That servitude, the humiliation that was offered up as a trade for pennies, was not for Baz. And since no employer would hire him, that left only one other option.

Ahead of him, a couple in raincoats and tartan scarves wrestled with their umbrella. He dismissed them as unlikely targets.

Baz had lifted two wallets today. The first one was a gift; it had hung out so far from the tourist's back pocket that it resembled a dog's lolling tongue. The wallets nestled reassuringly in Baz's front pocket now. Twenty pounds more, and he could get into a shelter for the week.

And then he saw her.

A little girl with elfin features weaving through the throng. Baz could tell she was neither trailing someone nor being trailed. In other words: alone.

On her back was a leather backpack. Even discounting the contents, the bag itself would be worth forty quid. With studied nonchalance, Baz stepped out from the mouth of the concrete overhang and began to follow her.

It turned out to be more difficult than he had anticipated. She was fast and took a circuitous route that left
him at times scanning the crowd to see where she had
gone. In and out she zipped, until he found the effort
of keeping up had covered his forehead with a film of
sweat. It was not easy to be inconspicuous either, he
was a head and shoulders taller than most of those
around him, and the twitches made those on either
side of him look over with concern.

Baz was beginning to consider giving up when she
stopped dead in her tracks and he almost collided into
her. Seizing the opportunity, he grabbed the pack with
one hand and one of her arms with the other, lifting
the item clear from her.

As some onlookers began to notice what was happening, he turned and headed quickly down a side alley.
But the girl would not let go. She clung to the bag, her
heels digging into the pavement with a determination
that surprised Baz. He turned around and lifted the
backpack clean off the ground, only to find that the girl
came with it, swinging up and colliding into his chest
like a human wrecking ball.

'Drop it, or I'll drop you,' he hissed.

The girl hesitated for a second and then dropped the
strap, tumbling back to the ground. Her hands were
clad in long-sleeved gloves, and she crossed her arms as
she considered Baz, not with hatred but with something else. It was almost as if she was sizing him up.

A few of the passers-by had stopped and were

looking at the strange sight: a brute of a man squaring off against an eleven-year-old. Baz could see that their fear would soon give way to righteousness. He turned on his heels and ran in the opposite direction.

He found an overhang in the concrete ceiling of the bunker-façade of the National Theatre and inspected his prize.

He unzipped the top and rifled inside.

But it was empty.

He frowned in confusion. A bad feeling had begun to gather in the centre of his chest. He turned the bag upside down and checked the manufacturer's label.

It wasn't even leather. It was a cheap knock-off. Not worth two quid.

It made no sense. Why put up such a fight over a worthless item?

And then it dawned on Baz. The realization was so far-fetched it couldn't be true. But just the possibility began to make him feel physically sick.

His muttering increased in volume and took on a desperate edge. He reached into his pocket with a trembling hand and checked for the wallets there.

They were gone.

He looked everywhere for her. It was fruitless, he knew. No one ever stayed in the same territory after taking down a mark. He was furious at himself, and his tics became more pronounced, his shoulders bouncing as if in syncopation to some silent tune.

He was almost back to the skate-park when a sight made him stop dead.

There she was.

In the exact spot he was in when he first laid eyes on her. She sat on a low wall, her legs kicking nonchalantly into the air as she watched him approach.

'You can have them back,' she said. 'I just want to talk.'

5

The heat from inside the café fogged up the windows facing the street, but the babble of voices and the hiss of a steam kettle from within sounded welcoming.

Baz pushed through the door, with Sara trailing behind him.

It was a small space, long and narrow like a train compartment, with booths running down each side. The restaurant was half-full and, as they entered, Baz looked around for a space. They sank into a pleather bench in the back.

They made an unlikely couple. Baz's frame filled the entire seat while Sara had to extend her feet in order for her toes to touch the floor.

Baz stared at her truculently.

'So?'

Before Sara could respond, a waitress materialized by their side.

'What do you want?'

'Full English,' said Baz, looking at Sara pointedly. This one was on her. 'And a cup of tea.'

'And what about you, love?' asked the waitress, looking at Sara.

'Nothing,' said Sara, shaking her head.

The waitress left.

'My name is Sara Eden,' she began.

The story she told was not dissimilar to the stories Baz heard from other young runaways. Men were pursuing her. Bad men. They wanted her for sinister, but unnamed, purposes. She had survived on the streets for a few weeks, but they were closing in. On her heels now. Could grab her at any time.

The story always ended the same way. With an appeal. A twenty-pound note would keep the predators at bay. Eyes would grow Disney-large, faces would become slack with innocence, chins would tilt minutely up. It was never clear how a sum of money that small would adequately defend a child from the massed forces of darkness pursuing it. But perhaps that was the point. They were just singing for their supper.

Baz half-listened, Sara's words receding into the background, like an overplayed song on the radio that Baz could finish from memory.

He kept one eye on the kitchen door, waiting for his breakfast to arrive. Whatever curiosity he had regarding the pickpocketing skills of this child was wearing off. He held up his hand to attract the attention of the waitress. He was becoming increasingly uncomfortable with how strange a couple they made as well, and the last thing Baz wanted was attention.

'. . . anyway, this is to start,' finished Sara, laying out five crisp twenty-pound notes on to the table. 'I'll give you another hundred if you agree.'

Baz's raised hand slowly dropped down to the table, a drowning man disappearing below the water.

She said she had a way to get cash. Quickly. In return she wanted something from him.

A trade.

She cut herself off when the waitress walked out of the kitchen with a steaming plate. The waitress slid it in front of Baz and laid a glass of water in front of Sara.

Baz snatched up his knife and fork and assaulted his plate with vigour. It had been almost twenty-four hours since he had last eaten, and his hunger had mutated into something else, overriding his conscious motor functions and shovelling food in his mouth faster than he could chew it.

When he had finished, he pulled out a bottle from his jacket and took a deep chug.

The alcohol burned as it went down, leaving a residue of warmth as if a pilot light had been lit inside him. Feeling fortified, his curiosity returned.

'All stolen money?'

'I didn't steal it,' said Sara, slowly, with authority. Eyes locked on his. A teacher correcting a pupil.

Baz was considering whether to believe her when the front door of the café opened, a shiver of glass and wood, accompanied by the buzz of the doorbell signalling a new customer. Baz turned around casually to see two men in suits enter and look around for a place to sit.

'So where did you get it?' asked Baz, turning back to Sara.

But now it was her turn to be distracted. She was staring at the men intently, watching their movements.

In the time it took for Baz to turn around, she had slid to the end of the bench, ready to propel herself out.

Baz's eyes flicked to the table and noticed something else.

Both knives on the table were now missing.

'Steady . . .' cautioned Baz, looking between her and the two arrivals. His new friend was becoming more interesting by the second. 'No need for you to do anything. That's where I come in, right?' He met her eye, nodding to calm her down, his words encouraging.

'It's not them I'm worried about. It's the ones that could be waiting outside,' said Sara, moving back along the seat to face him again.

Both her hands remained under the table.

'You used a knife before?' said Baz, looking at her with bemusement.

The dead-eyed look he received in return made his smile falter.

'OK, I'm listening. What do you want?' asked Baz.

The girl's request was a simple one. It required the threat of violence more than violence, and that was no problem for him. After consideration, he agreed, with one condition.

'I want the next hundred first,' he said.

PART TWO
Today

6

Today

Robert Waterman's phone buzzed.

He reached with his eyes closed, patting the side table by his bunk to locate it.

It was a physical battle to open his eyelids, but he managed a squint, staring at the blurred letters of the message as he held the phone directly over his face.

And then suddenly he was awake, as if he'd been doused with a bucket of cold water.

Waterman walked quickly out of the dorm room and along the wide central corridor that ran along the entire circumference of the bunker. Above his head, the barrel-vaulted ceiling glowed bright blue, simulating the time of day.

He pushed open the swinging doors on the side of the corridor and looked around the room, his eyes taking a moment to adjust. The illumination, which came from spotlights mounted on the ceiling and scores of monitors that bled LED lights into the space, made it difficult to see. In front of him, programmers sat at banks of terminals.

An intense-looking man in his thirties appeared out of the gloom, making a beeline for Waterman. He was well over six feet tall and so lean he stooped in on himself, his body curving in like a question mark.

'How long ago?' asked Waterman.

'A few minutes.'

Waterman didn't ask Ian Hunter why, if that was the case, he had only called him seconds earlier. He had bigger things to occupy his mind, like the fact that if he moved his head too quickly, stars appeared in his peripheral vision. As the leader of the intelligence analysis unit, he was in charge of tracking the unusual surge in electronic chatter over the past twenty-four hours. The intercepts hinted at a player on the scene planning something ambitious. A strike on a hard target like a British military base. And most disturbingly, inside the borders of the UK. The combination of threats had kept him standing sentry without rest before he forced himself to the dorm room.

'What are we watching?' asked Waterman. As always, he spoke slowly, his Yorkshire accent wringing the music out of each word.

Waterman's eyes raked the far wall, where a cinema-sized screen was mounted along with an array of smaller plasma screens that ran down either side. Continuous feeds were relayed on them, blinking on and off in rotation: CCTV from street cameras and private premises, satellite and drone surveillance footage, images hijacked from laptop cameras.

Two storeys above them, a vast network of neural computers sifted through unimaginable quantities of data, siphoned from the databases of British military intelligence and its overseas partners. In some cases, this was with the source's knowledge and blessing. In some cases, not.

'One through seven.'

Hunter's reply was terse. It had been like this all week. Hunter led the computer systems and IT unit and had been, until three days ago, a peer and friend. But Sam Taylor's breakdown had changed that. The fact that Waterman was only temporarily assuming Sam's role pending the appointment of a permanent replacement didn't seem to affect Hunter's inability to process that he reported to Waterman now.

Hunter pointed to the row of smaller screens on the right side of the cinema screen. On each was an aerial perspective, in monochromatic hues of grey, black and white, of a different military base. The images combined the ghostly clarity of an X-ray with the sharpness of a digital picture. Human figures the size of a thumbnail moved around, and the magnification was strong enough that he could tell which were women and which were men.

Waterman's eyes rested on another screen below the others, with an '8' inscribed on it. Its feed was of a different sort of facility. Four small hangars were arranged in a neat rectangular pattern, with a single runway splitting them in two.

Waterman was one of the few people who knew the location of the Scottish base known only as Camp Ultra. He knew whose headquarters it was but only learned of what was housed there this week, when his elevation to temporary head brought with it a new, previously unheard-of, level of security clearance.

He glanced at the console and chair sitting on the raised dais nearby, a force of habit. It was Sam's seat, and Sam always made the operational calls. A neat, meticulous man with an atomic sense of self-containment, Sam would carefully listen to every opinion before giving an order. But the chair was empty now, and today the faces around Waterman were looking at him instead.

Few coveted that chair. Certainly not Waterman, which made Hunter's ambition even more suspect. The Agency was created as a triage facility: a vault submerged into the foundations of GCHQ to which the top threats to the Realm were directed. A secret division; if the Agency was tracking something, then a potential strike was imminent. It was thinly staffed with the cream of the executive level from the sprawling institution above them. Job stints were intentionally short. Burnout was the eventual fate of everyone at the Agency.

And this period was the most nerve-shredding. This silence, the lull in chatter, was always the herald of an attack.

'Traffic has picked up again,' said Hunter. 'Something's happening.'

Waterman walked closer to the screens, his heart in his mouth.

'I see nothing on the feeds.'

The images of each facility had not changed, and tiny figures continued to move around the structures in slow patrols.

'Pull back the scope of surveillance by five miles,' said Hunter. 'Take in the surrounding areas.'

A few faces looked over at Waterman. It wasn't Hunter's role to take the lead.

Hunter walked to a console, typed into the keyboard and looked back up at the screens. They all went dark for a few seconds, and then the feeds reappeared, the aerial view now high enough to encompass the terrain encircling each of the British bases. They were barren, empty of activity. Nothing stirred.

'The attack's on Ultra,' said Waterman, his voice barely above a whisper.

He watched as a vehicle rammed the perimeter fence and burst on to the site, scattering the tiny figures. Flashes of white bleached out the screen, and when the images returned, further flashes consumed the aircraft hangars. When the light subsided, the structures were in tatters.

Waterman moved to a desk and picked up a secure phone.

The frenetic movement and bursts of light stopped, and a large, amorphous cloud, smoke from the explosions, now covered the majority of the screen, making it impossible to see what was going on below. Slowly, the smoke thinned and cleared as it was tugged in different directions by the wind, clearing the view of the base.

'Find Spokes,' said Waterman into the phone. 'Tell him F Squad's base has been attacked.'

There was no longer any motion on the screen. Bodies lay spread out across the ground, not moving. The roofs of the hangars were blown off, revealing the destroyed remains of four drones visible to the satellite. There was no sign of the attackers or their vehicle.

Waterman put down the phone and looked for a second at his hand.

It was shaking.

He knew without lifting his head that everyone was looking at him.

They had just collectively witnessed the worst attack on a military base on British soil.

He suddenly knew how Sam Taylor felt when he climbed the fire escape stairs, walked through the front door of GCHQ and started screaming at the top of his lungs in the car park.

7

Camp Ultra, Scotland

From Commander Daniel Spokes' perspective inside the enclosed jeep, F Squad's military base outside of Dornock appeared like a ghost kingdom out of the mist.

'One mile,' Spokes announced into the intercom, his voice barely above a breath.

Behind him, a convoy of jeeps bumped and rolled over the bracken-covered hillside. Four in all. The bulk of the Squad, returning from a mission. Above them floated a Lynx MK9A military helicopter, matching their speed and looking like a sinister Zeppelin tethered to their shells.

The Lynx would have provided a quicker route to the base, but its rotors would have obliterated any evidence that could exist there. And that was Spokes' mission. To see if the recent unwanted visitors to the base had left any clues to their identity behind.

More of the base materialized, as the wind blew at the fog. Its high perimeter walls now clearly visible.

Ten of his men had been at the base. All now dead.

He had seen the footage of the attack and he knew already that the attackers were seasoned. Even with the element of surprise, it was unimaginable for the occupants of one jeep to have taken the base with such speed. But as he played and periodically paused the footage before leaving, that's exactly what he saw.

His men's deaths were a tragedy, but Spokes' emotions were tightly in check, a dividend of being one of the most highly trained men in the British army. Although, technically speaking, F Squad was not the army at all. Indeed, if you had to be really technical, the Squad was off-book, its existence denied by the British government. Funding came from a black budget seen, as Spokes understood, by fewer than a handful of men in the country. They were the paramilitary unit of British military intelligence. Less than thirty men. All single: no dependants and no attachments.

His role was now to remove evidence of the armed drones F Squad maintained at Ultra before the Ministry of Defence regulars arrived, and then to pursue, apprehend and eliminate the attackers.

Spokes' father had been a regular in the British army stationed in Belfast. Sitting in the hallway of their house were an umbrella stand, a coat rack and the telescopic mirror his father used to check his car for bombs each morning. Life was war, and either you were prepared or you died.

They were less than a mile away now and he began running through the mental checklist he had for all operations: sniper sweeps, securing perimeters, splitting ground forces to divide any enemy still inside. Then the bomb search, in case the attackers had planted

IEDs for the search team. Only then, would the investigation begin.

'Halt,' said Spokes.

The convoy immediately decelerated and then stopped within a few hundred yards of where Spokes had given the order.

The voice of Simon Myers, Spokes' number two, squawked over the intercom.

'Do you have contact?'

'Just sit tight,' breathed Spokes.

He twisted his head to get a better view of the raised guard posts that made up the four corners of the perimeter chain-link fence.

The corners were all empty, other than the one at the north-west, where a lifeless body hung, half in and half out of the enclosure.

It was not the gruesome aftermath of the attack that had Spokes' attention. He was looking for something else: the one thing that could tell him the whereabouts of the attackers.

Outside, the only sound was the gentle humming of the engines as they turned over.

Spokes pulled a pair of thermal imaging binoculars from the seat next to him and stared through them at the ground surrounding the base. He could see the fence was breached; a great truck-sized hole was punched clean into the fabric of the enclosure wall.

Spokes kept up his review, aware that his men sat patiently, awaiting his lead. He was not going to rush; their lives were in his hands. Years of instinct had layered themselves into his system, like sediment in a stream, guiding the course and flow of his actions.

Through a gap in the buildings, he could see the smoking wrecks of the drones, their hulking remains collapsed on to the ground. Heat sources flashed on the thermal capture as fires burned amidst the wreckage.

He was making a mental inventory of everything he saw, while still maintaining his search.

And then he saw it: at the rear of the base, on the south side, directly opposite the tarmac approach road that ran into the north gate.

'OK, Simon, proceed with the sweep. Enter by the north gate.'

An hour later, ten bodies were lined up on the gravel floor of the base.

Spokes didn't need to wait for the evidence to know this was no ordinary terrorist attack.

First, each casualty had been killed with one clean shot. Ten dead, ten bullets. This was the most telling fact in itself. In a normal terror attack he would have expected an advance guard of one or two suicide bombers, followed by a wave of Kalashnikov-wielding madmen with a spray-and-pray approach to dynamic targeting. Corpses would have been ridden with bullets, and he would have expected to find one or two whose vital organs would have survived the inelegant shower. But there were none. Each man had been killed with a single clean shot.

Second, the weapons his men were carrying were

barely spent. That suggested an attack that had the element of surprise and efficient execution. It also suggested a fast-moving enemy.

Third, the weaponized drones housed at Ultra were not completely destroyed. That would have been the goal of terrorists: to put a large enough IED under each of the drones to blow them into a million pieces. But their shells were largely intact. The only damage to them were two clean craters on the top and bottom sides, where perfectly proportioned amounts of C-4 had blown out the guidance and surveillance units housed within the aircraft. The net result was the same, the drones were useless, but the route they took was precise and troubling.

As his men continued to scrub the site for more detail, Spokes walked to his jeep and climbed inside. He picked up his radio and switched on the scrambling device.

'Base, this is Alpha Four Bravo. We have a potential Code Blue.'

Blue was the code for an attack that was likely to have been perpetrated by a state-backed group in the guise of a terror attack. F Squad knew all about these: they were the unit committing them on behalf of the UK.

Spokes signalled to two of his men to follow him. They walked through the camp to the perimeter fence at the south, pulling the slashed chain-link to one side and walking carefully around the side of the two furrows in the earth.

This was the spot he was searching for when they first arrived.

Spokes nodded to the soldier carrying the digital camera. With a reflective hood to reduce brightness and anti-glare daytime colour reproduction, it was optimized and tested for any conditions. The man pointed it at the tracks running up to the perimeter fence. They were jumbled in places, different ridges mashing into each other, and in other places moisture from the mist had muddied the earth to partially cover them.

'There. That's not obscured.'

The route the attackers had taken was unmistakable. The photo would be able to pull an ID off the wheel sufficient to identify the tyre. And if they were in luck, that could lead to a vehicle ID. Spokes knew this was likely the end of the road of their line of enquiry. No vehicles were unique enough that the tyre track could lead them to the vehicle's users. But it was at least a start.

The soldier took multiple pictures with his camera and then plugged a lead from a satellite phone into the device.

'Let's see where these tracks go,' said Spokes, squinting at the horizon.

Ten minutes later, two jeeps were moving, following the trail across the moors heading north. In the front vehicle, Spokes peered out through the binoculars through the fog ahead of him. They were travelling at twenty miles an hour, a crawl for the fast-moving vehicles, but it was as much as Spokes would risk lest he lose track of the tyre marks ahead of them.

They were three clicks from Camp Ultra. As they

drove, Spokes was feeling more and more uneasy. He looked down again at the map open on his lap. They were leaving the known area of the Highlands, identified and measured by a dense sea of blue whirls and spidery lines. What lay beyond was blank space: a simple oasis of white paper, like the printer had jammed and left the rest of its job unfinished.

There was nothing out there. Nothing. And that meant that it was most likely a trap. It was the perfect place. The mist limited visibility to less than ten feet. Their attackers could be waiting in ambush right ahead, and he wouldn't know of it until they were on top of him.

Spokes shifted uneasily. He knew he needed to leave half his men with the bodies to protect the base, but the result was that they were now divided, and that left them exposed. Spokes knew who would win a firefight between his men and a handful of armed fighters but casualties were likely on his side. If he could eliminate the element of surprise, he might save some lives.

'Halt!' shouted Spokes.

The jeeps slid to a stop together, the last one skidding to the side to avoid hitting the vehicle in front.

Spokes stood up in the front seat and looked out. He then hopped out of the truck, indicating for the others in the following vehicle to disembark.

The tracks ran ahead of them. Spokes approached but slowed down as he saw what was coming. It made no sense, and yet it was there as plain as day.

The tracks simply disappeared.

The truck had vanished into thin air.

Spokes looked around in confusion and then walked back to his jeep and picked up the radio.

He was about to get back in the vehicle when he saw something flash on the horizon.

Spokes lifted his binoculars up and peered through them. He could see nothing at first, the mist hanging low to the ground and effectively blanketing the light source. Spokes waited, his eyes never leaving the spot where he had seen it. And then a gust of wind shifted the fog, causing it to drift, and he saw it clearly for the first time.

It was a box, the size of a household refrigerator, sitting in the middle of the moors.

PART THREE

1993

8

Lionel Dobbs tightened his scarf around his neck as he limped over Lambeth Bridge. A bitter wind was whipping down the Thames. On his right, dark clouds hung low above the iconic London skyline, and the impending storm was making his knee throb. He stopped and leaned against the railing, taking the pressure off his leg. He was still surprised by the fact that the injury was only a flesh wound. He had got off lightly. By all rights, he should be dead. The mother's botched attempt to de-programme the daughter must have made the child sloppy.

The doctor had given him a robust prognosis. There would be a severe restriction of movement for a couple of months; he wouldn't be able to lift his knee very much, if at all. But ultimately there would be nothing permanent, which didn't stop the fact that the pain was constant and at the upper edges of what he could bear. It only increased Lionel's resolve for what he knew he had to do.

He hobbled through the security doors of Thames House. It was three weeks today since Sara had disappeared, and he had come to dread the progress reviews at MI5's headquarters on the Thames.

What more was there to say? He had mobilized the

largest operation in the unit's history. Then he scaled further and used bribes and threats to co-opt police forces nationwide into their network. The web was complete. Now they just had to wait for her to fly into it.

He exited the elevator on the fourth floor and made his way down the corridor. At the end the door was open and he stepped inside. The office was large, and still filled with boxes from the occupant's recent arrival. Windows looked out on to the Thames. The thickness of the bomb-proof glass distorted the view, warping it subtly, like a carnival mirror.

The room's occupant sat behind his desk. Lionel had known this man for his entire professional life. They had started off as agents together, but a natural aptitude for leadership opened up a yawning gap between them, propelling his former colleague up the ranks and ultimately earning him the director general stripes, a month earlier, and this corner office.

'Has she come up on the radar again?'

Charles Salt spoke with the economy of a man whose next priority was more urgent than the last.

Lionel gripped the back of the visitor's seat in front of the desk. No one sat during Salt's meetings, which were famously short. His knee was still throbbing, and he felt light-headed.

'No,' he replied, shaking his head. 'The last time was the cash machine in Battersea. But we're pretty sure she's still in central London.'

'Make sure the code stays active.'

Lionel nodded. Of course.

Salt picked up a newspaper from his desk.

'What about the woman arrested at the house? Janey Small. Do you think she would know anything?' asked Salt.

'She's doing one year in Holloway,' said Lionel, shifting his weight to his other foot. 'We grilled her while she was in custody. She didn't know any of the details of Operation Orpheus. Or where the mother was. She was just some junkie ex-nurse the mother hired.'

'But, as the only link, the daughter will want to find Small,' said Salt.

'Of course,' replied Lionel, 'but she's not getting inside Holloway.'

'She won't need to,' said Salt. 'I arranged for Janey to be released. Yesterday. She's out. Spent the night at a halfway house.'

Salt tossed the newspaper into Lionel's hands.

Lionel felt heat prick under his shirt. Salt was getting directly involved. That meant Lionel had run out of time. His authority was now in question. He probably had weeks, if not days, to produce results or he would be permanently pushed to the side.

The newspaper was open at the middle pages, a large blue biro bubble highlighting a section of the print. As he read it, despite his discomfort, Lionel could not help but marvel at Salt's chess-game mind, always seeing multiple moves ahead. He looked up at his boss, trying to conceal any overt admiration.

'You placed this piece in the newspaper?'

The article was a masterpiece in spy craft, detailing

Small's release in such a breezy, journalistic style that no reader would suspect it was placed there. Even the mention of the halfway house, with sufficient detail for it to be identified, felt authentic. Above the piece was a black-and-white picture of a dead-eyed woman in her thirties, her slack, greasy hair falling by her sides.

'It should be enough to draw out the daughter. Maybe even the mother too, although she'll probably see it's a trap.'

'I'll head there right now,' said Lionel.

'Small's not there,' said Salt. 'The fool managed to get her hands on some drugs last night. Wound up at Guy's Hospital. The house is under instruction to direct anyone calling for her to the hospital.'

Lionel pushed off the back of the chair and hobbled towards the door.

'I want you to take support with you,' said Salt.

Lionel shook his head emphatically.

'I work alone, DG. You know that.'

'They'll meet you downstairs in five minutes,' said Salt, as if he had not heard Lionel. Sensing the meeting was over, Lionel headed for the door.

'One more thing, Lionel. I read your report,' said Salt, his voice dropping, 'and the answer is no.'

Lionel stopped in his tracks and turned to face Salt.

'That's a mistake,' he replied. 'She's too great a risk. In someone else's hands, she could be . . .'

'I want the daughter alive,' said Salt, emphatically.

A few minutes later Lionel stood on the pavement outside the building waiting for the detail to pick him up.

His world was unravelling. He sensed his reputation had taken a series of knocks over the past few months, but just heard the first tangible evidence of it. There was no point in trying to repair his relationship with Salt. His energies were best focused on keeping his eyes on the prize. Finding the daughter was the only way to reinstate his standing.

And not just finding her. Eliminating her.

It was Salt who had instructed Lionel to train her. And his genius had recognized what it would take to motivate her. So, Lionel formed a bond with the girl. Gave the fatherless girl a father. Gave a child of an unstable mother a context, a superstructure for living. And she took to it with a commitment that surpassed their expectations. Lionel taught her all he knew. Trained her like a new agent. Shaped her raw power into something efficiently lethal.

To Salt, the operation now was to get things back on track. But Salt hadn't been in the trenches, hadn't seen what Lionel had seen. Salt thought they had found the most powerful asset since Operation Orpheus was launched during the Second World War. Lionel knew better – they had created a monster.

And it was up to Lionel Dobbs to protect the country from her.

9

'It's for emergency situations. Afterwards, you're going to want to ask questions. But that's all I know.'

Sara looked at Baz, her eleven-year-old features stern. Baz shrugged.

'If it gets me the money, I don't care.'

'Good,' said Sara. 'First, we need a phone.'

They were on the embankment, sitting on a low wall, looking at the passers-by.

The voices in her head were loud this morning, a babbling chorus just under her perception, sounding like a crowd whispering to each other in a nearby room. Words leaped out at her every so often in an unsettling fashion.

Pssspsss . . . shhhshhh . . . dubdubdub . . . two two.

Baz surveyed the crowds in a professional manner. After a few minutes, he hopped off the wall and dived into the slipstream of a group of Chinese tourists following a guide carrying a raised flag.

Hsss . . . hsss . . . four four.

What seemed like a minute later, Baz materialized at Sara's side, a phone cupped in his hand.

Hmhm . . . tuttut . . . shsh . . . three seven.

'You said a hundred quid,' said Baz.

Sara pulled the elbow-length gloves up before she took the phone from Baz. She was still unsure what had spooked Penny and Lionel and caused them to take such elaborate precautions. Her mother would know, and until she found her, Sara had decided she wasn't going to take any risks.

Oh seven seven one two two four four.

The voices hissed the numbers, an incantation that ran in a loop over and over. She pressed the keypad of the phone in the same sequence, tipping the screen at an angle so it was obscured from Baz's view. She then pressed the call button and to her relief, as before, the line rang once and then disconnected. A second later a text arrived: SAINSBURY'S LOCAL 141923894814.

Sara looked around her quickly, her eyes searching the surroundings.

'We don't have much time. They'll be on their way.'

'Who?' asked Baz.

Sara looked over his shoulder and then pointed.

'Sainsbury's!'

A hundred yards behind them was the white-and-orange sign of the supermarket chain. Sara elbowed past Baz and sprinted towards it, caroming off tourists as she ran.

'Wait, my phone!' shouted Baz, running after her.

When Sara reached the shopfront, there was one person using the cash machine and two more waiting. She stepped to the front and addressed the line.

'Sorry, it's an emergency.'

The man in front looked at her with bemusement.

'Is there a "My Little Pony" sale somewhere?'

The smile curdled on his face as Baz ran up to them.

'You heard her. It's an emergency,' said Baz, stepping into the man's personal space.

The man held up his arms in surrender. 'All right, mate. Stand down.'

The woman using the cash machine left, and Sara stepped in and punched in the code from the phone.

The screen went blank for a few seconds, and then the whirring sound of cash being counted could be heard from within.

Sara looked over to Baz, who stared back speechless. Before he could ask a question, the mouth of the machine opened and five twenty-pound notes slipped out. Sara grabbed them and ran.

'Hey!' shouted Baz and launched after her.

Sara flew down alleyways and raced across squares, abruptly changing her course every hundred yards, zig-zagging as far as she could from the cash machine. She ran over a dual carriageway and saw the sloping decline ramp of an underpass nearby and sprinted down it, Baz's cries and heavy footsteps trailing her.

Once she was safely underground, she let him catch up. Baz could not speak at first and dry heaved, his torso bent double, his hands on his knees.

'One time they had a helicopter,' said Sara, as he caught his breath. 'We're safer underground. Here.'

She handed him the five crisp notes.

'One hundred pounds.'

Baz snatched the money from her.

'How . . . did that happen?' he blurted out between gulps of breath.

'It's for emergency situations. That's all I know,' said Sara, chewing her lip.

Baz looked at the notes in his hand with a sense of wonder.

'How long before we can do it again?'

'They'll be crawling all over the area now,' said Sara.

'Who's they?' asked Baz, his voice rising with frustration.

'I need to find my mother,' she said. 'She knows. She'll help.'

She fished into her jacket pocket and pulled out a page torn from a newspaper, carefully folded. Above the short article was the grainy photo of her quarry.

'I called the place this morning,' continued Sara. 'She's been moved to a hospital. They'll be watching her, so I need help distracting them. Are you listening?'

Baz took the newspaper from her hand.

'That's your mother?'

'No,' said Sara impatiently, 'Janey Small. She'll know where my mother is.'

Baz handed the paper back to Sara and took a deep breath.

'The bottom line is: you need help,' he said.

The statement surprised and disarmed her. The isolation of the last three weeks had seeped into her bones, keeping her in a constant state of fight-or-flight, separating her from the world. The acknowledgement of Baz's words was such a relief it brought tears to her eyes.

'Yes.'

'OK,' he said, 'what's the plan?'

PART FOUR
Today

IO

Bob Swift walked into the Arena. His four-hour sleep break, mandated every twenty-four-hour period, had been fitful, his mind jittering just below the surface of consciousness. As the newest arrival and the youngest member of the Agency, he was still having trouble leaving the rolling crises behind when he took his rest break.

Swift sat down at his desk and looked at the right side of his forty-two-inch monitor, where a separate window showed his in-box. He worked in the web-monitoring team, which patrolled the infinity of the Internet. A steady stream of new flags appeared constantly: new material on old pages, new pages on old sites, and new sites. A continual flow of information; over a billion websites, and three hundred million more added each year.

He looked at the latest flag that had dropped into the in-box.

It contained a link to a website that had been up and running for less than a minute. A 'crawler' – a software tool similar to an RSS feed that hurtles through the web searching for relevant material – had tagged it.

Swift scrutinized it.

The site had a clean and simple format, like the Google home page.

Underneath was a thirty-minute backwards count-down. The Agency's search algorithm had picked it up as a site with a high probability of risk.

Swift probed. There was nothing sinister on the site's face.

0:27:53.

He went back to the algorithm's reference and decoded the flag.

There it was.

A link to the official MI6 website.

0:26:12.

He checked the MI6 site to see if there was any related new activity.

Nothing.

He checked the link again. Swift thought for a second. A link was traditionally a cross-promotional event between two sites. A link from only one site was simply an appeal for attention from the other. A public 'shout out' as opposed to a private correspondence. The mystery site wanted anyone watching to know it had hailed MI6. As Swift was considering this, another flag arrived on the mystery site.

0:25:32.

He went to the algorithm immediately this time. A new link, this time to the MI5 website. He was reviewing the site for any clue to the mystery site's purpose when two more red flags dropped into his in-box.

Two more sites. Both UK military.

He stood up quickly.

0:24:15.

He walked through the cubicles of the rest of the Internet team towards the centre of the room to find Hunter. Before he left his station, the red flags were cascading in a heavy waterfall into his in-box. The mystery site was linking to every military intelligence site in the UK.

Daniel Spokes and his team parked their jeeps two hundred yards away from the box.

The bomb disposal team was on its way from London in a Lynx helicopter, having given him instructions en route on setting up a safety perimeter. Assuming it was a bomb – and that seemed a reasonable working assumption – it was best to wait for the professionals to deal with it.

Spokes used the broad rule of thumb that a thousand-pound bomb has a blast radius of two hundred yards. Assuming the box's function was only to act as a bomb, and all its capacity was used to house explosives, he guessed it must be in the range of a five-hundred pounder. He doubled the distance assumptions needed to be safely outside the blast impact and told his men to stay in their vehicles.

He kept his binoculars trained on the box. There was something strange about it that he couldn't put his finger on.

0:15:00.

'Do we know what the countdown is in reference to?'
Waterman looked at Swift with a blank look.

The young programmer had not been able to find Hunter. Unfortunately, the next up the chain was Waterman, and speaking to him was going to land Swift in hot water. The atmosphere in the Arena was poisonous since Sam Taylor's collapse and Waterman's battlefield promotion. Hunter's computer systems team had been at odds with Waterman's intelligence analysis unit ever since. But Swift didn't have the option of wasting precious seconds looking for his boss.

'I've looked into any global events that could tie into it, but there's nothing of significance. Should we take action?' asked Swift.

'Yes,' said Waterman. 'Shut it down.'

Swift jogged to his cubicle. The Agency had the technical and legal ability to exercise powers that were not available in the private sector, namely to hack websites and shut them down. The manner in which they did this was more direct than their hacktivist counterparts, who usually bombarded sites with denial of service attacks until the sites collapsed. Swift's group took the direct route, walking in the front door and shutting it down from the inside. The process required no court order and with most sites took less than a minute.

He sat down at his computer and started punching the keyboard. He hacked into the site quickly and then went through the registered files, deleting them one by one.

'Something's not right,' he muttered, loud enough for Waterman to hear, 'it's not coming down.'

*

The fog continued to make any close inspection of the surface of the box impossible. Spokes couldn't shake the creeping feeling that he should reverse the jeeps and drive back to Ultra as quickly as he could. His instinct told him this was a trap, but he had little choice but to proceed.

He dropped the glasses to his chest and checked the sky again. What he needed was visibility, at least to tip the odds more in his favour. The mist hemmed him in on all sides.

A gust of wind caused the vapour tendrils around him to eddy in waves, parting to reveal more of the landscape. He stared at the dancing swirls. The sight of them stirred something in him, a faint wisp of an idea that he reached for, but even as he pursued it, it fluttered away.

At face value, there was little he could do to influence the weather. And yet, he couldn't shake the feeling that there might be.

The box drifted in and out of view as the fog shifted around it, and as it did, that same idea fluttered up again, borne by a mysterious tailwind of neurological impulses that sparked through his brain.

Spokes stood stock still, as if any movement might cause the impending thought to waft away from him again. He realized he had stopped breathing. And then, with a mysterious drop, as if the idea had hit an air pocket, it settled directly in his palm.

The Lynx.

*

77

0:03:15.

As Waterman was moving towards Swift's desk, Hunter marched quickly past him.

'Step aside, Bob.'

Swift stood up, and Hunter took his seat, putting on a pair of outsized glasses and staring at the screen. The site remained there, the clock intact and running backwards at its steady speed.

Hunter looked up at Swift.

'Put it up on the wall.'

A minute later, the site was projected on to the large screen on the front wall. Swift could feel the tension in the room. The usual air of focused industry had been replaced by a sense of anticipation.

0:02:00.

'What's the countdown in reference to?' asked Hunter.

'We don't know. So far, there's only one thing we can be sure of . . .' said Waterman.

Hunter stared at the screen as the seconds ticked down.

'. . . and that's whoever is behind it wants our attention,' said Hunter, finishing Waterman's thought.

One minute to go.

Swift stood up in anticipation. Around him he noticed that others were getting out of their seats too and standing motionless, their eyes trained on the screen. Everyone in the room held their breath.

In the distance, he heard the *thud thud thud* as the Lynx approached.

Spokes' plan – that the downwash of air from the

helicopter would disperse the mist – was already working. The fog was churning, beating down into the ground and swirling outwards in a huge convex flow.

Spokes tightened his grip on the binoculars, readying himself.

Almost there.

He lifted up the field glasses and trained them on the box. He could see it more clearly now.

It was actually an inner container encased in a Perspex reflective outer casing.

Packed into the eight corners of the outer cube were thick wedges of what looked like C-4, from which a cluster of wires sprouted.

The chopper's blades were getting louder now, and around him the mist was shredding and evaporating, widening his field of vision, revealing more of the scrubland around him.

Ahead of him, something caught his eye. It was coming from the patch of ground where the tyre tracks ended.

Spokes squinted, doubting what he saw.

The air above the patch of ground seemed to be shimmering, like a mirage in a heat-haze.

He shook his head in disbelief.

He turned his binoculars in the direction, but the image warped and flickered, as if he was racking the focus of the glasses.

Then, with a flapping sound, the wheel of a jeep materialized from nowhere, standing upright in the grass.

'Shit,' muttered Spokes. He pressed the intercom. 'We've got a cloaking device.'

Britain was only one of a handful of countries that had cloaking technology. It was used on air and land vehicles, which employed carefully arrayed tiny glass panels to cover them, causing light to be bent around, making them disappear from eyesight.

The chopper was directly above him now. Its blades pummelled the air with such force it ripped off the moorings of the reflective tarpaulin covering the jeep. It sailed off across the moors like a bedspread torn free from a washing line.

The attackers' truck was less than twenty feet from Spokes. It had been in front of him the whole time.

Spokes scanned the interior of the vehicle, searching for assailants.

It was empty.

The mist had cleared now, and he could see clearly in all directions for a few hundred yards.

And it was then that he saw them.

There was not one box, but four.

Placed at intervals so they surrounded his convoy.

Their inner containers were made of dimpled silver metal casings, with black rubber seals that ran along their corners. They had no markings, other than on top, where yellow-and-black adhesive stickers covered most of the surface area.

The sign on the sticker didn't require any decoding. Spokes knew it as soon as he saw it. It resembled a stencil representation of a propeller, three blades attached to a central shaft.

The symbol of radiation warning.

0:00:01.

Spokes had turned and had taken the first stride back to his vehicle when the detonation caught his heels, lifting him up off the ground and throwing him into the windscreen of the jeep.

Screen one went blank.

It was the first movement in the site since it was first posted, other than the downward countdown.

After an extended moment, the site had returned to its home screen.

Words appeared, one by one.

I'M COMING FOR YOU.

The countdown underneath had a new number attached to it.

168:00:00.
167:59:59.
167:59:58.

11

GCHQ

The first thing that struck any visitor to the office was the wall behind the desk. The framed certificates were a visual journey through a truly exceptional career: distinguished service medals and commendations from ten years at MI5.

The chair behind the desk was empty, and Waterman could hear the sound of a phone call being conducted from behind the sliding patio screens.

Waterman walked through the doors into a small garden enclosed by high walls.

A tall, urbane-looking man in his fifties sat on a bench holding a mobile phone. He did not look up when Waterman entered.

'Not yet . . . no . . .'

Without waiting for an invitation, Waterman handed him a briefing note.

The man took the paper and looked at it absently as he talked.

'No, the government won't,' he continued into the phone.

He lifted the page as he read it, then looked up at Waterman, who nodded once, emphatically. The man's voice remained an aristocratic drawl as he spoke into the phone.

'I'm going to have to call you back.'

Sir Charles Salt, operational head of GCHQ, regarded Waterman for a long moment.

'Has anyone claimed responsibility?' asked Salt.

'No,' replied Waterman. 'Other than the warning on the website, there's been no direct communication.'

'Let's talk as we walk,' said Salt, standing purposefully and walking through the patio doors and out through the front door.

They walked down the main corridor that ran the length of the circumference of the building affectionately known as the Doughnut. The inside wall was floor-to-ceiling glass, through which Waterman could see sunshine bathing the inner courtyard. He was underground so much these days, the sight of the sun had a powerful effect on him, buoying him despite the circumstances.

'Spokes?' asked Salt.

Waterman shook his head. 'He took half of F Squad with him. They're all missing, presumed dead.'

Salt shook his head several times mutely. His step faltered, and he found himself looking through the window into the courtyard. Outwardly, his composure was unchanged, but Waterman could tell he was deep in thought. Salt pulled a packet of cigarettes out of his pocket and removed one, placing it between his lips.

'I haven't lapsed, if that's what you are thinking. Just like the taste,' he said, by way of explanation.

Salt began to resume his walk along the corridor

83

before stopping abruptly and turning back to Waterman, his piercing blue eyes holding him in their gaze.

'You know what's happening here?' he asked, as if the thought had just occurred to him.

Waterman shook his head. It was not for want of potential answers. But he knew his boss better than anyone else and learned long ago not to try to read his mind.

'Someone's declared war on British military intelligence,' said Salt, his voice incredulous.

He turned back without waiting for anything more from Waterman and led them through the circuitous route to the private lift that took them to the Agency.

'Spokes' theory was this was a Code Blue,' said Waterman when they arrived at the lift. 'Whoever did this had knowledge of Ultra's location, a cloaking device and dirty bombs. There's only a few state actors who could pull off something like this.'

'And all of them are meant to be our allies,' said Salt.

They stepped into the lift. There were three floors below them: computer systems, housing and an underground access road wide enough to accommodate large trucks. Their destination was even further below the access road, a floor only accessible by Salt and members of the Agency.

Waterman pulled a handheld device from his jacket.

'We do have a visual image. Five seconds of satellite footage that we managed to clean up.'

Waterman held the video player up so Salt could see it clearly. On screen, a black-and-white image of a vehicle ploughed through the army base's fence. Amidst flashes from explosions, the picture contrast shifted, and a lone figure dressed in black became distinct. It emerged from the vehicle and for a few seconds could be seen moving rapidly, an extended arm taking aim and firing even as it darted and rolled.

The lift trembled slightly, and a second later the doors glided open.

'Can we magnify it enough to make an identification?' asked Salt as he walked along the corridor under a brilliant azure-blue ceiling.

'Whoever it was wore a mask,' said Waterman. 'But I think I have someone who could help.'

Salt stopped in front of the doors of the Arena.

'One of ours?' he asked.

'No,' said Waterman. 'An old college friend. The best profiler I know. If anyone can tell us about this attacker, it's him.'

'Is he reliable?' asked Salt.

Waterman smiled ruefully. 'Reliability isn't the problem.'

'Then what is?'

Waterman scratched his beard.

'He hates my guts.'

PART FIVE

1993

12

The black Mercedes swung into the alleyway behind the hospital and parked behind a large skip.

Lionel knew the three agents in the car by face but had never spoken to them before. They were new recruits, part of a fresh crop that had been enlisted a year before. Square jaws, buzz cuts and calculating manners that seemed to inject threat into every interaction. He knew without needing to ask that they reported directly to Salt rather than to him.

The driver was Jonas, the one in the front passenger seat was Bonner, and he couldn't remember the name of the one sitting next to him.

Jonas turned off the car and twisted in his seat to face Lionel and the other man.

'There's three units here. They're covering exits on St Thomas Street, Great Maze Pond and Snowsfields. Remember: this is not a live-fire mission. She is to be taken alive.'

He twisted his head to make eye contact with each of them in turn, driving the point home.

'This is a ninety-pound girl, so one shot only. We stay in radio contact with the others. First to get line of sight engages.'

He twisted around, reached under his seat and pulled

out a black briefcase. The tumblers on the combination lock rotated under his fingers before he flipped the lid open, revealing four outsized black plastic guns resting in contoured depressions in the grey foam lining.

Jonas handed one to each man in the car.

'This isn't going to work,' said Lionel.

Jonas ignored him as he passed out the guns.

'Those are the orders,' said Jonas as he handed the last gun to Lionel.

'I'm the ranking officer here,' said Lionel. 'That gives me operational discretion. And I know the asset better than anyone.'

'You've got a problem with the plan?' asked Jonas.

'Firing on sight means an open-air confrontation. If we miss, she runs. Too many escape routes. She's eluded us for three weeks. We can't risk losing her again.'

Lionel could see that the logic of what he was saying was landing with Jonas. His hint at the risks of a botched mission being on Jonas' hands was a calculation. Salt had likely involved Jonas and his team as an insurance policy against Lionel's failure. And Jonas knew that too. The stakes were high for him, and failing Salt was not an option. If Jonas succeeded, he was likely to get Dobbs' job.

'So, what's your suggestion?' asked Jonas, his eyes flickering for a second.

'We let her into the building,' said Lionel, his voice devoid of emotion. 'The four teams then seal off all exits. I go in and find her. She knows me. There's a better chance I'll convince her to surrender. And if not, I'll take the shot.'

Lionel could almost hear Jonas' thought gears churning this time. The plan had the attraction of sealing the girl inside a building, so was tactically sound. Jonas' men were properly employed, as well, stationed at the exits. The icing on the cake was Lionel had the responsibility of capture. And a lame leg made this unlikely, so Jonas would get his asset and get rid of Lionel at the same time.

Jonas looked over at Bonner. 'Call the other units. Tell them the new plan.'

The food delivery motorcycle driver parked his scooter in front of the main hospital entrance and lifted the bike back on to the stand. Without taking off his helmet, he heaved the huge, black box on to his shoulder and walked up the hospital stairs.

Several doctors and nurses crowded around the front reception desk, talking on house phones. One doctor moved a phone from his ear to his chest and addressed the others.

'Ambulances four minutes out!'

The delivery driver wedged himself between them and flipped up his visor.

'Janey Small?'

A harried-looking nurse turned away from the group and ran a finger down a chart.

'D-4. Third floor,' she said, without making eye contact with the helmeted man.

Lionel stepped out of the car and walked down the alleyway towards the hospital entrance. There was no point waiting for Sara to arrive. He knew her better than that. She would never just walk in through the front door. He knew where in the hospital she was headed.

He walked past the skip, adjusting his path so the container blocked the Mercedes from his view. He pulled out the Taser Jonas had given him and tossed it in.

Lionel spoke into the microphone in his collar.

'I'm heading in. Get into position.'

As he turned the corner, he reached into his jacket holster, pulling out his personal Browning HP35.

Jonas would ensure the other teams stayed outside the hospital, guarding the entrances, which would give him the time he needed to complete the mission. He pulled a suppressor from his pocket, screwed it into the barrel, then slipped the pistol into the rear waistband of his jeans.

The delivery driver stepped into the lift and pressed the button for the third floor. As the lift began to move, he took off his helmet, carefully lowered the box to the floor and stood back and watched as the lid lifted of its own accord.

Sara's head emerged, followed by the rest of her body.

'I didn't see anyone suspicious on the way in,' said Baz. 'Maybe you were wrong?'

Sara shook her head.

'No, they're already here.'

*

Four ambulances parked in zigzag in front of the entrance stairs of the hospital, their rear doors open. Doctors and emergency workers streamed down the stairs to help disgorge stretchers from inside the vehicles.

A hospital security guard walked in front of Lionel and raised a hand.

'Wait here, please.'

Lionel reached into his jacket and pulled out his service identity card.

'Official business.'

The hospital security guard kept his arm raised.

'Sorry, sir. No one in or out. Those are my orders. Not until we get all the injured inside.'

Lionel's face darkened with frustration.

'Is there another entrance?'

The guard nodded, tilting his head behind him.

'At the rear of the building.'

Lionel looked up at the hospital. Sara was inside somewhere and, with the exits sealed off, wasn't going anywhere.

He turned away from the guard and spoke into his microphone.

'I want the front entrance sealed. I'm going in the back.'

The room was small, only slightly larger than the lift Sara and Baz had taken to the floor. It contained a single bed, as narrow as a door, and a worn chair. Pushed into the corner of the room was a wheel-mounted square monitor with an extendable arm that ended in a flat pad.

The person in the bed was less a body than a husk, sunken into itself, folds of skin hanging from bone like rags on a washing line. Its pallor was the yellow of cigarette stains. Baz stepped closer to the bed, then turned around to see Sara was frozen at the doorway.

Images were ripping through her, like air bubbles escaping from something submerged in deep water:

A faceless person pulling Sara into a smothering embrace.

Sara watching out of the corner of her eye as someone crushes a handful of tablets with the flat of a dirty spoon.

Sara being lowered into the warm water, her body displacing it and causing it to wash over her, forming archipelagos of her knees, chest and face. Headphones are placed over her ears, and she hears the metallic snap of the button that precedes the soft voice.

Then the lid is pulled over her, plunging her into darkness.

Lionel turned the corner of the building. The rear entrance steps were a short walk away. He looked around as he approached them. Two men standing nearby, ostensibly having a conversation, met his eyes and nodded.

Lionel lifted up the wing of his collar again and whispered into it.

'I'm going in. I don't want to see anyone else inside until I give the order.'

*

Sara snapped back to the present as she realized someone was talking.

'. . . communicate?'

A male nurse with a shaven head was now in the room. He stood next to Baz, and the two of them turned to Sara, as if expecting an answer.

'What did you say?' asked Sara.

Baz nodded to the nurse, who spoke gently to Sara.

Sara realized from his sympathetic tone that he presumed Janey was a family member of hers.

'She's had a stroke. This morning. Speech has been lost.' He pointed to the device in the corner. 'We brought that in . . .' he said, looking at Sara, as if gauging sensitivity.

Sara did not move. It was almost as if in Janey's presence she had become drugged again. The nurse continued.

'. . . it's for motor neurone sufferers. You put the pressure pad on a section of the body where there is still control. Pressure on the pad runs the cursor through the alphabet, the patient confirms with clicks.'

Baz had already begun approaching the machine. Sara looked over at him, seeing a compassion in him she had not seen before. He was stepping into the breach, trying to help Sara as she stood rooted.

Baz motioned for her to come closer. As she approached, Baz picked up a plastic chair that was pushed up against the wall and arranged it for her by the side of the bed.

From this vantage, she could see Janey in closer

detail. Her eyes were open, staring ahead through the visor of eyelashes created by her barely open eyelids. The eyes looked weak and unfocused, almost creamy, with the milky consistency of cataracts.

'Janey,' said the nurse, loud enough to make Sara jump.

Janey's eyes were immobile for a long moment and then slid sideways. Not one part of the rest of her body moved.

'The hearing is OK, but motor functions in the body are basically gone. What little movement potential there is might power the machine, but progress will be slow.'

Lionel walked down the main hospital corridor, looking for the bank of lifts. The building was a labyrinth of gleaming white passages that extended in front of him in each direction.

He stopped an orderly as he walked by.

'Lifts?'

The orderly pointed down the corridor to their left.

'They're at the front of the building. They might be in use now, because of that motorway pile-up. You might be better off using the stairs. They're on the left here.'

Lionel watched as the orderly walked quickly away. Nothing was easy. Three flights with his leg wasn't going to be a picnic. But there was little option. He was too close now.

He pushed open the fire escape door and stared at the concrete staircase heading up.

*

It didn't take long to secure the pads to Janey's right cheekbone. When the nurse was finished, he stepped back to let Sara retake her seat.

'I'll give you some privacy,' he said.

The machine was switched on and displayed the alphabet and a list of digits in three rows that ran the length of the screen. An electronic cursor circled the letter A, flashing on and off, waiting instruction from the pressure pad.

'Janey, where is my mother?'

'You might want to speak louder than . . .' started Baz, and then stopped as the cursor began to move slowly down the alphabet, wearily moving on to B and then C as if it was dragging a great weight behind it.

Sara looked up at Janey's face. The only visible indication that she was communicating were two veins that bulged on her forehead. Finally, the cursor landed on a number and stayed there, lighting up and fixing it with a border glow.

3.

Lionel reached the first-floor landing and looked up at the next flight of stairs. His right leg burned at the point of his injury, radiating in waves down to the knee.

He reminded himself that it was only a flesh wound. The fact reminded him that his quarry was not as deadly as he had feared. He needed to finish her, before her memory returned, and she became too powerful a threat.

*

Sara and Baz watched as the cursor reappeared at the front of the alphabet. This time it did not move for a long time, enough that Sara looked up at Janey and then back over her shoulder at Baz. He, in turn, shook his head in confusion and waved his hand up and down to indicate they should wait. Sweat was now running down Janey's forehead and hanging like stalactites from her eyebrows.

3.2.7.

The cursor reappeared again at the front of the alphabet and then hung there, not moving.

'C'mon,' urged Sara.

Lionel reached the second-floor landing. His leg was now numb, which helped progress. He picked up his pace, leaning on the balustrade for support, and began to take the steps two at a time.

3.2.7. F.O.R.

Baz turned away from watching the machine to smile at Sara.

'Looks like it's working.'

Sara did not return his smile. In the last few seconds, images and sounds had begun pouring into her mind, taking her focus out of the room.

A lone motorbike rider careened towards her, the engine growling like a pack of angry dogs. The sounds and images were accompanied by a twisting feeling of dread in the pit of her stomach.

'We need to leave.'

'We're almost there,' protested Baz.

'Someone's coming,' said Sara, standing up.

Baz watched as the cursor dragged along the alphabet, heading for an unknown destination. He tore his eyes away from the screen to the laminated floor map that was screwed to the back of the door.

'There's internal stairs at the end of the corridor,' he said, turning back to the machine and staring as the cursor hobbled onwards. It finally rested on a letter.

'It's a T,' said Baz.

Sara shook her head, her eyes fixed on the floor map.

'The internal stairs won't get us out. We need an outside fire escape. There's one next to this room.'

She pulled open the door and motioned him through.

'Let's go. We're out of time. It's Fortune. 327 Fortune.'

Baz stood reluctantly and, with a final glance at the machine, followed her into the hallway.

They ran down the corridor and pushed through an exterior door marked FIRE ESCAPE at just the moment the door of the internal stairwell swung open.

Sara and Baz clanged down the metal stairs, taking them three at a time.

Each time she landed on a step, Sara looked behind her instinctively at the closed fire-escape door on the third floor, waiting for it to fly open. But it remained closed.

They were on the first-floor landing now, and close enough to the ground that she could see the alleyway below them. It was empty, and Sara turned to Baz and allowed herself a smile. He responded with a whoop of exhilaration, his voice rising higher, and Sara whooped too, feeling her heart rate soar at the prospect of escape.

Suddenly the sound of Baz's cry rose in pitch and volume to become a strangulated parody of what it was before. She turned around in time to see the entire surface of Baz's body shudder as if he was having a fit. He collapsed on to the staircase and rolled down the remaining stairs, his body entwined in thin metal wires that appeared from nowhere.

Standing at the bottom of the stairs were three men dressed in black leather jackets and carrying what looked like large fake-looking plastic guns.

One of them stepped forward, his hand held up.

'Sara, you can't run. There's only one way out of this, and that's with us.'

She ignored them, jumped the remaining stairs and crouched down where Baz was lying at the foot of the stairs, unconscious.

Lionel looked down at Janey Small's frail figure. Her sheets were damp with sweat, and her breathing was shallow and irregular.

Next to her, a video monitor was linked by a sensor that ran to her cheek. A cursor was moving, communicating to an absent audience, propelled forward by the last remnants of Janey's energy. It lurched through an alphabet in a crawl until it settled and lit up the borders of one letter, completing a message.

3.2.7.F.O.R.T.U.N.E.

D.O.N.T.

Lionel knew the question to which the first line of the message was the answer. It would lead the girl to where it started.

If he moved quickly, he might even beat her there.

He watched Janey's face as she kept propelling the cursor forward. Her face was slick with perspiration, and pearls of sweat hung from her eyebrows.

D.O.N.T.T.R.U.S.

Lionel took hold of the pillow on which Janey's head rested and pulled it out gently, letting her head fall back on to the mattress.

D.O.N.T.T.R.U.S.T.H.E.R.

The girl must have left before Janey had begun this second line of the message. Too bad. She would have to learn the hard way the truth about her past.

'Goodbye, Janey,' he said, his face expressionless.

He gripped the pillow at either end and pressed it into her face, his arms locked down, driving the back of Janey's head deep into the mattress.

'What did you do to him?' asked Sara.

'He's going to be fine,' replied the man. He reached behind him and pulled a pair of handcuffs from his belt. 'Put these on, Sara.'

The air around Sara began beating loudly, and then everything seemed to slow down. She could hear her own breathing, loud and rasping in her ears. It was as if she was standing in a vacuum chamber, set apart from the world around her. Outside, every sound was becoming amplified, from the clink of the handcuff bracelets as they touched each other to the creak of the man's leather jacket as his arm reached for her in exaggerated slow motion.

Sara reached a hand out towards the handcuffs. The man continued to move towards her, like a deep-sea diver, slowly and as if battling extreme pressure, while her movements were lithe, freed from the apparent density of the atmosphere around her. By the time she clamped the restraints on to his wrists, she could see the surprise only just beginning to register in his face, one muscle at a time.

A sound like a tyre exploding on her right made her pivot. She turned in time to see two darts attached to wires launch from the gun of the man on her side. The darts flew through the air, like two lazy flies cruising in her direction. Sara stepped back and twisted easily to the side, watching as the twin projectiles sailed by in front of her, lighting up the air with static charges as they flew. They hit the third man square in the chest. At first, nothing happened. Then the man's hands began to shudder, as if he was trying to take flight. The flapping became more agitated as his arms and torso began to convulse.

The air pressure around Sara was building, causing her ears to pound with such force that she had to blink back the pain.

The man who had just fired the Taser dropped the gun in slow motion down to his side and began to reload.

Sara turned to face the man in front of her, who

shouted in rage and lunged at her, his hands pinned together by the handcuffs. She ducked low and crashed the heel of her palm into his Adam's apple before he registered the movement. He gagged reflexively and fell to the ground.

The pressure continued to build around Sara, and it was only then that she realized she had been holding her breath the whole time. She exhaled, and at the same instant the world around her collapsed and then resumed its normal speed.

She found herself lying on the ground, looking up at the remaining man. His finger squeezed the trigger as the gun aimed directly at Sara's chest. She closed her eyes, wincing at what was to come.

Then she heard a loud metal crash and opened her eyes to see Baz standing over her with a discarded metal pylon in one hand. The man was lying on the ground directly below him, out cold.

Baz looked at her in amazement.

'How did you do that?' was all he could say.

'Do what?' asked Sara, clutching her head in pain.

'I've never seen anyone move . . .' He faltered, too confused to continue. He helped Sara get up and took a step back, looking at her.

'Who are you?' he said finally.

The question was so direct that it wrong-footed Sara. She looked back at him, her face slack with incomprehension.

'I have no idea,' was all she could manage.

*

A commotion outside distracted Lionel from his labours. He let go of the pillow and walked to the window.

In the alleyway, three storeys below, he could see Jonas, Bonner and the other agent writhing on the ground. Next to them stood Sara and a mountain of a man.

Some instinct caused Sara to look up and she met Lionel's eyes. She stared at him for a second, her expression inscrutable, and then began to run with her colossal companion in tow.

Lionel turned and moved quickly across the room. He took one final look at Janey as he passed the bed. Her face was mottled blue and grey, and her mouth was half-open as if in a silent scream.

He leaned over her and unplugged the machine, causing the monitor to go blank.

'Close off the streets around the hospital. They're on foot in the alleyway,' he barked into his collar.

He pulled the gun from his waistband and clutched it in his hand.

13

'This way!' shouted Sara, running down the alleyway towards the main road. Baz followed her, holding his left arm across his body, loping at a slower speed, trying to shake off the effects of the Taser.

Above them, the sounds of a helicopter could be heard, but as Baz looked up to scan the sky, all he could see were low-flying clouds.

Sara reached the intersection first. The alleyway abutted a cobbled pedestrian street a few hundred yards long. Throngs of people crowded the pavements in front of pubs and cafés.

'C'mon,' said Baz, through gasping breaths, as he caught up with her and then ran on to the thoroughfare.

'Wait!' said Sara, grabbing his arm. 'Look.'

Baz followed her pointed finger to the end of the street, where two black Mercedes cars screeched to a halt and men in black leather jackets piled out. At the other end of the street, two more cars shuddered to sudden stops and ejected a crowd of men.

Baz and Sara had not been spotted and watched as the men formed lines, like a search party, at either end of the street. They began to walk towards each other, sieving through the crowds, their eyes searching each pedestrian's face.

A clanging sound behind Sara made her turn. Lionel Dobbs stepped out of the rear hospital doors and began walking towards them, his eyes locked on Sara.

There was nowhere to run.

She and Baz could neither go forwards nor back. This was it. There were too many to fight this time, even with the mysterious abilities she seemed to have but couldn't explain. They needed something else to help them. Some divine intervention or at least some distraction.

A few yards away, a mobile phone rang somewhere in the crowd. It jolted Sara back to the present.

'Quickly, the phone,' said Sara.

'Who are you going to call?' asked Baz as he pulled it out.

Sara snatched it from him and pressed a sequence of buttons.

The men were a hundred yards from them on each side now, ploughing through the walkway, leaving no face unscanned.

Sara shook the phone impatiently.

'C'mon, c'mon.'

Finally, a beep signalled the arrival of a text.

Sara immediately dialled the number again.

'We need to go, now,' said Baz.

'Not yet,' said Sara.

Lionel couldn't believe his luck. Sara and her companion stood at the end of the alleyway, not moving, as if waiting for him.

Maybe she was tired of running. Maybe she had given up.

Lionel looked at the pedestrians milling behind Sara. There were too many witnesses to complete his plan here. He would need to adapt.

Sara pointed to places along the pedestrian walkway.

'Do you see them?'

Baz nodded, a look of realization spreading across his face.

Lionel was less than a hundred yards from them now. There was no escape.

Sara gave Lionel a final look and then disappeared with her companion around the corner.

'Got you,' said Lionel with a measure of satisfaction.

He limped methodically forward. There was no need to rush now. He had flushed them out, into the hands of the other units.

He knew what would come next. They would be apprehended and separated. Salt would enlist Lionel to interrogate the man to see whether he had gleaned anything of Operation Orpheus during his time with the girl. If so, he would need to be eliminated.

Lionel's plan would need to wait. There wasn't much he could do while the girl was in custody. Salt would want to keep her close to him. But Lionel knew they would need him eventually. No one knew her better than him. And when the call came, he would pick his time carefully and then take her to somewhere remote.

It would be quick; he wasn't a monster. It was nothing more than threat containment.

The exercise today had aggravated his leg, and white-hot pins and needles slowed down his pace. They didn't need him, though. The other units would have her by now, so his presence would just be supervisory.

He finally reached the end of the alleyway and turned the corner. But nothing could have prepared him for what he saw.

The entire street was filled with people fighting, a chaotic mêlée of swinging arms and butting heads. The mob included women and children, who all clambered over one another. The lines formed by the two teams had dissolved, and agents were scattered, struggling against the street riot like swimmers battling violent tides. Covering the whole scene was a storm of confetti that blew over and around the angry, snarling crowd. Nearby, two bicycles were entangled, the riders battling it out on the cobblestones as the same confetti swirled around them.

The snowstorm hung low to the ground, but gusts of wind pushed it upwards. Lionel's eye tracked the paper shreds as the wind caught and blew them in eddies and vortices up and towards him.

One shred separated itself from the rest and danced through the air. It flapped towards him and he snatched it mid-air.

'Christ,' said Lionel.

It was a twenty-pound note.

They were all twenty-pound notes.

14

On either side of the road was a string of forlorn terraced houses. At one stage this must have been council housing. The designs were cookie-cutter: cottage-cheese exterior walls encasing small, two-storey dwellings with thick windows containing fracture-proof glass. Worn grass gardens separated the front doors from the street.

'There's only one street in London beginning with Fortune.'

Sara stared at the street, willing a memory to return.

Each front garden had some form of debris lying in it: a doorless fridge, a semi-burned couch, a tattered flag. It looked like a demilitarized zone.

'Shall we find 327?' asked Baz.

'Through the back,' said Sara.

A few minutes later, Baz crept down the alleyway that ran behind the back gardens of the row of houses.

'It's that one there,' said Baz, looking over the tops of the fences and pointing to the penultimate house on the row.

The rear plots of each house were worse than the fronts, resembling refuse tips more than gardens. Abandoned items such as rusting bedsprings lay on worn patches of scrub grass. Rear windows were smashed, boarded up or covered with grime.

Number 327 was no exception. The house looked abandoned. No lights were on inside. It resembled nothing more than a filthy shell.

'They'll be coming, won't they?'

Sara said nothing.

'How long?' asked Baz.

'Soon,' was all she could reply.

Baz put his fist on the handle of the back-garden gate of 327 and rattled it, but the door remained wedged.

'Must be rotted shut,' he said, taking a step back and looking around for another way in. He shrugged his shoulders.

'Only one way,' he said, lifting up his knee and pointing to the top of the fence.

Sara accepted the offer and climbed up, grabbing the lip of the wooden slatted fence. It was still a foot above her head, and she strained to pull herself up.

'Here,' said Baz, sliding a cupped hand under her right armpit to lift her up. The action caused the sleeve of Sara's t-shirt to ride up, pressing his fingers against the bare flesh of her upper arm.

'No!' screamed Sara.

Baz recoiled, letting Sara fall to the ground, where she rolled into a foetal ball and curled up against the wall. Both her hands gripped her temples, and she squeezed her eyes shut, rocking her body back and forth on her tailbone. Baz could hear a soft whimpering sound coming from her.

'Sara?'

Baz took a step closer. A thin stream of blood was

coming from Sara's inner ear, dripping on to her shoulders.

'It wasn't your fault,' said Sara, looking up at him with sightless eyes.

'What did you say?' he asked, his stomach lurching.

Her hands shot out and grabbed Baz's arm, the movement so blindingly fast he cried out in shock. He tugged his arm back, but her grip was strong.

'It was an accident . . . the sun was too bright . . . there was no way you could have seen him . . . it was an accident . . .'

The force of it took Baz by surprise, physically winding him and bringing stinging tears to his eyes. He never mentioned that day to anyone. The facts of it were hidden even to him. The moments seemed to have separated and drifted around each other, like a kaleidoscope, making recollection impossible. All he could see was the brilliant bright light, flashing in his eyes, obscuring everything around him. He remembered his breathing becoming erratic as he lifted up the rifle and pulled the trigger. The sound was muffled, like it was taking place far away, the resound distant and cushioned. He could feel the discharge kick into his shoulder. He pulled the trigger again and again. He waited, but the only sound was his tattered breathing in his ears. He craned his neck forwards, peering through the sun's brightness. And that's when Billy had fallen into his foxhole, choking from the bullet that had passed through his windpipe. Every day since then he had stared directly into the light, trying to see if he could find any clue to Billy's cloaked presence within it. And now, it was as if the scene had been reconstituted for the first time. Each pixel arranged itself into place and he was there again, looking into the light. And all he could see was a brilliant glare. There was no sign of Billy. It would have been impossible to see him.

For the first time his tics and twitches subsided. A memory flashed in his mind of him and Billy sitting in the back of the Jeep Commando, heading to town on leave, uniforms pressed, the sun shining on Billy's upturned face as it creased in laughter at a joke.

He was quiet for several seconds and slowly became aware of his surroundings. He was sitting on the stone path.

The shuddering of his shoulders was more subdued, like a punctured tyre slowly deflating.

He reached out a hand to where she was still sitting hunched in a ball on the concrete floor.

'Sara.'

She did not move.

15

As she sat there, more and more static close-ups mauled her consciousness:

. . . sitting on the hard leather of a jeep seat, bouncing along a dirt-track road . . .

. . . the grainy wood feel of a rifle butt in her hands . . .

. . . lips drawing on a cigarette, the nicotine filling her lungs, both calming and stimulating at the same time . . .

The visuals and sounds were superimposed on the alleyway, like a film projected on to a painted canvas.

It wasn't just the outside world that was different. She was also herself and yet she was not. Her extremities felt heavy and unworldly, and when she lifted her arms, they lifted both in the alleyway and in the superimposed world. As she passed her hands experimentally in front of her face, she seemed to experience double vision. A beefy pair of hands flickered in front of her, overlaid on to her own.

The full-throated rattle of an engine echoed in the air around her, and just beyond them, a voice broke through.

'Sara, Sara.'

Her name hung in the air, like two repeating chords played on a piano, over and over. She groped her way through the fog of her consciousness, her mind still jangling, moving from one world to the next.

'Sara, Sara.'

She opened her eyes and found Baz looking at her with concern.

'Are you OK?'

The other world was receding further and further with each moment, its colours washing away as the shapes and edges of the alleyway returned with sharp focus. The sounds of the other world were the faintest whisper now, and the superimposed world faded to nothing. In front of her stood Baz, his bulk filling the width of the alleyway.

The look of concern on his face touched Sara. She held out a gloved hand and allowed him to lift her up.

'I'm . . .'

She didn't finish her sentence. She stopped, staring over his shoulder at Lionel Dobbs, who stood ten feet behind Baz, his gun raised, its barrel pointing at Baz's head.

'No!' screamed Sara.

Her shout merged with the report from the gun, although the gunshot was muffled, the sound of a carpet being beaten with a single swipe.

Blood and viscera splattered across her face and clothes before she could swipe her head away, and Baz's body was thrown into the side of the fence, tipping the entire wall into the garden.

Sara looked down at him. The top half of his head was missing, replaced with a stew of hair, blood and brain.

Lionel limped towards her.

'Let's go inside, Sara. No sudden moves.'

Sara willed her legs to move, but they were rooted to the concrete. She could feel the panic paralysing her. Her fingers began shaking with an increasing tremor that spread to her wrists and arms. Soon it would take her over completely.

She squeezed both hands into fists and forced a breath into her lungs. Her chest rose and fell, and the action seemed to break the spell. She lurched to the side and ran.

A fencepost near her head exploded into splinters, and she clattered over the fallen fence into the small garden of number 327.

On either side of her were the two low fences that separated the garden from those on either side. The fence on her left had tilted to the side with the collapse of the back enclosure and she veered in that direction and vaulted over it into the next-door garden.

Lionel climbed over the damaged back fence and stalked into the garden of 327.

'There's nowhere to run, Sara.'

He hobbled quickly to the broken adjoining fence and stepped into the next garden.

16

Lionel entered the garden in time to see Sara disappearing over the far fence. He raised his gun and squeezed off two more shots, thumping them square into the panels just below the spot where she had disappeared.

He stopped to listen, waiting for the sound of a falling body. But there was just silence. He couldn't hear any movement, which meant that she was either dead, injured or was hiding just the other side of the fence.

He tucked the gun into his waistband and limped across the balding grass. A sense of sadness was blooming in him. It was not the fact of killing a child. He knew she was no ordinary child, even though it seemed that the mother's deprogramming had neutralized some of her power. It was the loss he felt at what could have been. If the daughter had trusted him, it could all have been so different. He breathed deeply to fight the anguish in his heart. He was at fault too. He had let feelings develop in him that clouded his judgement. Her condition had drawn something out of him, and the methodical hunt of Sara was as much a hunt to kill that which had escaped as it was to contain her threat. With the firing of the last shots, both were now terminated.

His mind was so far away that he was halfway across the garden when he heard them.

The sound was like several chainsaws firing up at the same time.

He looked over and saw three creatures sit up, bodies stiff, shoulder blades raised, eyes trained on him.

He couldn't recognize what sort of animals they were at first. Their frames were huge and misshapen, with thick welts of crude stitching knitting together missing chunks of flesh.

Their faces were the stuff of nightmares: the upper lip was missing from one, giving it a ghoulish, skeletal look; another was missing an eye.

Dogs: fighting dogs.

Their antecedents had been bred and interbred so many times it was impossible to tell what breed they were but, when standing, their heads were level with Lionel's chest.

Fear lurched in him with such force it knocked the breath from his lungs.

He froze, not moving a muscle. The dogs eyed him warily. Their muscles shimmering beneath their pockmarked skin, ready to propel them forwards.

With infinite care, he began reaching behind him for his gun, his eyes locked on to the dogs, his hand moving slowly.

The dogs did not move, but their snarling increased in pitch and volume, and their bodies flexed and strained as if against invisible leashes.

He stopped moving his hand, leaving it suspended in the air.

Something in his peripheral vision caught his eye. It

looked like a child's doll at first, red and white debris pulled apart and lying in patches on the grass. And then he saw the head and realized it was a house cat, torn to shreds for sport.

If he went for his gun now, he might be able to get one of them, but the others would be on him before he could re-aim. His only chance was to make it to the fence and leap over.

Keeping his eyes on the dogs, he began to walk purposefully forwards.

On cue, they separated; two of them moving in opposing arcs towards him while the other one stalked towards Lionel slowly.

'Sara,' he hissed, his mouth not moving.

The dogs were closer now, less than ten feet.

'Sara.'

Lionel looked over his shoulder at the lead dog, who was now stationed directly behind him. The other two dogs were on either side of him, snapping their teeth and lunging.

He made a decision – he could make it. It would take one leap, he would favour his good leg, lift it high enough on to the top of the fence, the momentum would carry his centre of gravity over, and he could topple on to the other side.

He took a final look at the dog behind him and broke for the fence.

Immediately the dog behind him jerked forwards, its mouth open and teeth bared.

Lionel pushed himself off his left foot as he ran towards

the fence, then raised his right knee and stretched out his arms to grab the top.

Only his knee didn't lift far enough. It couldn't. It was still frozen, the scar tissue from Sara's attack robbing it of the precise amount of strength it needed to lift high enough to clear the fence.

He collapsed in pain on to the grass. Above him, Sara's head appeared above the fence, looking down at him with an unfathomable expression.

Lionel looked up at Sara, his mind scrambling back to the night in the safe house and the flesh wound she had given him, a wound that seemed to miss the mark one month ago and yet now robbed him of exactly the amount of strength he needed to escape. Before his mind could think through the implications, he screamed.

'No!'

They were the last words he said before the dogs set on him.

17

Sara ran out of the gate at the bottom of the garden and into the path she had walked down earlier.

She was waiting for it to hit her. The sight of Baz's blasted head, the wet splatter of his blood and brains on her face. The sight of Lionel set on by dogs, their huge animal heads shaking to pull pieces of his body apart.

Behind her, two men lay dead.

Her heart raced, and a queasy feeling roiled inside her.

She hunched over, waiting for her stomach to spasm and gorge to rise. Nothing came out, and she spat on to the ground.

She staggered down the path, placing her palms on to the fence walls for balance. Ahead of her lay Baz's body, his still form lying in a pool of red-black blood.

Her stomach twisted again, and she felt blood rush to her head, making her feel woozy and light-headed. She weaved through the garden of 327 and gripped the door handle of the kitchen. Her mouth flooded with saliva, and she doubled over, waiting for the vomit to appear.

Behind her, she could hear the sounds of dogs chomping on wet flesh.

When the tide of sickness never arrived, she pulled down the handle and pushed the kitchen door open.

The kitchen was filthy. Piles of dirty crockery lay stacked on the counters, and black mould sprouted in the corners of the cupboards and floor.

'Mother! Are you here?'

Her voice echoed through the house.

In the living room, the only pieces of furniture were a stained couch that ran along one wall and a chipped coffee table.

Sara's breath was getting more and more shallow, on the edge of anxiety, and she didn't notice the motorcycle helmet sitting on the coffee table until she was almost at the front door.

She walked back slowly and looked at it for a long time, as if expecting it to disappear like a mirage.

She reached down and picked it up. The outer casing was large and bulbous, but the interior padding created a much smaller cavity. She realized it belonged to a woman.

And that's when she heard it.

The sound of water.

Coming from upstairs.

Someone was running a bath.

Sara climbed the stairs slowly, her breath coming in shallow wheezes, walked along the landing and stood in front of the open bathroom door.

Inside, an attractive woman in her late thirties, dressed in a black leather motorcycle one-piece, sat on the edge of the bath as the taps ran, filling the tub with water. Her long brown hair fell over one shoulder.

Sara tried to speak but couldn't catch her breath.

'Show me your hand,' said the woman.

Sara looked back at her, confused.

'Your hand, hold it up,' the woman demanded.

Sara held her hand in front of her.

'Look: there's no tremor any more,' said the woman. 'That sickness you're feeling. It's adrenaline. You're not traumatized. You're energized.'

Sara realized the woman was right. The things she had witnessed should have engulfed her in a wave of horror. But the wave never arrived. She crouched down and forced herself to take several deep breaths.

'Who are you?' she said at last.

The woman looked at Sara, as if for the first time. Her eyes were dark, with an intelligence in them that took everything in.

'You already know who I am.'

Sara nodded, as if to herself.

'How did you know to find me here?'

'The same way you knew you'd find me here,' her mother replied.

18

'Sit down. We are going to finish what we started.'

The bath was almost full, and her mother turned the taps off, letting silence return to the house. Next to her, a long slab of corkboard rested against the far wall.

'Why did you make me forget?' asked Sara, stepping into the bathroom.

Her mother looked away, her eyes alighting on something at the other end of the bath.

'Look what's still here,' she said to herself.

She reached out and picked up the four, yellowing scraps of paper that were resting on the edge of the bath, the edges fishtailing up.

'I sat here for the first few hours. Watching you. That first time,' she said, as if in a dream. 'Doodling. You always loved anagrams.'

She held up the words for Sara to look at.

Phoebe. A. Wife. Rests.

Sara stared at them for a few seconds before looking up at her mother.

'Beware. Of. The. Spies.'

'Good girl,' smiled her mother. 'Take these.'

She held out two tablets in the palm of her hand.

'Your name's Phoebe,' said Sara. 'I remember now.'

'Too late,' said Phoebe. 'It's time to forget.'

'I don't want to forget,' said Sara. 'I want to go with you.'

'They'll find me, eventually,' said Phoebe. 'They'll try to take me back. But I won't go back.' Emotion crept into her voice. 'I won't go back. Ever. And nor will you. It's too late for me, but I can give you freedom.'

Sara held up her hands and fought to keep the panic from her voice. 'Mother, listen to me. I don't know what we're running from. But whatever it is, we can fight it. Or run from it. Together.'

Phoebe stopped and looked at her.

'You have no idea who we are dealing with. Just take the tablets.'

Sara took the tablets and threw them at the wall.

'I want some answers. Now.'

Phoebe stood up and pulled the blind away from the window, peering through the frosted glass.

'We don't have much time, Sara. You have to trust me. This process will take a few hours. And they are already looking for you. They'll come here, eventually.'

Sara shook her head in confusion. She was crying now, her cheeks wet with tears, their taste salty where they ran into the corner of her mouth.

'What's wrong with you?' she said, her voice incredulous. She looked at her mother in dismay. The woman standing in front of her was inaccessible, focused on only one thing.

'You've already begun to remember,' said Phoebe.

'Each day you're coming into more of your power. They won't stop until they find you. Sara, look at me.'

Sara brushed her tears away roughly with the back of her forearm and looked at her mother.

'Don't trust me,' said Phoebe, 'trust your heart. If you still don't think what I'm telling you is right, we can leave together right now.'

Phoebe stretched out her hand to Sara, palm upwards. Sara looked at her mother's hand with trepidation for a few seconds and then reached out and held it in her own.

She had no idea how long they were connected. It could have been a few minutes or several hours. When she finally broke contact, Sara backed away as far as she could until her back hit the bathroom wall.

'No, no, no!' was all Sara could whisper to herself.

What she had seen continued to throb through her like an electrical current.

'Here,' said her mother. Her palm was outstretched again, this time with two more tablets sitting within it.

Sara looked back at her with apprehension and then nodded to her mother.

She watched as her mother crushed the two tablets with the flat of a dirty spoon and dragged the powder across the tile into a glass of water.

Sara drank it, swiftly, in two gulps, in case she changed her mind. She took off her jeans and top and walked towards the bath.

Before she could get in, her mother stopped her and pulled her into an embrace that was so tight it startled her.

Sara buried her face in her mother's hair and inhaled its scent, desperate to store as much of it away as she could.

And then it hit her. The memories she had experienced when she stood in front of Janey's hospital bed. They were not memories. They were what was unfolding in front of her, right now.

Her mother released her, and Sara moved towards the tub without looking back.

She sank into the warm water, the pads of the earphones pressed to her ears, her mother's taped words like a lullaby in her head.

Above her, Phoebe lifted the corkboard in her arms.

A profound sense of surrender washed over Sara, a hundred times more powerful than the final tug of sleep at the end of each day.

Before the lid blacked out all light, a thought occurred to Sara, and she mumbled to her mother.

'What's my real name?'

Before she heard any reply, strange sounds and images swam into her disintegrating consciousness as the final residues of her memory began to fade, like a sand structure washed away with the tide.

Then the world went black.

19

'I don't believe it.'

The words groped towards Sara through the darkness. And then suddenly the lid was pulled away, and her whole world was blinding light.

A shadow loomed over her.

'It's her again.'

Sara winced as she opened her eyes and stared directly up. The policeman's face was mottled red as he bent over the tub and stared at her.

Strong hands lifted Sara out of the bath and wrapped her in a towel. A woman with thick-rimmed glasses stood next to the policeman, staring at Sara as if she was an apparition.

'Do you remember me?' asked the lady, finally, her voice shaky with emotion. 'I'm Claire. A month ago? I found you. Here.'

Sara looked at her blankly.

Claire was about to say something else when the policeman pointed to a pile of clothes on the floor.

'Get her dressed,' he said.

Claire hesitated, swallowing her words, and reached down and picked up the jeans. As she passed them to Sara, a plastic bag fell out of the rear pocket and dropped to the floor.

The policeman picked it up, holding it up to get a better look.

'It's the things we found with her last time,' said Claire. 'The locket and the picture of the man.'

She took the bag from him and handed it back to Sara.

Sara walked down the stairs, numb. She tried to remember how she had arrived at the house, but her memory dead-ended ten minutes before. Her mind was a flat battery, turning over silently.

Claire and the police officer flanked her on either side.

Sara could hear the police officer whisper to Claire.

'What's going to happen to her?'

Claire's voice was artificially upbeat, as if she knew Sara was listening.

'I'm going to apply for an emergency protective order. Give the state custody. We're going to find her somewhere safe, far away from here. No one's going to get to her again.'

PART SIX

20

1997

'What happened, Sara?'

The counsellor's office was both cosy and anonymous at the same time. Posters of boy bands adorned the walls, soft toys spilled out of a chest in the corner and a foot-tall Buddha statue smiled benignly from the edge of the desk. The room resembled the love-child of an office and a girl's bedroom, a simulacrum of intimate personal space relatable to all. Boxes of tissues sat on every table.

The counsellor's face was the subject of much derisive conversation over the lunch tables of the school, but in truth few girls left her office dry-eyed. That face was perfectly created as a catalyst for tears: eyes perpetually brimful of pity, mouth trembling in anticipation, voice quavering with infinite understanding.

They had surrounded Sara in one of the school hallways an hour earlier. The corridor was a noisy river of children, whose chatter ricocheted around the enclosed space, causing kids to raise their voices to be heard, which echoed even more loudly around them, creating a loop that kept ratcheting up the volume.

There were three of them: one alpha and two others.

No one noticed when they yanked Sara out of the stream into a recessed area near a water fountain.

'She wants to see your lunch money,' said one of the beta girls, nodding to the alpha, who was a head and shoulders taller than the others.

Sara crossed her arms protectively, hugging her satchel to her chest.

The alpha's arm whipsawed outwards, like a cobra striking, smacking into Sara's bag and gripping the strap.

Sara didn't know what made one of the beta girls gasp. And then she looked down and found one of her own arms was extended, the fist embedded in the armpit of the alpha, the other hand holding on to the alpha's hand, two fingers circling the wrist.

The alpha looked at her, face darkening with anger, other arm rising.

Sara watched the scene play out as if she was an observer to it, like it was someone else's hand gripping the girl's hand, and then someone else's arms push-pulling with a single pump, dislocating the girl's shoulder with a sickening pop.

A pregnant pause, and then a scream that mingled pain, outrage and self-pity in equal measure layered itself on to the deafening chorus around them.

'Is there someone you are angry with, Sara?' asked the counsellor, her voice as soft as a feather bed. 'It's OK to be angry.'

Sara didn't feel angry. The only emotion she felt, which accompanied her throughout each day like a shadow, was a sense of amputation. It was like she was missing a limb. Or like she was a child from a children's story, kidnapped from the royal family and raised as a pauper, who cannot explain the yearning she feels when she stares up at the palace walls. This was not the life she was meant to be leading. Some essential part of her had been taken, and the person left behind was strange, with a nature she could not understand.

'We can talk about things here, Sara,' continued the counsellor. 'This is a safe place. No judgements. I know about your special background. Talking about it is the best way to heal.'

But Sara didn't want to talk about it. How can you tell someone that you only have four years of memory to rely on? She was an infant housed in a teenager's body. How can you tell someone you just met that you know they live in a small flat with a salmon-coloured carpet, alone other than a Siamese cat who shares each evening meal with her? Sara doesn't know if these thoughts are real or not, but has learned the best way to avoid trouble is to keep her mouth shut.

'Well, are you going to say anything, Sara?' A note of disappointment crept into the counsellor's voice.

After a period of silence, the counsellor sat back in her seat, a look of despondency on her face.

21

2000

Tick tick tick tick tick.

Sara stared at the wall of the headmistress's study. Its entire surface was covered with clocks. They beat asynchronously, creating overlapping waves of sound that washed across the room.

One particular clock transfixed her. An old-fashioned Swiss, complete with two miniature wooden platforms. A carved female figure with braided hair in a dirndl stood on the extended right platform. Sara stared at the other side of the clock, where the left platform stood empty, projecting out from a tiny dark doorway.

'Sara?'

Sara couldn't take her eyes off that opening. There was something terrifying about it. Anything could be crouching in the darkness, waiting to come out.

'Sara.'

The voice was louder and broke the spell. Sara turned around to face the headmistress. She was in her sixties, dressed in black jacket and trousers. Her face was large and round, the main features disproportionately gathered together in the centre, leaving a wide perimeter of flesh underemployed.

She was standing behind her desk, staring down at a piece of paper.

'Sit down,' she said.

Sara sat. She recognized the paper. It had been torn out of her exercise book an hour earlier, seconds before the class erupted into chaos.

'This school was built to house girls with troubled pasts . . .' began the headmistress, walking to the window and looking out. She still had not made eye contact with Sara. '. . . so I wasn't concerned by your history: expelled from three schools in three years. I looked at your admissions file. All that brawling, with students and teachers. I recognized an anger in you that I've seen in other girls abandoned by their families. I felt I could help.'

Sara disconnected from the headmistress's voice. She was still struggling to comprehend what had happened in the classroom. She had been staring out of the window, the teacher's voice drifting in and out of her consciousness, merging at times with the drone of the lawnmower outside. Sara's hand idly doodled in the margins of her exercise book, scribbling patterns in an easy, hypnotic flow as she watched the gardener perched on the ride-on lawnmower execute lazy figure-eights in the grass. Then the teacher appeared over her shoulder and was wrenching the book from her grasp, and all hell broke loose.

'Do you know what you wrote, Sara?' asked the headmistress, meeting her eyes for the first time. She walked slowly back to the desk and lifted up the scrap of paper.

Sara's mouth was dry, and she fought the feeling that was rising up in her. It started in her chest, like a bird trapped inside the skeletal cage of her ribs. It fluttered and beat around inside her, banging into the bones and organs in a state of agitation. It crowded out the air from her lungs and kept her breathing in shallow gasps.

She took an involuntary glance back at the Swiss clock, staring into the shadow of the opening.

'One of the staff speaks Arabic,' said the headmistress. 'They translated it for me.'

Sara looked back at the desk. She could see the paper now. A densely printed cursive script covered the top half of the page. The writing meant nothing to her: just a decorative font with no meaning.

'It's a martyr's confession, Sara.'

The headmistress looked at her closely, as if the essence of her could be gleaned from her features.

'When did you learn Arabic?'

Sara held her eye but didn't respond. She doesn't speak Arabic. At least, the person she believes she is does not speak it. But she has long ago given up the search for a demarcation line between who she is and who she is not. There is the person she thinks she is, and there is the other person. A being that lives in her shadows. A creature who could emerge at any time and fracture any sense of normality she has.

'I . . .' she began, and then petered out.

'As a last-resort school, expulsion is against our credo. But you are eighteen in three months,' said the headmistress. 'Consider yourself suspended until then. That means you don't need to come back. I thought I could help you. I was wrong. Whoever you really are is worse than I imagined.'

Sara turned to leave. She had stepped over the threshold of the door when the clocks on the wall began pealing, striking the hour with an atonal concert of bells and chimes. She stopped, rooted to the spot, staring at the Swiss clock and the dark portal. The blonde girl was retreating, and something else was emerging from the shadows.

Sara watched, her mouth dry.

'Goodbye, Sara,' came the headmistress's voice.

On the right side of the clock, the female figure was almost gone. And on the left, two extended wooden arms were coming into view. The fingers were stretched and twisted, like the gnarled branches of a tree.

Before she could see what emerged, the door slammed shut.

The driveway of the school inclined down towards the main road, where it dead-ended in a set of high steel gates.

Sara walked towards the main road with a purpose.

This school had as little claim on her as any of the others in the last six years. They all blurred together in her memory.

Before she reached the gates, she left the road and ducked into a dense bush. By the base of the trunk was a collection of flat stones arranged into a heap.

Sara kicked the piles of stones, dug off the top layer

of soil and pulled out a dirt-encrusted backpack she had buried there the day she arrived.

With school over, there was nothing left to stop her now.

Her path was clear.

She needed to unlock the secret of her past.

And inside the backpack were the only clues she had.

22

The white strobe pummelled the walls of the nightclub.

Sara looked through the tinted window to the dance floor, two storeys below, where clubbers silently bobbed and churned.

The office was a black box tucked into the upper reaches of the converted warehouse, like a birds' nest folded up into the corner of a roof. An aerial gangway projected out from its front door to the middle of the ceiling, where it met a circular staircase dropping down to the floor.

'This is the full kit.'

She looked away from the window and returned her attention to the boy. He was in his late teens, with a shaven head, emaciated frame and dirty t-shirt – the calling cards of the hacker, more focused on the mind than the body. Clear, blue, intelligent eyes stared at her from beneath a high forehead. She had forgotten his name since their meeting yesterday; there seemed little point storing away what was obviously a handle.

He waved a hand across the desk – lying there was a passport, driver's licence and phone – and picked up each item, turning it over in his hands like a collector as he described the artisanal efforts that went into creating it.

Sara found she was zoning out, catching only brief phrases of his commentary, like listening to a radio station that was drifting. A sense of unease had been dogging her all day, a feeling that something had happened in the last twenty-four hours that would have terrible consequences for her, like a wave displaced by an undersea earthquake that builds in size and speed as it rolls inexorably towards a beach where bathers sit watching a flat sea.

He had finished speaking and was looking at her, waiting for a response. She forced herself back to the present.

'And the things I showed you yesterday?' she asked.

The boy shook his head. 'Not much.'

He leaned over his laptop, his fingers lightly flicking the keys.

'FRS is just developing now . . .' He squinted into his laptop screen.

'FRS?' asked Sara.

'Facial recognition software,' he explained. 'It wasn't a bad picture,' he said, looking up briefly.

Sara walked around the desk. On the laptop screen was a digital copy of her Polaroid, sliced into cubes through a superimposed grid. The boy had toyed with light and contrast, tightening the images. The man's face was clearer, sharper, and she could see for the first time the colour of his eyes. Ice-blue.

'But I checked the registers. Nothing.' He tapped the return button and stood up. The image disappeared.

'What else can I try?'

The boy inclined his head to one side and then another, like a street vendor deciding whether to accept an offer.

'Your best solution now is time. The FRS will develop. Two, three, maybe five years. Maybe more.'

The enormity of the time frame spread out ahead of her, giving her a dizzying sense of vertigo. Each time she felt like she was getting close, her prize pulled away, like a magnetic children's toy whose pieces repel each other when they come in close proximity.

The boy was talking again, pointing to a new picture on his laptop: her locket and chain.

'. . . told you yesterday. It's plastic, not worth anything. I recognized the design. It's an ancient symbol, a protection from evil. Now the number . . .'

He toggled a switch, and multiple perspectives of the locket flashed on screen until it settled on a close-up of the underside.

'I don't know if you've seen this, but it's got some sort of code printed on it: 515195140126923. Nothing came up on the registers for this either. Could be a distributor's serial. Or a manufacturer's stamp. But even assuming it is one of those, it won't get you any closer to who gave it to you.'

Sara visibly deflated. The boy's reputation as an identity thief and procurer was unrivalled.

She remained standing in front of him. Something he had said had snagged a tripwire in her mind, alerting her to something, although she wasn't sure of what.

'You told me you wouldn't show these to anyone

else,' she said, groping towards the alarm system sounding like a growing klaxon in her mind.

'I didn't,' replied the boy, bristling.

'But . . . you just said you did a web search . . .' replied Sara, still unsure of what she was trying to say.

The boy relaxed visibly. 'That's not public. I use topline VPNs and DNS redirectors. No way anyone could trace my searches back. You don't have to worry . . .'

Sara didn't hear the rest of his reply. Her focus was snatched by an electric shock that started in the base of her spine and spread in concussion waves, flowering up along her upper back and neck. Her head dipped, a reflex, as if someone had crept up behind her and had taken a swing from behind. She spun around, looking in shock at the empty room.

Sara fought for breath, her heart rate spiking as fight-or-flight responses fired throughout her system. She ran to the window and looked down.

At first, she saw nothing other than flashes of light. Then, on the ground floor, she saw them. A group of men in suits scanning the crowd, heads swivelling, searching the space.

'There's no need to freak . . .'

His voice trailed off as he joined her at the window and followed her gaze. The men had regrouped and were pushing through the crowd towards the base of the stairs leading to the office. Two bouncers blocked their way, and a mute but hostile exchange was happening.

'Is there another way out of here?' asked Sara.

'They have nothing to do with . . .' started the boy.

But he didn't take his eyes off the window. Below, the bouncers were keeling over, tipping over the balustrades, and the men were moving up the stairs, the flashing light of the strobe making it seem like their bodies were teleporting forwards in tiny increments. They would be at the front door of the office in seconds.

'Shit,' said the boy, his assured demeanour faltering.

He ran behind his desk, stood on his chair and reached for a clasp embedded in the ceiling.

Sara looked back through the window. The men had reached the top of the stairs and were looking directly at her from the other end of the aerial walkway.

She swivelled and saw the legs of the boy disappearing up into the hatch door.

A thudding sound was getting louder and louder in her head, overpowering her ability to think. It swelled, thumping in her chest and tingling down her arms and legs. The gap between the concussions was getting longer, matching the interval of her breaths.

She willed her legs to move. The feet stamping on the metal gangway were loud enough now to be heard over the music. But something was disconnected in Sara, her body was no longer receiving signals from her mind. She looked up at the hanging hatch door, tantalizingly close, willing herself to dive on to the desk and spring up into it.

The sound in her head was deafening now, crowding out all other noise, leaving her in a cocoon swaddled in a primitive heartbeat. She noticed that time was down-shifting gears, grinding to a crawl, every ion in the room seeming to vibrate in slow motion.

And then the door was opening, swinging inwards, pulsing with the time-lapse effect of the strobe, arcing with the ricochet force from a horizontal stamp with a heavy boot.

Sara stood in the centre of the floor, frozen, her eyes wide, watching as the men surged inside, flowing like water into the room. They broke over her, a rock in the centre of a stream, and carried on to the desk, where they peered up into the black square above them. First one, then another hoisted themselves up, disappearing into the boxy maw, while the final man rushed out through the front door, pounding back along the metal bridge, leaving Sara standing amidst visible slipstreams left in their wake that hung in the air around her like stardust. She traced them with her eyes, the only soundtrack to the silence being the systolic-diastolic beat in her ears.

Sara took an enormous involuntary inhalation, the deep survival breath of someone who had been oxygen-deprived to the limits of their ability. The world folded in on itself, and, with an audible pop, the music came crashing back.

She looked around her in confusion. The door was shut, and heavy boots were again clanging towards her, like the needle of time had skipped its groove. For the briefest of moments, the stardust hung in the air, a shimmering trail left by the men's invasion of the room seconds before. She looked at the slipstreams and realized what she needed to do.

*

Bonner, Jonas and Page kicked down the door and burst into the Portakabin that functioned as the office of the nightclub. GCHQ had tracked the IP address linked to the Orpheus-related searches to this geo-location.

Furnishings were perfunctory – a desk, a filing cabinet, stacks of servers – and there were no corners in which to hide. Their eyes were drawn immediately to the hanging attic door, swaying slightly. From his crash through the door, Bonner vaulted up on to the desk and wedged his shoulders into the cramped space in one fluid movement. Jonas followed and Page, hearing the muffled order from Bonner, turned and ran back the way they came to close down any exits.

Sara crawled out from under the desk. Above her, she could hear the two men crawling along the floor of the attic on their hands and knees.

Before she left, she took the various accessories of the personality the boy had made her – passport, phone, driver's licence – and threw them in the wire bin by the desk. That identity was burned. And she knew now she could not trust anyone else in the future. If she was going to stay ahead of those pursuing her, she would need to teach herself how to live off the radar.

23

Sara sat on the roof, her feet hanging over the edge.

From her eyrie, she could see the spiked skyline of the City and the low-slung neighbourhoods of the West End.

She had discovered her refuge weeks before, after a random memory popped into her mind. A poetry class at school. Sara staring out of the window at rain-sodden playing fields. Her only recall of what was taught was a single line still lodged in her mind. *Only the birds leave no footprints.*

It was the answer to a problem that had been plaguing her since she had arrived in London.

And so now she spent as much of her time here as possible, above the reach of the half a million CCTV cameras that blanketed the capital's streets.

Ten floors below her, nightingales were singing in the trees that lined the pavement.

Dusk was settling. It would soon be dark, and she would need to find a place to sleep.

Each night brought the same choice. Hotel or empty house. The streets were never an option for Sara. She considered herself home-free rather than home-less.

She reached into her jacket and pulled out the wedge of paper, unfolding it several times. Her sketch of the city wasn't perfect but was accurate enough to pinpoint the location of each of the sites.

She had stumbled on to the first of them a few days ago, unconsciously, during one of her long walks. Her feet had begun moving of their own accord, veering off in a new direction, as if the sudden stimulus of her surroundings had hijacked her navigation system. More curious than scared, she had let herself be led. Ten minutes later, she was in a part of London that she had never been in and yet, at the same time, felt oddly familiar. It was like inhabiting a fully realized moment of déjà vu.

She eventually stopped in front of a derelict building in south London, an abandoned pub, and prised open one of the boarded-up windows.

Her steering mechanism guided her through the shelled-out interior to an empty room at the back.

It was behind several loose bricks above the fireplace.

A black metal box.

She pulled it out and looked around her, half expecting to see someone step out of the shadows and reclaim their prize. But the building was silent.

She opened the box, not breathing, unsure of what horrors her unconscious mind may have guided her to.

To her surprise, what lay inside were several passports, a brick of fifty-pound notes, a stack of plastic drivers' licences held together with an elastic band and another stack of credit cards held together with a black bulldog clip.

Sara emptied the box out and crammed the contents

into her pockets before pushing the container back into the crevice and refilling the space with the bricks.

She was too smart to use the identities or credit cards. Whoever had left them there would no doubt be monitoring them, able to trace the new covers.

Leave no footprints.

But false identities could be altered, photos replaced and electronic tags or chips stripped out. As a last resort, there were plenty of fences who would pay good money for them as is.

She took five notes from the brick of money and checked into a hotel that night, treating herself to starched sheets and a stocked mini-bar that tinkled merrily when the fridge door opened.

When sleep finally claimed her, her dreams were vivid. They guided her, like a ghost, down walkways in London to multiple locations. It felt as if the dream lasted all night, and she woke up feeling washed out. She shook the feeling off and grabbed a pen and paper, writing as much down as she could before the images in her mind evaporated like mist.

They were all dead drops, scattered around London like a dark version of an Easter egg hunt. Empty cisterns in public toilets, flues in disused chimneys.

She knew her time was limited. Now she had found one of them, they would be watching the others. She had given herself a few days to raid each one.

It took her hours to reach the park, even though it was less than a mile away from the roof where she was sitting.

She increased the counter-surveillance each time, walking in circles and doubling back on herself many times, keeping an eye on her reflection in store windows, seeking out a tail.

When she finally walked into the park, the tree branches were silhouetted against moonlight, swaying like arabesques in the wind. The air felt sweeter in here than outside, although it could have been her imagination.

She walked along the perimeter path that hugged the railings separating the urban oasis from the street. Other than the ambient hiss of the park at night, the only other sounds were her footsteps, crunching out and releasing into the air, reverberating in the stillness.

After ten minutes of walking, she was sure there was no one following her and began to look for a path to the centre.

And that's when she heard it.

The echoes of her footsteps had shifted and changed, a different sound emerging, like a layer peeling away revealing . . . a heavier footstep behind her.

Someone in thick leather soles, coming up at a fast pace.

Sara looked over her shoulder, and the other footsteps stopped. There was no one in sight, although much of the park remained cloaked in shadow. She glanced quickly around and then resumed walking again. After a pause, the other footsteps restarted, faster this time, beating out a pulse.

Sara broke into a run, furious at herself for being lulled by the seeming stillness of the park.

The other footsteps became quicker and heavier, and a male voice squawked something indistinct into a radio.

The exit was in front of her now, an ornate wrought-iron gate half open, and she lunged through it, her peripheral vision registering the two cars speeding towards her from opposite directions.

She cleared the pavement in two strides and sprinted across the street.

'It's her!'

A blur of movement in her vision, and suddenly there was a car sliding in front of her, jerking forward with the force of a sudden stop. Sara kept moving, the momentum carrying her over the bonnet, somewhere between a roll and a slide, as the front doors popped open and men spilled out.

'Don't fire!' cried a voice nearby.

She swung to the left and ran down a side street, moving by impulse, her eyes barely taking in her surroundings, the world around her a jarring mess of colours.

She could hear car doors slam as half the pursuing force piled back into the vehicles while the others kept up the foot pursuit.

The street was narrow, and ahead she could see a blank brick wall.

A cul-de-sac.

There was no choice but to keep running. She didn't dare look behind her, but she could hear the steam-hiss of their breaths as they gained ground.

Up ahead was a side alley, and she twisted and entered

it at full speed, suddenly aware how narrow it was, a tapering canyon.

Behind her, a voice was narrating her movements, relaying them to the vehicles, prompting them to a new destination.

The alleyway elevated ahead, hump-backing into a pedestrian bridge.

She could see to the other side of the overpass, where two cars scissored to a stop at the other side, cutting off any escape.

She was out of choices.

She launched herself up the incline, sprinting to the apex. Behind her, trailing feet feeling like they were close enough to clip her heels.

She heard it before she saw it.

A clattering, rushing sound and a flash of silver below her.

Ahead, men in suits were running towards her from the other side. They were less than ten yards away now.

'There's nowhere to run, Sara!'

She grabbed the railing, taking a deep breath and vaulting into the darkness, her body floating, the stars above her and the rushing train below, for a fraction of a second seeing the faces on the bridge staring down, and then the speeding roof hit her like a missile and she was holding on with everything she had, the bridge flying away at speed behind her.

24

One year ago

The woman walked down the gravel path that cut through the centre of the trimmed quad in front of the university science park.

She was tall, with long chestnut hair drawn into a ponytail. Pods of bearded students looked up from plastic tables to watch her as she passed by.

Her beauty had been an uncomfortable fact that had settled on her in her late teenage years, like a deformity she could not remove. She had no time or inclination for romantic attention, so the ubiquitous male stares were not part of a reality she wished to share. She wore no make-up and did as little as possible to enhance her genetics. A blank mien was the only thing she painted on before she left the house each morning.

As she walked, she pulled the pill bottle from her bag and shook it into her cupped palm. The feeble rattle from the container indicated she needed to find a way to refill it again. She would worry about that later. She popped two tablets into her mouth and swallowed with a practised flick of her head.

The voices in her head had been hissing all morning.

During childhood, those voices had ruled her, making

her doubt her sanity, separating her from the pack, isolating her. But leaving school had not denied her an education. She had seen to that. *The Handbook of Clinical Psychopharmacology* was a fixture in most public libraries and had become her most trusted counsellor. It advised, among other things, that antipsychotics were the main medicine used to treat schizoid voices.

It turned out Risperidone and Olanzapine could be found in most high-street chemists, where security is low at night and break-ins infrequent and rarely investigated. A carton of orange juice was the accompanying ingredient, Vitamin C being an effective delivery agent, guiding drugs immediately into the bloodstream. She had become a chemist in her late teenage years.

The effect of the drugs was pleasing to her, making her feel snug, insulated. Her mind, continually pressed against the windows of her eyes like a child watching a street parade from a bedroom window, now sat back in a place deep inside her skull. It was like an overstuffed chair had been built deep inside her head for her to sink into and watch the world go by.

Her hyper-alertness, the sense that she was connected to everything and everything was connected to her, had dampened. The memory of her teenage years – the psychotic breaks, the isolation, the paranoia – all felt distant now, a lawless border town that had been one stop in her long journey.

She kept walking at the same pace to the marble front stairs of the university science buildings. The front door was locked through an automatic key swipe system. She pulled out an electromagnet the size of a snail's shell and placed it on the white box housing the swipe system. She flipped a switch on the top, and the device magnetized with an audible hum, suctioning itself to the white casing of the key card system. After a few seconds, the locking system shut down, and the heavy front double door popped and drifted open.

She pushed through the doors and walked through the ornate, cavernous entrance hall and up the second set of stairs leading to the second floor.

At the top of the stairs, the corridor stretched out in both directions, and in front of her was a glass case containing a list of offices and their occupants. She pulled out her phone and checked a name against the list and then turned and walked down the left-hand corridor, the heels of her boots striking the marble floor and echoing off the walls.

She stopped in front of an office, which had the name 'Doctor Oliver Seers' stencilled on to the crenel-lated glass. She knocked on the door three times with the heel of her hand rather than her knuckles, a confident knock.

'Yeh!'

The voice from within was young, and the accent mid-Atlantic.

She opened the door and walked inside. The interior of the room was as far away from an academic's room as you could possibly imagine. The room was large and dominated by three long lab benches piled high with computer equipment and monitors: enormous stacks of self-assembled hardware, wires springing out at all angles. Almost every square inch of the floor was covered with servers and memory stacks, other than a trail that led from the door to where he sat. The hum of the computers was matched only by the chilly buzz of the air-conditioning units perched on tables. Crumpled cans of energy drinks littered the floor.

The man sat on a high stool, his fingers clattering on the keyboard in front of him. In scruffy trainers, ripped jeans and baggy t-shirt, he looked more like a young offender than an academic.

'Oliver Seers?' she asked.

'Yes,' he replied, looking at her absent-mindedly.

'I hear you've just made a breakthrough on a next-gen FRS.'

'Sorry, who are you?'

Sara Eden closed the door behind her and then locked it.

A look of apprehension passed over Seers' face.

'This is a restricted-access building. You're not allowed . . .'

Sara walked through the stacks of equipment towards his desk. She then reached into her pocket, slowly enough that it caused him to flinch, and pulled out a thick stack of £50 notes.

'Your department just experienced thirty per cent cuts: a tough time for researchers. All I want is one search.'

Seers looked at her for a second, wavering, then reached out and put his hand over the stack.

'The AI in typical facial recognition software is pretty low-level,' said Seers, his demeanour visibly more relaxed, 'other than small variations, it's usually matching like-for-like. We put in an additional AI layer that uses data forecast models that take into account the effects of ageing.'

'A short way of saying that would be, if I had a picture from twenty-five years ago, you could match that with a picture of the same man today,' said Sara.

'Yes, I mean, the software isn't complete yet, there's still some bugs, but essentially . . .'

Sara nodded and pulled the dog-eared photograph from her pocket.

'OK, so we need to digitize it first, with this scanner.'

He lifted the lid of a portable scanner nearby, placed the photograph face down and then closed the lid. A border of bright light ringed the scanner and a second later he flipped open the lid and handed the photo back to Sara.

'OK, now we just run the picture through all open databases on the web.'

'When shall I come back?' she asked.

'No need, it's done. There was only one hit . . .'

Sara could not see the screen from where she was standing, but she noticed that Seers had gone quiet. He then turned around and looked at her in confusion.

'Looks like that guy is now the head of military intelligence in the UK.'

Seers shifted uneasily as he looked at the picture in Sara's hand.

'I should probably log this search and get your name.'

Sara took a step towards him, and Seers instinctively took a step back. He was taller than her, but there was something in her demeanour that made him anxious.

'What's his name?' she asked.

'I'm going to have to ask you to leave now,' stammered Seers.

Sara leaned over him and looked at the screen.

'Charles Salt,' she read, 'thank you.'

PART SEVEN
Today

25

Heathrow Airport

Caleb Goodspeed looked out of the window of Dr Adina Porter's office. The view was commanding, taking in the entire breadth of both runways. From where he was sitting, the tails of aircraft moved across the bottom border of the window like plastic sharks' fins. A memory popped into his head – his last flight from here, a trip to Barbados – and he swallowed hard to maintain his composure.

Porter pursed her lips and regarded Caleb with cool professional detachment. Everything about her exuded poise and professionalism: from her Chanel trouser suit to the framed photographs on her credenza of her shaking hands with international dignitaries.

'You probably know why I asked you back here, Caleb,' she said. A perfectly manicured scarlet fingernail picked up a piece of lint from her otherwise immaculate leather desk and flicked it into the air.

'Actually, I don't,' said Caleb.

'You're not a very convincing liar,' she smiled. 'Two years ago, you called me out of the blue and told me my new programme of training officers to detect suspicious passenger behaviour would fail. I chose to ignore your advice. And now we have this.'

She lifted up the newspaper on her desk between her thumb and forefinger as if it was germ-ridden. Caleb didn't need to read the headline, he had seen it earlier that day. A damning report on the fifty-million-pound initiative had been leaked to the press.

'You were right,' she said. 'It failed. I've brought you back so you can tell me why.'

Caleb's eyes flicked over to Edward Freeman, the associate head of security at Heathrow Airport and Porter's number two. His eyes had not left Caleb since Caleb had first walked in. Caleb's Nikes, combat trousers and t-shirt probably didn't help. Freeman looked like he had been pressed from a corporate mid-level executive mould: rail-thin, blue suit, Windsor tie, not one hair out of place and shoelaces double-tied and of equal length. The only movement was the pencil wedged between his index and middle fingers, which wiggled frantically like a hyperactive metronome.

'You were trying to do something that can't be done,' said Caleb. His voice was gravelly and raw, and he cleared his throat before continuing. 'Spotting disguised threat requires intuition, not observation. That can't be taught. It's genetic. The only way that programme would have worked is if you'd hired me to source the right people for you.'

Freeman gave Porter a sideways glance and a raised eyebrow.

'You doubt that I could?' asked Caleb.

'I do,' said Freeman, his voice more forceful than his slight frame would suggest. 'The programme didn't fail because we didn't have the right people. It failed because it was a nineteenth-century solution to the problem. The right answer, the only answer, is technology. We need an upgrade in our software.'

Caleb stood up and walked to the window. In front of him the control tower rose up like a metallic mushroom from the concrete bulk of the main airport building.

'Is that the control tower?'

Freeman spoke before Porter could answer.

'I know where you are going with this. No, it's not fully automated. And yes, we still use controllers . . .'

'Of course you do,' interrupted Caleb. 'The risks are too high not to. Artificial intelligence can never match real intelligence.'

'That's not . . .' started Freeman.

'A hundred billion nerve cells,' said Caleb. 'That's how many the brain has. More than the stars in our galaxy.'

Porter smiled, enjoying the performance, but Freeman's face tightened even further. Caleb pressed on.

'Our brains can make a billion billion calculations per second. A million times faster than the fastest supercomputer today. What if I could prove AI can never match human intuition?'

'That's an empty promise,' said Freeman. 'How can you do that?'

Caleb nodded to the computer sitting on Porter's desk.

'Find me a recent example where your screening systems missed a threat. Show me a picture of the person. I'll tell you what one of my people could have told you.'

Freeman gave Caleb a thin smile.

'Now that's a decent offer.'

He leaned over to Porter and whispered in her ear. She nodded a few times and then typed on the keyboard until she found what she was looking for. She twisted the monitor around.

On it was a pristine, colour digital picture taken by a security camera embedded in a ceiling: a bird's eye view of a young man walking through a metal detector. Behind him was a packed line of travellers waiting their turn. He was in his early twenties, dressed smartly in a blazer.

'Adnan Shawab,' said Freeman. 'A detonator and C-4 found in his briefcase. Our behavioural detectives missed him.'

'Sounds like your baggage screeners missed the explosives too,' muttered Caleb.

Freeman nodded in irritation. 'Touché. Anyway, lucky for us we did a random search.'

'Where was the flight going?' asked Caleb.

'Boston,' replied Freeman.

'The bomb was planted on him. He knew nothing about it,' Caleb responded without a pause.

'How could you possibly . . .' stuttered Freeman.

Caleb ignored him. He dug his hands into his pockets and walked back to the window. 'Three, or four . . . maybe even five. That's the real question.'

He looked back at Freeman, as if just noticing he was in the room.

'Five,' Caleb said definitely, nodding his head. 'That's the answer. Well, the actual answer is three. Look for number three.'

Freeman stared back in confusion.

Caleb then answered slowly, as if to a child. 'Adnan is one of five children. It was the third one that planted the C-4 on him.'

Dr Porter raised a perfectly shaped eyebrow.

'Impressive, Caleb.' She twisted around the screen.

On it was a black-and-white still of a boy in his late teens being dragged out of a house by two masked policemen.

'Fawaz Shawab. Adnan's seventeen-year-old brother. Arrested a few days later. So how did you know?'

Caleb walked over to the computer and tapped a key to recall the prior photograph.

'Look at that face,' he said, pointing to Adnan. 'That's not the face of anyone planning something diabolical. It's studious. And no kid that age dresses like that for a flight. It's too formal. That's a varsity jacket he's wearing. I was going to guess Harvard or Yale. You said he was flying to Boston. So, Harvard. The blazer, it's a uniform, a badge he wears, like a pennant of distinction. He's defined by it. He's not going to blow up a plane. So, the explosives must have been planted. But by whom? We'd normally look for suspect affiliations. But we all know Adnan wouldn't keep that sort of company. The person who did this was family: someone he could not choose. Let's dig deeper. Look at the shoes and the trousers: they're threadbare and they don't fit. Hand-me-downs. This is a smart kid but not a rich one. The family's poor. He's carrying an unusual briefcase. It's a doctor's case: old, but kept in great condition. It's not something you'd buy on purpose, not if you were a foreigner trying to fit into an elite American school. Someone gave it to him, and it never leaves his side. Father, I would say. Shawab is an Egyptian name, a popular one. So, I'd say he's the son of an Egyptian physician and the case is a gift from a proud father. Now here's the tricky part. Proud fathers often mean neglected siblings. And Adnan has them. Quite a few. He's the eldest: academic overachievement is almost always a first sibling trait. So how many others? This was a middle sibling, resentful and radicalized because of the family's economic troubles. Being the middle of five is exponentially more impactful than being in the middle of three, so I guessed five.'

Freeman looked at him, stunned.

'Jesus.'

Dr Porter twisted her swivel chair towards Caleb, in the process turning three-quarters away from Freeman.

'OK, Caleb. Where do we start?'

Caleb took a pen and slip of paper from his jacket pocket and wrote something down, then folded the paper in two. Neither Porter nor Freeman took their eyes off the folded piece of paper that Caleb kept in his hand.

'Step one,' said Caleb, 'you walk me through your

current security measures: armed units, canine teams, baggage screeners and air marshals. Step two, I help you hire appropriate consultants from my network.'

'We're not talking about psychics, are we?' asked Freeman, his face souring. 'The press will string us up if they find we're using psychics.'

'There's no such thing as psychics,' replied Caleb, flatly. 'Anyone who says they're psychic is either lying or mentally ill.'

'How much is this going to cost, Caleb?' asked Porter, keeping things on track.

Caleb placed the folded piece of paper on her desk and pushed it towards her. As she read it, for the first time her poise slipped, and a flicker of anger ran across her face.

'You can't be serious,' she said, looking up at Caleb in surprise.

Caleb walked to the door and opened it. Before he left he turned back to them.

'How much is your passengers' safety worth to you?'

26

Caleb's Range Rover purred as he drove down the corkscrew ramp from the airport car park.

The pitch had gone well. Porter would string out calling him as long as possible, he knew that, just to make a point, and the negotiation would be noisy, as it always was when a client realized Caleb's services were essential. But the job was his.

Caleb twisted the steering wheel, letting the car glide on to the exit road leading back to London. As he did so, he slowly allowed the mental tap he had fastened before the meeting to loosen, releasing the anxieties that had preoccupied him this morning to return.

You are one in a million, Caleb.

He could still hear his mother's voice, clothing the phrase in her sing-song voice.

That was her way of describing his remarkable ability to see beneath the surface of things. It was a proud mother's way of naming something she could not understand. And prescient. After years of studying the fields of intuition, Caleb discovered her phrase was a near-perfect description of the percentage of the population with similar skills.

This month was the tenth anniversary of the launch of his company. The start had not been auspicious. His partner and former best friend had bailed on him at the eleventh hour, almost collapsing the company before it started.

The betrayal turned out to be a blessing of sorts, fuelling Caleb's desire to make the venture succeed. His abilities quickly put him in demand, but then a challenge surfaced that would become his perennial problem: finding others like him.

It turned out it took an intuitive to spot an intuitive. It began with a clue – maybe an unguarded expression, maybe some pattern in personal history. Sometimes it snagged Caleb without him even registering it consciously. But the moment it did, he plunged in immediately, a deep data dive into the person's background and history. Extraordinary empathic ability was like a radioactive isotope, leaving hot traces in its wake: schooling, likes and dislikes, relationship history, all data points became binary to him as they were processcd to see if the person was unique. A sensitive. With a threshold amount of biographical information, Caleb had learned to spot a fellow member of the tribe in seconds.

But quantifying ability didn't turn out to be the problem. The issue was finding enough candidates so he could beat the odds. *One in a million*. The phrase now haunted him.

With his small consulting network already straining to capacity, and without an ability to find the required million subjects, the Heathrow job was a pipe dream.

Caleb's mind was brought back to the present by a

black Mercedes E Class sliding into the lane in front of him, close enough that he pumped his brakes and lurched forwards in his seat. There was something unusual about the car that Caleb couldn't put his finger on. Without lingering on it, he swore under his breath and checked his mirror to see if the fast lane was safe to overtake.

At the same time, an identical Mercedes accelerated along the fast lane and drew alongside Caleb's car. It had the same tinted windows as the car in front, making it impossible to see inside.

Caleb then realized what he had missed before. The bodies of both cars hung low to the ground. That meant their shells were armour-plated, bullet- and bomb-proof.

He looked into the rearview mirror to see a third car pull into position immediately behind him, and on his left a fourth car appeared from nowhere and drove up parallel to him.

He was boxed in.

The passenger window of the car on Caleb's driver's side glided down, revealing a granite face and a weight-lifter's body jammed into an Armani suit. The man's jacket was open, exposing a shoulder holster and the thick black handle of his gun. He jabbed a finger towards the next exit ramp.

The Mercedes convoy moved as one, sliding across the lanes, corralling the Range Rover and herding it towards the off ramp.

Caleb guided the SUV with care, trying to keep within the tight space the four cars created. His heart pounded in his chest as his mind scrambled to stay ahead of the situation.

Making enemies was not difficult in the private security business. Indeed, it was inevitable. He made a living from thwarting the plans of very bad people, and they rarely took kindly to it. Within the last six months alone he could think of a handful of people who would want him out of business. Permanently.

Observe and analyse: the first step was to know who he was dealing with.

The cars were expensive. Armour plating isn't cheap. This wasn't the cortège of your average gangland thug. The manoeuvre they were executing was not easy either. The drivers were professional, not just muscle taking wheel duties. The man in the passenger seat: there was no sadism in his face. It wasn't the look of someone savouring a prospective kill. It was the blank face of someone communicating an order. This convoy was charged to get Caleb somewhere, to someone exercising the power. But everything about the person behind it remained hidden.

His antenna for threat had kept him safe so far, and he cursed himself for drifting off in a reverie.

His eyes flicked down to his car phone, and he snatched it from its cradle and dialled the police emergency line.

'Can you hear me? Hello?'

The line was dead. There was no static, nor clicks of a call trundling over an exchange, just silence. The phone may as well have been dead. With a chill, he realized they must be using a jammer.

As they approached the exit ramp, two of the cars drove in front of the Range Rover and two dropped behind. The lead cars stopped at the roundabout and then took a turning that was signposted as a dead end.

A mile further, a chain-link barrier separated the road from a private airfield. The procession of cars stopped, and a man exited the front car and unlocked the barrier, pulling the gates open.

The airfield was abandoned. Tarmac stretched out in every direction, its surface raised above the surrounding marshland like a concrete tabletop. The only structure was an enormous aircraft hangar in one corner, which the cars now drove towards.

Caleb considered peeling away from the other cars and making a break for it. But it would have been useless. The surrounding swamp meant there was only one way in and out.

They drove through the open hangar door and parked, sectioning off the SUV and forcing it to stop. Caleb stepped out of the car. It took his eyes a few moments to adjust to the dark interior.

The vast hangar was empty, other than a table set up on retractable legs in the middle of the space.

A man sat on a folding chair behind the table. He was tall, well over six foot, and built like a bear, with a bushy beard that was long enough to obscure his neck. An iPad lay on the table in front of him.

'Hello, Caleb. It's been a while,' said the bearded man cheerfully.

'Robert Waterman,' said Caleb, shaking his head. 'That explains the cloak and dagger.'

'Would you have come otherwise?' asked Waterman. 'No.'

Waterman paused, segueing.

'I was sorry to hear about Tara, Caleb.'

His tone was heartfelt, but Caleb didn't respond.

'You know why you're here,' said Waterman. 'I need your help.'

Caleb shook his head.

'The answer is still no.'

'Try being a little less self-righteous, Caleb,' urged Waterman. 'What happened was a decade ago. I had a family. The government offer was too good to refuse. Would you have done any differently?'

Caleb said nothing, and Waterman let the moment hang before he broke away and lifted the iPad in front of him.

'Tell me what you can about this. If nothing, then you won't see me again.'

'Should you be showing me secret material?' asked Caleb.

'We vetted you,' replied Waterman.

Caleb looked over, despite himself. It was a black-and-white film, taken from an aerial view, of an airfield: buildings set around a single runway. A truck burst through a perimeter fence, followed by flashes that lit up the screen. A lone figure exited the truck and darted around, firing at the figures guarding the base. The clip lasted less than ten seconds.

'This attack took place yesterday on a British army base in Scotland,' said Waterman.

'I didn't read anything about it in the papers,' said Caleb.

'Nor will you,' replied Waterman.

'And you want to know who did it?'

Waterman didn't reply.

Caleb shook his head and sighed. 'I don't work for free, but getting rid of you for good is worth it.'

Caleb took the iPad from Waterman and pressed play, stopping the clip several times to look at the frozen footage. He then handed it back to Waterman.

'Looks like you've lost some top-secret equipment.'

'Explain,' said Waterman.

'The attacker killed three soldiers in the clip I saw. But didn't fire directly at any of them. He was aiming at the spot they were moving to. The only explanation is you must have a weapon with some form of predictive targeting device. And the attacker stole it.'

Waterman tugged at his beard meditatively.

'What can you tell me about the attacker?' he asked after a long pause.

'Based on the body movements, it could be a man or woman. I would say between late twenties and early thirties. A killer by trade: there's no hesitation or remorse. One of yours gone rogue?'

'I'd forgotten what our interactions were like,' said Waterman.

'Thank you,' said Caleb.

'It wasn't a compliment,' said Waterman, his face

draining of humour. 'To respond to your theory: there is no secret handheld weapon with a predictive targeting device. But now I think I know who did this. And you can help me track them.'

Caleb shook his head. 'Forget it, I don't work for the public sector.'

'We will make it worth your while,' said Waterman.

Caleb turned and started walking back to his car.

'I'm not interested,' he said over his shoulder.

He had almost reached the hangar doors when his step faltered, like something had just occurred to him. He turned around to face Waterman.

'OK, I'll do it.'

Waterman looked at him with suspicion.

'I haven't told you how much yet.'

'I'll find a way to make it work.'

'Will you?' asked Waterman sceptically, his eyebrows raised. Without taking his eyes off Caleb, he walked forwards, closing the gap between them. 'What are you up to, Caleb?'

Caleb shrugged his shoulders.

'Fine, if you don't want my help . . .'

'Hold on,' said Waterman, raising one huge hand, 'I never said that. Tomorrow morning. 10 a.m . . .'

Caleb nodded and began walking briskly back to the car.

'. . . no games,' shouted Waterman to his retreating back, 'this isn't about you and me any more.'

But Caleb had already gone.

27

GCHQ

Caleb was lost.

The maze of corridors within GCHQ was bewildering.

He checked his watch. He already knew he was late for his Waterman meeting, now just rechecking the extent.

He had arrived at the gates of the sprawling military intelligence complex an hour earlier but hadn't anticipated the bomb and K-9 vehicle searches or the airport-style X-ray screening inside the central atrium of the main building.

By the time he walked through the secure lobby concourse, sun-drenched courtesy of a vaulted glass ceiling, he was already late.

Behind the reception desk, a huge royal crest was carved into gridded sandstone: lightning emerging from the base of the crown and striking the planet, the letters GCHQ emblazoned across the globe.

The receptionist had given him instructions where to meet Waterman, but that was fifteen minutes earlier. He was about to retrace his steps when a young man, dressed similarly to Caleb, down to the khakis and trainers, still in his early twenties, came around the corner and approached him.

'Dr Goodspeed? I was sent to find you.'

The young man handed him a thick set of papers.

'We just need to take care of a formality first. It's the Official Secrets Act. Signing it will give you clearance.'

'And if I don't?' asked Caleb, looking at the stack.

'Then this is as far as you go,' said the young man in a neutral way.

Caleb considered this. Signing the OSA was the last thing he wanted to do. He took the pen and reluctantly put his signature on the paper. The young man took the papers and slipped them into a pack across his shoulder.

'Thanks. Follow me.'

They passed through another set of security gates and turned left to follow a long corridor. One wall was floor-to-ceiling glass, through which Caleb could see an interior courtyard covered with manicured grass.

'Do you know much about GCHQ?' asked the young man, making conversation.

Caleb responded without taking his eyes off the view.

'You're the organization responsible for providing signals intelligence to the British army. You intercept emails, calls and social media messages. Twelve billion phone calls, two hundred billion emails and fifty billion social media messages each day. To analyse it all, you've created a secret supercomputer in your basement that can break the exaFLOP barrier: a billion billion calculations per second . . .'

They had stopped in front of a bank of eight lift doors.

'. . . which is where we are presumably going today,' said Caleb, pressing the 'down' button.

A lift door opened, and Caleb stepped inside. The young man remained outside, looking thrown.

'That's . . . well . . . yes . . .' he said, the lift doors cutting him off in mid-sentence.

The only evidence of the lift's movement was the slightest of vibrations. A few seconds later, the opposing door opened into a reception area, with corridors leading in both directions.

Caleb heard heavy footsteps coming, and a few seconds later Waterman walked into view. It had been less than twenty-four hours since they last saw each other, but the towering Yorkshireman already looked older, his eyes sunken and bloodshot.

'The UK has five categories of warning, known as threat levels, that are used to signal to the public an impending terrorist attack . . .' Waterman began without ceremony. 'This way.'

They walked down a curving corridor, a blue line running down the side of the wall, broken by intermittent arrows pointing in their direction of travel. A line of breadcrumbs, thought Caleb, in case anyone became lost in the maze of identical corridors that made the facility into a labyrinth.

'. . . the fifth and final level is referred to as Critical. It means an attack is imminent. When we go to that level, maximum security measures are put into place.'

He stopped in front of a door – Caleb noticed that the blue arrow line ended at the frame – and punched an eight-digit code into the security keypad. The door retracted, sliding into the wall.

'All cultural, business and transport centres are on the highest security measures. This way.'

They stepped through into a wide hallway. If the areas of GCHQ Caleb had seen so far took their aesthetic from off-the-peg corporate interiors, then this new zone was straight from a hi-tech catalogue. Black walls with recessed lighting stretched out in each direction, absorbing the light so it was impossible to tell how long the passageway was, giving Caleb the momentary feeling that he had stepped through a portal into deep space. The neutral grey carpet had become a metal grille over which they walked. Waterman raised his voice to be heard over the clatter.

Caleb noticed that the temperature had dropped since they had left the lift. As Waterman spoke, his breath was coming out of him in an icy vapour trail. Wherever they were going, it was colder than a meat-locker.

Up ahead, the walkway dead-ended in a metal door.

'Why are you telling me this?' asked Caleb.

Waterman turned around and held Caleb in his gaze.

'I informed the head of GCHQ about the likely suspect in the Ultra attack. We went to Critical this morning.'

28

Waterman's hand hovered over the keypad mounted on the side of the door, hesitated and then dropped back down. He turned around to Caleb.

'Look . . . before we . . . I just want to . . . I meant what I said . . . about Tara.'

He stood there, not moving, waiting for a response.

Caleb's stomach twisted in knots. This was the last thing he wanted.

He didn't talk about Tara. Not with other people. And certainly not with Waterman, here, stuck in a basement with no escape routes. The truth was that the only way he, someone with an almost limitless ability to empathize, made it from day to day was by placing Tara's memory behind a high-walled enclosure he had painstakingly built. Behind those walls was so much grief he feared it would overpower him, tearing him apart and leaving nothing remaining. So he learned to ignore it, like the father and children who go about their daily routine while a mad mother paces in their attic.

He looked down at the ground, avoiding Waterman's eyes and praying for the hiss of the retracting door. But Waterman's hands remained by his sides, and Caleb realized he was waiting.

He looked up at last and, to his surprise, saw his old

college friend looking back at him, encased in the adult man he had become. A sense of nostalgia stirred in Caleb, like walking into an overgrown estate and seeing traces of the manicured garden you used to play in as a child.

Doing his best to contain his internal agitation, Caleb gave him a grudging nod.

'Thanks.'

'What happened?' asked Waterman.

Caleb took a deep breath. So this was it. It was all going to have to come out now. And to his enemy. The man who betrayed him. But even as Caleb rehearsed this well-worn narrative, it sounded false to him. Waterman didn't have a malicious bone in his body, and Caleb knew that hating him had served its purpose, like a runner imagining he is being chased by a phantom gang in order to reach his top speed.

'I don't know,' said Caleb, the words coming out before he had a chance to check them. 'She hadn't been well for some time.'

Why won't anyone believe me!

High-pitched screams were floating now over the enclosure walls, piercing him to the core.

'She always was rather . . .' Waterman searched for the right word. 'Highly strung.'

If Waterman noticed Caleb's ratcheting discomfort, he wasn't showing it.

They were hiding. In the crowds. I saw them.

In Caleb's heart, the enclosure foundations were shaking, causing the ground to ripple and the tops of walls to teeter.

'It got worse at the end . . .' said Caleb, his eyes pricking with tears, surprising him. 'She stopped taking her . . .'

'I heard they found her . . .' said Waterman, overlapping.

'OK,' said Caleb, louder than he expected, the word bursting out, 'are we going to get started any time soon?'

You were never good with your own feelings, Caleb. It's always been easier to read others.

Hairline fractures were running up the side of the walls he had worked so hard to fortify. Her voice was louder now, clearer, her Irish lilt lending a musicality to the words.

Waterman looked at him for a moment and then ran a hand through his beard in embarrassment.

'Of course, sorry.'

He pressed the code on the keypad, and the door slid open.

Caleb watched Waterman enter over the threshold. The pain of repressing his emotions was physically manifesting now, like he'd swallowed a bag of broken glass that scratched against the inside of his chest with every breath. He inhaled slowly, squeezing his fists in silent admonition to himself to keep his shit together.

Once he crossed the threshold, it took Caleb a few seconds to process what he was looking at.

'The largest server farm in Europe?' asked Caleb, pulling his jacket tighter around him. He welcomed the distraction of new subject matter.

'Comfortably,' nodded Waterman.

They were in a cavernous underground hangar.

'We keep it at ten degrees,' continued the Yorkshireman. 'That's why it's so cold.'

Caleb looked at the white stacks humming around him and, despite the anxiety that still jangled his nerves, felt the hairs begin to bristle on the back of his neck. The floor space looked to be the size of four football fields. Rows and rows of evenly spaced white server stacks spread out in front of them. If memory space were physical space, then housed in these plastic casings were galaxies, whose infinite reaches would take millions of years to explore, even travelling at light speed. Ever the hacker at heart, Caleb was transported by the cosmic nature of digital space in front of him, capable of housing the sum total of human knowledge multiple times over in some side pocket to its memory while it maintained its daily duties.

Computers are safe for you, aren't they? You can programme them, they aren't messy.

Waterman kept walking along the near wall.

'We're going in here,' said Waterman.

He pointed to a door in the corner of the room, its outline barely visible as a micro-thin line in the otherwise gleaming wall. Caleb prised himself away from the sight of the servers and followed Waterman.

29

The room was claustrophobically small after the end-less stretches of passageway they had covered. Barely larger than a family car, it contained one armchair and a front screen that covered the back wall. A projector was built into a box screwed into the floor.

'We use this room for siloing information from the mainframe,' said Waterman. 'Data is dropped into here for viewing, but it's only a one-way connection. The door will be locked while you are here.'

Caleb reached down and picked up a plastic remote control. There was no other input device in the room: no keyboard, no mouse, no audio-feed microphone.

'Trust that low, huh?'

'You're the proverbial fox in the hen coop, Caleb,' said Waterman, taking the remote control off him. 'Take a seat. You said you wanted to help?'

Caleb sat down, feeling the back of his shirt press against his skin. It was sodden with sweat. He ran his palms along the fabric of the chair as surreptitiously as he could.

Talking about Tara had opened a fissure in the walls. The memories of that day, each one like a shock troop from a vast army massing on the other side, began step-ping through the breach.

Ping. Ping. Ping. The chirrup of his phone, announcing the arrival of text messages. He shifts in his seat, the leather squeaking underneath him, it is as if he has curated this memory to last for ever, he slips a finger into his pocket, feeling the raspy wool on his hand, knowing that he will see a ladder of texts all from the same sender, his needy, hysterical wife, the mad woman in the attic.

'So, you think one person is enough of a danger to raise the threat level nationwide?' said Caleb, struggling to bring his focus to the matter at hand.

The texts stop, leaving Caleb in silence. He goes about his day, the quiet registering with him, like the awareness of the presence of an absence. Then the banshee-shriek of the phone, like a call to arms, and the time he took to answer it would stretch out for ever in his memory.

'Let me show you,' said Waterman, picking up a remote control and pointing it to the screen.

30

'This is the only footage we have of the operation called Orpheus.'

Caleb stared as footage appeared on screen: an operating table in the middle of a room, shot from a static perspective. Three whitewashed walls and a fourth that was covered by what appeared to be hospital screens on wheels.

A Herculean act of will was taking place within Caleb. He was tethering his eyes and focus to the front wall of the stuffy room as if breaking contact would leave him forever lost at sea. He was being asked to perform the task he excelled at, projecting himself into the synthetic reality of recorded images, reading those who lived within them, reclaiming their two-dimensional traces into three-dimensional lives, skills he used on strangers but was not able to use on his own wife.

The images were black-and-white, and the quality was poor, a digital copy of an analogue image. Twenty years old, maybe more. The picture was framed awkwardly, tilting slightly to the left, giving a skewed perspective on the room, as if they were seeing things through a discarded camera that was still rolling film.

'What you are going to see actually happened,' said Waterman, not taking his eyes off the screen.

After a few seconds a door opened and a young girl entered, wearing medical scrubs. She must have been less than ten years old, with intense black eyes that stared out from a face dusted with freckles. Untamed brown hair tumbled on to her shoulders.

A thick-set, bearded man in an open-necked shirt carrying a briefcase followed her in and closed the door behind them. Through a porthole, Caleb could see a woman watching them from the other side of the door. She was in her early thirties, attractive. The similarities between her and the girl were striking: black shark's eyes nestling on top of high cheekbones and a ski-slope nose.

Take a seat.

The bearded man looked at the girl and nodded towards the table.

Caleb's mind concentrated on the images, breaking things down, synergizing, doing his best to screen everything else out.

'It's a mother and daughter, civilians,' started Caleb. 'The man isn't the father. But like one. The professional voice and tone he is using with her is for the camera. He's close to the girl. A mentor. This recording is for an official audience. To prove something. The man is a believer, but others he works for are not. The mother is consenting to whatever is happening, but there's something about her . . .'

He hesitated. Was it real or was he imagining it? The perennial problem with intuition: is it really there or only in my head? There was something about the

187

mother's eyes, wide open, staring, the faintest hint of a dislocation from what she was seeing. Or was he remembering Tara, and painting a patina of his own on what he saw? The similarities were there, no doubt.

'. . . she's schizoid . . .' said Caleb, looking at Waterman for support.

Waterman nodded.

On the screen, the man turned and walked directly towards the camera until his body filled the screen, blocking out the view of the room. He bent over, his face filling and fish-eyeing the lens. His shoulders twitched with the effort of some off-screen adjustment, and the camera tilted back.

The man turned around and walked back to the table.

This next part is very important. It all needs to be recorded by the camera. Do you understand?

Caleb listened to the man's words, the action playing out on screen compelling enough that he suspended further analysis.

The man bent down to open his suitcase and reached into it. He held up what he had retrieved, addressing the camera.

Two coins.

He turned back to the girl, addressing her.

Close your eyes.

He placed the coins on the child's closed eyelids.

Hold them, please.

The child followed the man's directions with the seriousness of an acolyte. Caleb could tell her movements were unrehearsed. She hesitated before each action, unsure of what was coming next. She brought up her index fingers and placed one on each coin, holding them while the man returned to the briefcase and removed an amorphous lump of material.

Putty dough.

He twisted the dough into two pieces and then placed one piece over each of the coins, moulding them gently with his thumbs until they completely covered the eye sockets of the child. The man stood back to survey his work.

The result was chilling.

The grainy quality of the image smoothed out the child's features so she resembled a sightless mannequin.

The man then returned to the briefcase and lifted a wad of material.

Bandage roll.

The child remained completely still as the man placed one end of the bandage on the bridge of her nose and then began to wrap the cloth in circles around her head. When the strip had run out, the upper part of the child's head had been completely covered.

Caleb's attention was fixated on the screen. He kept storing the continual feed of intuitive information from the film into a cache in his brain, unwilling to interrupt the drama he was watching.

One more item.

The man lifted a thick black sack from inside the briefcase and placed it over the child's head. The child's torso emerged ghoulishly from beneath the black sack.

The bearded man turned to face the camera.

This is the first test of Orpheus. 30 May 1990.

He then whispered something inaudible to the girl.

'Watch this,' said Waterman.

The man took two steps back and put his hand into his pocket. He threw his hand in the air, releasing four coins in a shower towards the child. Faster than Caleb's eyes could track the movement, the girl flipped down on to the ground and snatched the coins, both hands punching the air with lightning stabs.

Caleb looked around at Waterman in complete astonishment.

'Play that again.'

Waterman shook his head.

'Watch what's coming.'

Wait. What are you doing?

The mother spoke for the first time, the pitch of her voice rising in alarm. Her voice sounded digitized, and Caleb realized she must be speaking through a loud-speaker from the other side of the door.

The man had pulled a pistol from beneath his jacket and was walking to the hospital screens.

Calm down, Phoebe. This is something your daughter and I have been working on. No cause for alarm.

He pulled the screens backwards, concertinaing them and revealing that the room in which they were standing was one corner of a much longer space. Positioned at intervals were three hooded men tied to chairs. They sat motionless, bodies slumped and propped up by thick rope wrapped around their torsos.

No! Baby, stay where you are.

The woman's voice was shrill, panicked. Both of her hands were pressed to the inside of the glass, her palms white.

The bearded man walked quickly to the door and flipped a switch housed in a panel on the wall. The woman's voice cut off immediately, although Caleb could see her mouth miming increasingly frantic cries.

I thought you would be proud.

He addressed the camera.

Orpheus, show me what you can do.

He balanced the gun in the palm of his hand and then threw it high in the air. The next few seconds happened so fast Caleb's brain struggled to catch up with what his eyes were registering.

The gun was snatched in mid-air, the girl was moving, rolling, kneeling, a shot was fired, the report deafening in the enclosed space, the head of a detainee jerking backwards, then two more head shots, then the gun was sailing in a long parabola back in the man's direction.

Caleb glanced at the woman standing on the other side of the door. Her face was wet with tears, and her shoulders were heaving with sobs. Both fists hit the glass with a slow but steady drumbeat.

The man walked to the chairs in the deep recessed area of the room and took off the masks one by one.

They were dummies; sackcloth stuffed with straw.

'You think the kid, now an adult, attacked your base?' asked Caleb, breaking away from the screen and turning to face Waterman.

'What do you think?' said Waterman, looking at Caleb in a measured way.

Caleb took a deep breath and then blew out a low whistle.

'How do you know this film is real?'

'The man is Lionel Dobbs. MI5,' said Waterman. 'The film was shot at a safe house in England. The tape has never left our possession. It's real.'

'Why isn't the mother a suspect?' asked Caleb.

Waterman stiffened. 'Why do you say that?'

'Because she's like the girl. They have the same abilities,' said Caleb.

Waterman looked back in surprise. 'How do you know that?'

Caleb ignored the question.

'Tell me more about Operation Orpheus,' asked Caleb.

Waterman shook his head. 'I can't.'

'Up to you. You're the one wanting answers,' said Caleb, sitting back in his chair.

Waterman chewed his lip meditatively and then gave Caleb a tentative nod.

'Started in the Second World War. Concerned a particular family, tracked through the generations. But it was abandoned after the child escaped. Been missing ever since. That's all I can say.'

Caleb turned back to the screen, where the footage had cut to a different scene.

A white room, as bare as a cell, shot from a stationary camera in a ceiling corner. A timer in the corner of the screen tumbled over, recording fractions of seconds.

The child sat on the floor at the far end of the room, still in her surgical scrubs. The impediments had been removed from her eyes. She held a handkerchief in one hand and dabbed periodically at her ears, which appeared to be bleeding.

The mother paced in the centre of the room, her arms tightly folded. Her movements were erratic, and she cursed and mumbled to herself. She suddenly veered and ran towards the camera, fixing it with an intense gaze and screaming at the top of her voice.

'You lied to me! This is not what we agreed! We are not your prisoners!'

Caleb picked up the remote control and paused the film. It froze on a close-up of the woman's snarling features, her face contorted into a rictus of fury.

Caleb scrutinized the remote control.

'Can we close up on the image?'

'The mother?' asked Waterman.

'No, the girl.'

Waterman pointed to a button on the remote and Caleb toggled it several times until the screen magnified the image of the girl so it filled the screen.

A locket hung from the girl's neck, and on her arm was a design – a tattoo or a birthmark – in the shape of an infinity sign.

31

Waterman re-entered the Arena, deep in thought.

He had left Caleb in the screening room, poring over the footage, stopping, starting and rewinding the film with the remote control.

As Waterman walked back to his desk, Bob Swift rushed over to him.

'I think I figured out how the attacker got hold of weapons-grade radioactive material,' said Swift, holding up an iPad.

'Let's hear it,' said Waterman. Piecing the clues together was the only way to trace back to the source. However, Bob Swift didn't work for him. He worked for Hunter, and Waterman wouldn't put it past Hunter to lead him down a false trail, even when the stakes were as high as they were.

'Look at this,' said Swift. He flicked his finger across the surface of the iPad. A series of photos swiped by, commercial cargo vessels run aground on jagged rock outcrops.

'Three ships went down a month ago, in different areas off the coast of Scotland. Each wreck was a week apart.'

'Evidence of foul play?' asked Waterman.

'None,' said Swift. 'They just ran aground.'

Waterman was beginning to get restless. Over Swift's shoulder he could see a pile of reports sitting on his desk for review. In case his working theory about the attack on Ultra was wrong, he needed to piece through the whereabouts of every foreign agent working in the UK.

'I presumed the carriers would be insured through Lloyd's of London,' continued Swift, oblivious to Waterman's mounting distraction, 'so I brought up the claims.'

Swift scrolled down on his iPad. A new set of images appeared on screen: shots of the vessels beached onshore, a close-up of a jagged hole sliced into the bow of a ship, and then a different perspective on another ship with an equally gaping slice in its hull. Underneath the photos was a photocopy of a document with densely printed text.

'The findings were that the ships ran aground,' said Waterman, peering closely at the extract of the Lloyd's claim form. His patience was reaching an end. 'I haven't got time for this.' He pulled away and began to head for his desk.

'The accident reports . . . they all have the same conclusion,' Swift called out after him. 'The lighthouses were dark at the time. There were no beams to guide the ships.'

Waterman was only half-listening now. He lifted up the top report and scanned it.

'So I thought, what are the odds of three lighthouses in three different parts of the coast all failing in two weeks?' Swift continued, oblivious, following Waterman to his desk. 'There weren't any power outages at the time.'

Waterman shook his head. Muttering, 'No, light-houses work on independent generators . . .'

He never completed the sentence. An expression washed over his face that was so surprising that Swift stopped what he was saying.

'Are you all right?' he asked Waterman.

'Those lighthouses were built in the 1970s,' said Water-man. 'The power sources at the time were all nuclear . . .'

'Strontium-90,' continued Swift. 'Same as the mat-erial in the dirty bomb.'

'He raided the lighthouses,' said Waterman, 'and without any power, the ships ran aground.'

Waterman grabbed him by the shoulder and shook him.

'Good work, Bob!'

Waterman looked around. Hunter was in the far cor-ner of the Arena, leaning over the workstations of two analysts. Had he known, he would have taken the infor-mation straight to Salt, bypassing the Agency chain of command.

Waterman put a hand around Swift's shoulder and directed him towards the front cinema screen.

'Pull up the locations of the three wrecks.'

Swift's iPad was linked by Bluetooth to the central control network in the room. He tapped the surface, and a second later a map of Scotland appeared, blown up to fit the size of the screen. Three red spots appeared on the coastline, with dates superimposed above them.

'It looks like he hit the lighthouses one after the other, moving west to east,' said Waterman.

'There's one more lighthouse left on that part of the coast,' said Swift.

Waterman tugged on his beard meditatively.

'We should do a recon,' he said at last. 'Send F Squad. What's left of them.'

32

Caleb sat in the stillness, having paused the projector the moment Waterman left.

In front of him, the frozen image of the young girl stared at him.

Caleb wiped his eyes with the back of his hands and took a third shaky breath.

That face.

There was something about it he couldn't fathom.

It was enough to pull him from his pain.

Throughout the film, the girl had remained a mystery to him, despite his best efforts. Everyone else he turned his formidable attentions to was an open book, and yet this child was an enigma. Her face remained a two-dimensional representation, pixels on a screen, announcing . . . nothing.

What did the adult she was to become want? This was Waterman's question. Caleb stared at the picture, his eyes sliding off the screen each time, failing to find a purchase. He literally had no idea.

He toggled the remote control and tightened the image on to the locket. There was a design on the front he didn't recognize, multi-coloured concentric circles. And some form of writing on its underside. He froze the image and saved a copy, tightening the resolution.

It was a number string.

515195140126923.

The numbers meant nothing to him.

He pulled his handkerchief from his pocket, blew his nose and then checked his watch.

He was running out of time. He needed to start.

He bent forwards, looking at the raised platform that housed the remote control and projector. It was covered in the same fabric that carpeted the floor. He reached out and felt along the seam until he found a patch that was loose enough to slide his fingers under. He gripped the end and tore it from its base, skinning the platform of its covering and exposing what lay beneath.

The projector was housed in a plastic casing bolted down by four screws. Caleb took a pen from his pocket and pulled the clip from the cover. The bevelled edge had served him well before in similar situations and he slid it into the cross-groove of the nearest screw and began to twist.

Once the four screws were removed, he placed them carefully in his pocket and lifted the shell up and away from the projecting unit. As he hoped, there was a USB port next to the projector that had been hidden by the cover.

Caleb pulled a wired USB silicon roll keyboard from his inside jacket pocket and plugged it in.

The keyboard and USB connection would give him the

ability to interact with the processing unit of the projector, but not much more. In order to be able to access the main neural network in the facility, which was his intention, the reason he was here today, something just short of magical was needed. A series of siege-busting weapons would be required to plough through the fierce firewalls that ringed the virtual city walls of the military facility.

Caleb pulled out the flash drive from his pocket and plugged it into the port in his keyboard. The top of the drive glowed white as it whirred and disgorged its contents into the wafer-thin processor attached to the keyboard, along the USB wire and into the projector unit, like a syringe of nanites injected straight into the bloodstream of a sleeping patient.

Caleb knew the facility had the most vigorous virus checks on the planet.

But no alarms would be triggered if no virus existed.

Like the Stuxnet virus, which infiltrated and attacked the Iranian nuclear facility in 2010, Caleb had carefully built the virus in three separate parts – a worm that drove the attack, a rootkit that hid its nature from those watching and a link file that automatically replicated copies of the worm.

The three parts tunnelled in separately, below the watchful gaze of the defence systems, and only assembled once they were inside the firewall. Even now, they were spreading through GCHQ's neural system, replicating like germs working their way through a host body, seeking control centres and modifying codes to build a bridge through which Caleb could enter.

The risks were high, Caleb knew. The consequences of breaching the Official Secrets Act were serious. They would throw him into a secure military cell whose walls he could touch with both arms spread wide and leave him there for decades.

But it was worth it.

Waterman had given him the idea, when he told Caleb he had been vetted.

The test administered by GCHQ and the other arms of British military intelligence to vet citizens was the most comprehensive in the world. The data points harvested on each person covered almost every aspect of their psychological make-up and personal history. This data would reduce the margin of error for review to almost zero. With access to their vetting files, Caleb would be able to search for those with the same skills as himself. If he couldn't find anyone here, then he might as well shut up shop.

33

'They're a few minutes away from the lighthouse,' said Swift.

Waterman pointed a finger at the front wall. The analyst fed an instruction into the computer and immediately a line of four screens running along one side of the wall flickered on.

The images took a few seconds to coalesce into something intelligible: live feeds of cramped spaces filled with heavily armed men in uniform.

'We're relaying through helmet cams.'

A second later a map of a section of coastline around Inverness appeared on a large section of the wall that was still dark. The occupants of the Arena watched transfixed as two flashing blue lights pulsed along a sinewy grey track that hugged the coast.

Two more helmet cams blinked on, relaying feeds from the front seats of the vans. Their views were washed in the green and black of night vision. The vehicles drove without front or rear lights, navigating purely on GPS and the short distance ahead of them that was reclaimed from darkness by the goggles they wore.

The Arena watched as the two trucks moved through the pitch darkness, surrounded by a bubble of green light that only they and the occupants of the front seat could see. The blackness hemmed them in on all sides, lending the bumpy road the feeling of a lunar landscape.

The four monitors running down the left side of the screen relayed the feeds from the helmet cams: Cam One, the front seat of the leading van; Cam Two, the cramped rear; Cam Three, the front seat of the following van; and Cam Four, the rear cabin of the following van.

The views of Cams Two and Four were almost identical: tiny, packed quarters full of assault team officers, luminous pupils shining like cats' eyes.

'Patch me through to Myers,' said Waterman.

Waterman had never met Myers but had reviewed his file. Like the others, he had no dependants. A Scotsman with five years of SAS training and before that two tours in Afghanistan.

Swift nodded, and seconds later an audio link opened, leaking the sounds of weapons being prepared, a chattering chorus of clicks and bolts, into the Arena.

'It's Waterman, can you hear me?'

'Clearly.'

The voice that responded was confident, assured. If Simon Myers had any trepidation about his own battlefield promotion, he wasn't showing it.

'Intel led us to this lighthouse. But that could have been intentional. Do you understand what I am saying?' said Waterman.

'Yes. We'll exercise maximum caution,' came the off-screen reply.

'Look for trip wires, IEDs. Assume nothing,' said Waterman. He had begun pacing nervously, tugging at the end of his beard.

The flashing blue dots were almost on top of the lighthouse now. On the map, the building hung precipitously over the edge of a cliff, straddling the powder-blue representation of the sea and the forest green of the land.

'This is close enough.' Myers' voice crackled over the speakers.

Cams Two and Four showed the men in the rear of both vans lurching forwards with the momentum of the sudden stop.

The four cams wobbled and shook as the team prepared for the assault.

Cams Two and Four suddenly went black as the back doors flew open on both vans.

And then they were running.

Cams One and Two showed a pack of men in a tight group, automatic weapons held out in front of them, running to the bottom of a fire escape. In front of them was an emergency exit door, and above them, a metal ladder hung from the suspended grille platform of the fire escape.

Cams Three and Four showed the assault team running across a wide area of tarmac that ringed the perimeter of the tall, cylindrical structure that rose like a finger into the sky. The lighthouse was dark, the beam off, and there was no evidence of occupation.

On Cam Four, the commando at the front of the pack – Myers – could be seen lifting his hand, and the cam plunged down, huddling with the rest of the team in a sudden crouch. For a second, Cam Three twisted its perspective, looking directly at the balaclava-hooded officer carrying Cam Four, a tiny lens mounted on the side of his helmet.

Myers pointed to Cam Four, clenched his fist three times and then pointed at the front door. Two men peeled from the group, wedged a crowbar in the door, then launched their bodies against it, splintering the lock. After two firm but surreptitious shoulder barges, the door gave and creaked open.

On Cams One and Two, an identical operation was unfolding. Two of the assault team were running their fingers along the edges of the metal emergency exit door on the ground floor. One of them silently indicated to the other, who slid the blade of a knife in and jemmied it open. Behind them, one of the unit stepped off the knee of another and caught hold of the bottom of the ladder, lifting himself up.

Cam One now relayed a feed of the ascent up the fire escape metal ladders. On each floor, the camera would swivel sideways, looking through the windows into the gloomy interior. On the cam, the assault officer's reflection could be seen, machine gun pressed into his shoulder, muzzle tracing an arc around him.

On Cams Three and Four, the leader pointed upwards with two fingers of one hand and tipped them towards the interior of the building. The two feeds from the cameras jiggled as the pack moved quietly forwards. As they stepped over the threshold, the monitors plunged into darkness for a second before night vision washed the screens into deeper hues of green and black.

34

Caleb leaned back in the chair, running his fingers through his hair in frustration.

It had taken him less than an hour to scour the first file of vetting forms, which covered the bulk of the analysts within GCHQ. He knew he would recognize what he was looking for the moment he saw it. It could be a fact or biographical detail or a pattern that could be seen in perspective, like unfocusing one's eyes and seeing the rivers that run down the spaces on the page of a book.

But there was no one even close.

He drew back and looked at the other files, which were represented in a three-dimensional bar chart, a series of blocks of different heights clustered together, making Caleb feel like he was on an aerial route over a Manhattan grid of buildings.

By the time he finished with the third file, he was beginning to get concerned. Statistically, he knew that the odds were against him. Less than a million people had security clearance in the UK, so the chances of finding the *one in a million* were tight.

He drummed his fingers on the side of the chair. He had little option but to proceed at this point, having already taken the risk. But maybe he needed to look more closely at the files before opening them, to see whether the sections under which they were categorized were more likely to contain what he was looking for.

Caleb began to type, his fingers flying over the soft keys, the three-dimensional grid expanding and shifting to display the file names.

And that's when he saw it.

A set of files with a strange logo on them.

He didn't recognize it at first. It looked like an error, as if the space key had been skipped, leaving two identical letters squashed together.

Then he realized what he was looking at – an infinity sign.

Most forms of data encryption work through an algorithm that scrambles the text until it becomes a randomized stream of characters. Without a passkey, the data will not yield its secrets.

The initial Data Encryption Standard (DES), smashed with relative ease by hackers, led to a series of innovations designed to advance the standards of encryption. DES became Triple DES; the popular Twofish became Blowfish.

For Caleb, they were as easy to get into as a wet paper bag.

The US government's Advanced Encryption Standard (AES) was the current apex of protection and had not yet been cracked. Or at least was not known to have been cracked, although Caleb knew of several hacker networks that had done so but were waiting for a plum enough prize to steal before alerting the authorities they had the keys to their data kingdoms.

It was AES that wrapped and encrypted each of the GCHQ files.

The hacker methodology was ecumenical to any encryption method. Software targeted the encrypted data by randomly guessing millions of potential keys, and since an incorrect key results in an excretion of nonsensical data, the hacker knows by default that the key just used was wrong. Hacking was literal, every slash and swipe clearing a path forwards through the brush.

It took Caleb less than five minutes to find the key to the infinity sign file.

The data that was produced was less than the other files. A short burst of names and addresses without any other vetting information.

Caleb was about to discard the file and look at the next one when something struck him as peculiar. The list of names seemed strange. None of the first names seemed to be a match for the surnames. Daisy Haddad, Montague Kryzinski. And several of the first names contained curious anomalies in their spelling. Peterr, Simmon.

Considering a fresh approach would be best, Caleb resumed the hacking routine, and a few minutes later, a new set of results was received, also a list of names with no other information.

It was as he reviewed the second set of results that something dawned on him.

This 'infinity sign' file might be wrapped in honey.

Caleb had heard of honey encryption before – it was cooked up in a corporate lab somewhere in the US by a group of bearded conservative academics with entire pen sets sticking out of the breast pockets of their short-sleeved shirts. An older nerds' revenge.

The encryption tool was built with an additional layer of security. When an incorrect key was guessed, the system would respond by sending fake data to the hacker, but data that appeared to be real. Since the data wasn't a meaningless stream of randomized characters, the hacker wouldn't be able to conclusively dismiss the recent result.

Without knowing what type of data was enclosed in the protected file, it was impossible to know what was real and what wasn't.

The only option Caleb had was to review each result and search for anomalies, but with hundreds of thousands of keys tried every second, it would be like sifting through a haystack looking for straw-shaped needles.

Caleb stared at the results, lost in thought. There was only one way to crack a file wrapped in honey. He would need to guess the content of the file. If he knew what the file contained, he could separate the false results from the successful hacks.

He rubbed the end of his chin, considering his next step. Waterman would be back soon, and Caleb needed to be disciplined about his search, working through as many files as he could. But the fact that this file was wrapped in honey suggested it contained something more precious than the others. It was the only file protected with the experimental encryption tool.

Caleb knew he had to hack it.

And he had a clue to what was inside.

The infinity sign.

It could be a reference to many things – indeed it even had a peripheral meaning in coding language. But Caleb kept coming back to the image of the little girl on screen and the mark on her upper arm. The file had something to do with the girl. He knew it. Assuming he was correct, what he needed was some other piece of data which may likely be inside the file, which could be used as a way to test the validity of the data returned.

He picked up the remote and rewound the film, stopping periodically until he arrived at the moment he was seeking.

This is the first test of Orpheus. 30 May 1990.

He stopped the tape and rewound it again.

This is the first test of Orpheus. 30 May 1990.

He pressed the volume button and watched the bars climb on screen, a static din filling the room.

The man's whisper to the young girl was audible now, but barely.

Happy birthday, by the way.

Caleb paused the tape.

The girl was born on 30 May.

Caleb changed the structure of the hacking code to seek any keys returned that featured 30 May.

He began the hack again and, to his satisfaction, seconds later, the final bar unlocked and a river of code ran down the screen.

He was in.

It was a list of names.

Hundreds of names.

All women.

He looked at each one, seeking the imprimatur GCHQ used that showed they had been vetted.

But there was none.

Strangely, none of the names were vetted.

Out of curiosity, he typed the first name into Google on his phone. She was a hairdresser living in Richmond. He continued to do this; the second was a lawyer in the City, the third was a flight attendant. They seemed to not have any connection to each other. A random list.

The final Google search caught his eye. The flight attendant's birthday was listed as 30 May 1983 on her Facebook page.

This must have been the data that had allowed the honey wrap to be removed.

On a hunch, Caleb googled the other two women and checked their social media pages.

They were also both born on the same day: 30 May 1983.

Caleb looked down the list. There were about two hundred and fifty names there. All women. All born on the same day.

He'd stumbled on to a unique file, hidden within the vetting files. A file with no GCHQ employees, no one with security vetting. They were just random women with one thing in common – the day they were born.

He was about to exit the program when a name leaped out at him. It hit him with such force that he felt physically winded and stared at the screen for a full minute before breaking his trance. It was only then that he made the connection with the date.

He recognized the name.

It was Tara's.

35

F Squad stood in the lobby. The main stairwell was circular and rose out from the chessboard floor. From the ground, they could look directly up the atrium to the ceiling six storeys above them.

'Silly string.'

Myers' voice floated through the speakers.

One of the assault team pulled a canister from his backpack and walked towards the stairs. Using a technique the British army had perfected in Iraq, the soldier sprayed the foam threads at the bottom of the stairs from a position ten feet away. Cam Three stepped forwards, looking closely at where the foam landed, seeing if it had been snagged by any invisible tripwires.

'Clear,' whispered another voice, and the team moved slowly up the stairs.

The assault officer repeated the exercise, firing the canister at the stairway every few yards and then examining the debris.

'Halt,' hissed Myers.

The team froze, twisting their heads in his direction in unison. On Cam Four, Myers could be seen pointing a gloved finger.

Cams Three and Four craned upwards.

Above them, fluorescent paint had been daubed

on to the wall, covering it in a message that ran all the way down, from the first-floor landing down the corkscrew staircase, a garish graffiti in letters ten feet high.

YOU WILL DIE HERE

No one moved.

Then above them, a sound could distinctly be heard slicing through the silence.

A tearing sound.

Like scissors slicing through a thick cloth fabric.

Myers cocked two fingers towards the stairs, and the team continued moving, silently on their toes, spraying foam ahead of them as they went.

As they ascended, the sound became louder and began to take shape.

It was the sound of something, or someone, coming down the stairs.

Slowly.

Cam Three ran around the stairwell, on to the first-floor landing and then up the second tier of stairs.

Halfway up the second flight the cam suddenly halted, poised at a point where the stairs shielded him from being seen by whoever was descending.

The muzzle of the machine gun swung into view as it took aim at a space in the centre of the stairs.

The feet kept scuffing their way down, like an insolent metronome.

They were on the point of coming around the corner of the stairs now.

Any second.

In the Arena, Waterman approached the wall, moving now to the vertically aligned cam monitors. He stepped up close, until he had an intimate view of each of the four cams. At this distance, he could see Cams Three and Four were shaking slightly. Minute vibrations that could hardly be noticed: the result of a heart pounding like a trip hammer inside a bullet-proof vest.

On Cam Three, a gloved hand came into view, gently taking hold of the safety catch of the machine gun and releasing it.

The sounds were almost on top of them now.

'Steady,' muttered Waterman to himself.

The hand clasping the gun on Cam Three moved from the safety catch to the trigger.

As it did so, a metal slinky appeared around the corner, furling and unfurling itself in a caterpillar curl as it hit each step and then descended to the next.

No one moved as the slinky slithered down the steps, under the bridges formed by their legs, and around the corner.

Waterman looked around to the others in the Arena, who were staring at him in confusion.

'Keep going,' urged Myers' voice.

Cam Three and Cam Four resumed their creeping ascent of the stairs. Past the second floor and on to the third. Then the fourth, until they were moving faster and faster, building a rhythm, closing the gap between them and the looming ceiling.

They reached the final landing. A single door lay at the end of a short stone corridor. Inside was the light room.

A hand reached out on Cam Three and tested the door. It was unlocked.

They were in the two-storey lens room of the lighthouse. Above them, a rotunda wrapped itself around the building and in the centre of the room, a huge mechanism rose from the floor, like the inside of a clock laid bare. On the top sat the dormant lens of the lighthouse, sitting on a rotational axis.

Cam One showed the lens room from the perspective of the fire escape. The assault officer wearing the camera levered up the window from the outside, and Cam One and Cam Two slipped inside.

All four of the cams now fed images from different perspectives of the vaulted room.

The interior was large enough that the walls were cloaked in shadow, refusing to yield their secrets, even to the night vision. The cams rotated their views around the room, searching.

A voice came over the loudspeakers.

'All clear . . .'

And then Myers was screaming.

'On your right, on your right!'

Waterman tried to follow the cams as they veered wildly from side to side.

And then, for a fraction of a second, he saw what Myers saw: a group of masked men standing in the shadows, aiming their weapons right at F Squad.

Gunfire erupted in the enclosed space, a deafening clatter that rained down glass fragments with such force it was as if the roof was collapsing.

'Ceasefire! Ceasefire!' screamed Myers.

The din ratcheted down immediately, save for a final errant burst of fire that ended with a crash at the other side of the room.

'Enough!' shouted Myers.

Something had caught his eye, and he walked slowly from the centre of the room to the outer perimeter, directly towards where the armed men were lying in wait.

Waterman watched through shuddering cams, still agitated from the firing frenzy. He fought back the urge to scream into the microphone and call off the mission. His role was purely intel and support, but he had never felt so helpless as he did now.

Myers disappeared into the shadows, where the overhang of the roof above cut off any light. An aching silence extended in the room. Over the speakers, those in the Arena could hear the collective breathing of the unit, as deep and regular as a tidal flow, as they worked to regulate their emotions.

'Cam One and Two, on my side.'

Waterman breathed a sigh of relief when he heard Myers' voice.

Both cams walked towards him, their night vision flickering to brilliant green to accommodate the movement into darkness.

The first thing that Waterman saw blindsided him.

Myers was standing in front of an armed man, less than a foot away.

Waterman's every muscle clenched and he struggled to find his own breath.

And then he looked closer.

It wasn't an armed man at all, but a reflection: of Myers.

The cams twisted, taking in the walls for the first time.

'Mirrors,' breathed Myers. 'There are mirrors everywhere.'

36

Caleb sat in the darkness of the tiny room, too afraid to draw breath. He suddenly knew what he was looking at.

After the girl from Operation Orpheus had disappeared, GCHQ must have pulled out all the stops to find her.

Assuming that the girl used her skills to go underground, GCHQ had set the search conditions that it knew.

They were looking for a girl born on 30 May 1983.

There were two hundred and fifty-three female babies born on that day in the United Kingdom that were still alive. And one of them was Tara.

Military intelligence must have had them all under surveillance, waiting to see whether one of them was their child assassin in hiding.

A cold dread crept up Caleb's spine.

The destination of his line of thought was obvious now, but Caleb slowed down, squeezing the brakes and testing his underlying reasoning. Maybe it was a junk file? Maybe it was planted there on purpose by GCHQ for him to find?

The policeman had stood stock still in their bedroom, one of Tara's diaries open in his hand. Caleb could see the handwriting over his shoulder, wild and sloping, as if tilting with the weight of the madness in the words. Government agents were after her, hiding in the shadows.

Caleb scrambled down mental corridors trying every door other than the one waiting open for him. But none of the doors opened. Finally, he realized he had no other choice.

Tara was right. She was being followed.

Caleb stared at the girl's face on screen. Her escape, almost thirty years ago, had set in motion the chain of events that had ended, among other things, in Tara's death. There was no direct link, no culpability flowing from one to the other. But these two women were part of the same story. A narrative with an overlapping set of actors, a shared history that ended in tragedy for the fragile Tara and a life in hiding for the girl. All the women on the list were co-opted into the same drama, suspended in a web of meaning spun from the same strands.

When he and Tara had met, Caleb was an optimist, which meant that to him the world was an enormous organic education machine, constructed to help him evolve. People and experiences were propelled into his path when he most needed them. The secret of life was not in creating opportunities, but in recognizing them when they were sent his way by the benevolent software on which the universe runs. Life was like falling backwards on to a bed of feathers. He had to worry for nothing because everything was provided.

And then Tara became out of sync, a bug in the system, something he could neither fix nor explain. Why had the universe made her this way? To what higher ground was all the paranoia and panic she brought to the world meant to take them? The bug could not be fixed, so the software had to be rewritten from scratch.

The universe was suddenly no longer intelligent, responsive to his needs, but cold and unfeeling. Not even cruel, as this would presuppose intelligence and intention. Just random. A series of events with no code to combine them. Before his mind could process her death, he built the high enclosure walls and devoted himself to work with a purpose that bordered on mania.

But now, for the first time in a long while, the world seemed no longer cold and random. Tara's death had something to do with this girl. Life seemed powered once more by an intentional code, connecting events, pulling them together and, in this case, keeping secrets, hiding them from sight. A code that could be hacked.

He needed to find out about this girl, what made her special and why she was being hunted.

37

Waterman looked in disbelief at the images of hundreds of men, reflections of the unit, projected and refracted from every surface. Someone had, with infinite care, arranged mirrors to cover the entire perimeter wall of the lens room.

As if stirred by the same thought, all four cams tilted upwards at the same time and stared at the huge domed roof. What they assumed was a solid structure was in fact a greenhouse of glass held together by metal lattices. The outside of the rotunda had been boarded up, turning each interior pane of glass into a reflective surface facing inwards.

'The whole place is a hall of mirrors,' muttered Waterman, shaking his head and looking around.

On the cams, F Squad stood in confusion, their light machine guns tipped up. The room seemed to contain an entire battalion of them, brilliantly lit in deep greens and blacks, spilling into every corner of the room.

'Why would . . .'

Waterman's sentence was cut off by a loud humming noise that seemed to emanate from deep inside the lighthouse. On the cams, the Squad began to move towards the perimeter of the room, backing away from the source of the noise.

And then there was a dazzling flash.

Instantly, the four cams were washed white, the delicate sensitivities of the night vision blasted by the blaze of light.

'Someone switched the lens on . . .'

Waterman twisted away from the wall of screens to shield his eyes. Swift was standing by his side.

'The mirrors are trapping the light and reflecting it,' said Swift.

'It's an ambush,' said Waterman, cold dread creeping through him. 'To blind them.'

The screens on the front wall of the Arena looked like they were windows looking out on to a star going through a supernova. Thick fingers of brilliant light stabbed through the darkness in the Arena like projector beams in a darkened cinema.

And then Waterman heard it.

Single shots, like a car backfiring slowly and methodically.

Myers' voice could be heard shouting off screen.

'Take off your night vision.'

Everyone in the Arena held their breath as the cams were stripped of their infra-red overlays.

The light crept back into the feeds, which resembled retinas blasted by a camera flash. All the while, the sound of the shots continued. After a few seconds, vague shapes and shadows of the interior bled back into the cams, finally coalescing into a sight Waterman was dreading.

The bodies of the remaining members of F Squad lay scattered around the floor, not moving.

'Robert.'

Waterman turned to find Hunter standing with an iPad in his hand.

'Not now, Ian,' said Waterman.

He turned back to look at the devastation on screen.

'You need to see this,' insisted Hunter.

Waterman whirled around. 'I don't know if you've noticed, but British intelligence's military unit has just been wiped out. We are being hunted. What is more important?'

Hunter held up the iPad to Waterman's face and he spoke slowly, as if explaining something crucial to a child.

'We're being hacked. Right now. The breach is coming from inside the computer room.'

38

Caleb sat in a cell five feet high, four feet wide and six feet long.

Dimensions designed to force a detainee to crouch while standing and curl up while sleeping. The purpose of the cell was punishment as much as containment.

A simple mattress sat on a bedframe. There were no sheets or coverings, and the mottled bedding was a landscape of stains that resembled a marine map of an island chain. The only other item in the room was a toilet, which lacked both a lid and a seat and whose blue water stared at him indecently.

Waterman stood with his arms crossed, leaning against the door. Outside, an armed guard stood watching, automatic weapon slung across his chest, hand gripping the base.

'Why, Caleb? Just tell me why?'

'You were looking for the girl all the time, weren't you?'

Waterman exhaled noisily.

'We had nothing to do with Tara's death.'

'Didn't you?' replied Caleb. 'Are you telling me that you didn't know Tara was on the list? You knew she had nothing to do with the girl.'

Waterman took a step closer to Caleb, his voice dropping.

'Look, Caleb. This is serious. You just hacked into GCHQ. You could be in a cell like this for the next fifteen years. I'm sorry for what happened to Tara, but her problems started long before she appeared on that list.'

Caleb stared at Waterman. He was remembering now what had kindled and then stoked the schism between him and his old friend. Below the bluff, kindly, big-bear exterior, there was a hardness to Waterman. A flint-like core that would not be tempered by appeals to friendship or emotion. Caleb realized it was what made him so suited to being a spy.

'I'll make you an offer,' continued Waterman. 'You tell me what you learned about the girl, and I'll see if I can get them to drop the charges.'

Caleb considered this. He didn't doubt the sincerity of the offer. The country had gone to its highest threat level once this girl was suspected of being the attacker of the base. Waterman would do everything in his power to find her. And whatever anger Caleb had for Waterman right now, he knew he had to get out of this cell.

Caleb sat into the creamy leather seat of his Range Rover. His infiltration of GCHQ had not been successful. He had not found any candidates with high intuitive ability and, as a result, his business was likely sunk. But, strangely, the thought didn't trouble him. He felt as if his obsession with work was behind him, as if he had come out of orbit from the dark side of the moon. He had a new purpose now.

He was going to find the girl.

He had told Waterman most of what he knew. That the girl trained at such an early age she would feel her childhood had been taken from her. That she would want to find the person responsible. And that this was likely the man in the video, Dobbs. He didn't tell Waterman that none of this came from a reading of the girl. In all but one respect, she remained impregnable to his skills. His deductions came from the way the others in the room had interacted with the girl, picking what he could from their responses.

Before Caleb pressed the ignition, he opened the glove compartment and pulled out a pen and paper, writing down the information he had memorized while he was in the silo room. It was details he had found, shortly after hacking Dobbs' personnel file and discovering he was dead. They pertained to his supervisor, the watcher behind the screen for whom the video was made. He would be the girl's quarry.

There was one thing he had managed to deduce about the girl. It was obvious to him but he was sure Waterman and the others had not picked up on it. And knowing it meant Caleb had to find her before they did.

Waterman stood in the large reception room of GCHQ, hands in his pockets, ruminatively biting his lip, watching Caleb's car drive away.

He knew Caleb was hiding something from him, that Caleb had made a discovery while he was in that room he was not sharing. Waterman had considered leaving him in the cell, sweating him for longer. But it would be a distraction. The clock was ticking and, anyway, Caleb didn't have a monopoly on intuition. Waterman had a hunch about Orpheus too. She would come here, to GCHQ. Dobbs was dead, and Salt was the only remaining agent from Operation Orpheus still living. She would hit him here, at their base. She'd taken out the drone unit, their aerial support from the sky, which had almost killed her last week, and F Squad, the only military unit at their unique disposal to defend them. The hunt ended here.

He needed to increase security at the facility.

He let his eyes slide over from the road to the green hills that surrounded the facility.

Somewhere out there Orpheus was waiting, biding her time. Where was she hiding?

PART EIGHT

39

Tom crouches on the floor of the cell, his back to the wall.

Other than a hole in the floor for human waste, the room is empty.

A bare cube.

He rubs his head, still woozy since waking up a few minutes ago on his back in the middle of the floor.

He catches something in his peripheral vision.

A plaster on the back of his hand.

How did he get here? Remember. He must remember.

Running. He is running. An evening jog. Randomly taking corners, lost in the flow. There is a car. He remembers a car. Front wheel on a jack. Driver kneeling. Tom stops, jogging on the spot, asks if he can help. Then something bizarre. Driver stands too quickly. Tom feels a sting.

He drops his arm and takes a closer look.

Peeling away the plaster: a tiny speck of congealed blood, sitting on a pin prick.

Blackness. Then bright light. A hood is removed. He's in a room. Never seen it before. It's large. Dominated by three large planks of wood. No, too wide to be planks. Doors. Detached doors. Arranged into a U-shape. A workstation. Supported by bricks.

'Help . . .' Tom croaks. 'Help . . .'

Makeshift desktop surface is piled high. Enormous stacks.

Self-assembled hardware, wires springing out at all angles. 'Follow. The. Instructions.' His captor's voice is electronic, human but filtered. Coming from behind him. He twists to catch a glimpse, but can't move. Thick rope binds his torso to the chair back. 'Follow. The. Instructions.' Tom throws his body in every direction. Frantically. Only his hands are free.

There is a piece of paper in the corner of the room. Tom drops to his hands and knees and crawls towards it.

It's in fact several pages, stapled together. He turns it over in his hands, an image flashing in his memory.

He bends over the work desk. Tapping on the keyboard with uncertain fingers. Looking back and forth between the pages, filled with instructions, and monitors arrayed in front. A website. The instructions are to build a website. An untraceable one.

Tom tears the pages off, one by one, letting them drop to the floor, until only the stub remains. He looks closer at what binds them.

It is a thick staple.

The website is done. Tom twists his head to see if his captor can see. The room appears empty. He screams wildly. And then there's the sting again.

The staple has been straightened out into a jagged strip. It has taken some time, and Tom wipes the blood from his fingers on to the wall.

He grips the staple and slides it into the tiny space between the thick electronic lock and the door jamb of the cell. He pokes it until he can feel the other end hit the solid wall of the bolt. He waggles the material, probing for the end of the bolt. Beads of sweat form near his hairline as he feels the staple warp and buckle under the pressure he is putting on it. This is his only chance. And then his thumb slips forwards and he feels the makeshift pick slide in between the bolt and the strike plate. The door unlocks with a satisfying thunk.

But twenty minutes later he has not moved and is still staring at the door.

He should have escaped.

By now he should be far away.

Maybe it is the drowsiness, but something is stopping him – a memory – nagging at him, as persistent as the throb in his head.

He has been running. But his direction is not planned. He is taking streets at random. He, Tom McLeitch, the best firewall builder in Scotland, and the only man who could have done that job. And his captor is waiting for him. How? Tom doesn't have his phone on him, so there is no GPS to track. And he is miles away from his apartment.

Tom makes a decision and undresses, putting his clothes and shoes in a pile. He then scours his body, and then his clothes and shoes, looking for a tracking device. He is not going to escape only to be caught again.

He finds nothing.

He squats naked on the cold floor, his palm pressed to his forehead, as if the pressure might squeeze the answer out. His ear is cocked to the door, listening for any sound.

Tom considers whether there is more than one abductor. He shakes his head. That wouldn't explain how his kidnapper had been waiting in a car on a street that Tom had never been down before and only turned into on a whim.

Then he hears it.

So faint he thinks it could be a mosquito. But it's too cold for mosquitoes. It's a car. And it's approaching.

He pulls on his clothes and shoes, pushes open the door and scrambles out. He's in a dank corridor. Opposite him is another room. The door is ajar, and he can see the monitors and hardware he was forced to use. At the end of the corridor is an exit, framed by white light, and he hits it as hard as he can in full pelt, enjoying the feeling as it swings open and clangs on the far wall.

He doesn't stop until he is in a thicket of trees, a hundred yards or more away. He throws himself down on to the ground and twists to face the direction he has come.

It looks like a disused bomb shelter. Only the roof can be seen, peeking out about a foot above the grass: hidden from sight.

The engine noise is getting louder now, and he thinks he sees flashes of something through the canopy of trees.

He bolts upright and sprints.

Ten minutes later, Tom stands at a T-junction, his chest heaving from exertion. The topography around him has changed from dense woods to fields and hedgerows.

He looks at the two roads that stretch out in opposite directions. He takes a deep breath and takes the left turn.

Ten minutes later, Tom stands on the side of a main road, at the point where the route he was following merges, his thumb extended, waving down passing cars.

One stops, and a window rolls down. Tom approaches the car hesitantly, in a wide arc, waiting to see who is inside.

But it is only an older man, in his sixties, asking where Tom is going.

'Wherever you are,' he replies, getting in.

The man is retired, driving back from visiting family in Aberdeen. He chats nervously to fill the silence, his eyes occasionally flitting down to Tom's bleeding fingers, while Tom stares silently through the window at his side mirror, checking the cars behind him.

No one is following.

The driver lets Tom out in the middle of town.

'The police station is down that alleyway and on the right,' he says, in answer to Tom's question, before driving off.

Tom walks quickly down the alleyway, his mind doing its best to remember the route here. The bunker was no more than five miles from where he is now. The police could be there in fifteen minutes or less.

He is so immersed in his thoughts that he does not notice the person walking towards him from the opposite end of the alleyway. By the time Tom looks up, the other person is less than a few feet away.

A hand reaches for Tom with terrifying swiftness, the palm gripping Tom's face. A chemical smell jams itself up his nose with the force of two fingers, and he drops to the ground like a puppet with its strings cut.

40

Orpheus returned to the bunker, parking the truck a discreet distance away, its green tarpaulin covered by the canopy of trees.

Orpheus carried the programmer's unconscious body back into the bunker, deposited it back into the holding cell and then checked the computer room, eyes taking in the environment, searching for any damage.

Nothing had been touched. The monitors continued to display the countdown on the website, and on two side screens, floating bars of code pulsed out, like the LED lights on an amplifier, chronicling failed attacks on the website by the security services.

The rear room would need to be checked.

Orpheus walked to the end of the passageway and lifted the full-length boron suit from the steel peg on the wall. Two pairs of gloves – for inner and outer wear – lay on the stool nearby. The last piece of equipment, a full face-piece with self-contained breathing apparatus, dangled from a second peg.

It took several minutes to ensure the suit was on correctly and there were no breaches. When satisfied, Orpheus moved slowly to the door at the end of the passageway, which was vacuum-sealed and locked with a heavy metal bar that rested across the centre of the frame.

The bar was heavy, even for Orpheus, and opening it required launching a shoulder at the edge of the handle with considerable force. Once unlocked, the heavy door pushed open with a sigh, as if the room was reluctant to disclose its secrets.

Inside there were three rows of lead ingots, stacked high. Each one was the size of a child's coffin, with industrially thick walls that were ribbed in ridges on the side.

Everything was secure.

Before leaving, Orpheus paused on the threshold of the door and listened. It was impossible to tell whether it was imagination or not, but at times Orpheus was sure the contents of the containers seemed to hum.

PART NINE

41

Cheltenham

Sara looked out of the bus's window through successive chain-link fences towards the massive circular building.

It resembled an airport terminal more than a spying facility, with exterior walls of glass and sleek, modernistic flourishes on the roof.

She was surprised how close it was to the rest of the town. Rows of detached residential houses sat less than a few hundred yards from its border, and a narrow river snaked through fields and estates to its south.

Only the security cordon that wrapped itself around the perimeter of the facility gave any clue to what was happening inside.

She was in a specially designated bus, ferrying employees from the front gates to the staff entrance. It stopped at the first checkpoint; four armed officers moving through the vehicle, inspecting ID cards and checking them against a register. One of the officers led an Alsatian down the aisle of the bus.

Sara knew from her research that the security measures her fellow passengers could see were not the only protections. Anti-aircraft guns were positioned below the line of sight on the roof of the facility, and the armed units guarding the building took up an entire wing.

Somewhere, behind the fortifications, was the person who had the answers. To her childhood and to who she was before her life and mind were taken from her.

The rest of the day was spent in HR processing.

Getting the job had not been difficult. It was an administrative position with low-level security clearances. The construction of an identity was easy. After years of being hunted, it had taken her less than an hour.

The challenge lay in finding a way out of the facility once the job was complete. Her identity would be burned, and she would be left deep within an impregnable fortress. It was this dilemma that she wrestled with in the months of planning.

The bus passed the final gate, over the sprawling car park and to the employee gate, shuddering to a stop.

Her research had been meticulous. She knew every aspect of the orientation process for employees at her level. In a few minutes, they would be shepherded from the vehicle and led through the door. They would each be handed a security badge hanging from a necklace of green ribbon and a map of the interior of GCHQ. Fingerprinting and identity questionnaires would follow, interspersed with security seminars and short breaks of machine-poured coffee and awkward mingling.

She alighted from the bus and watched the other

new arrivals weave around her as they walked into the building, a ripple of nervous conversation moving among them. Before she followed, she took one last look behind her, wishing that time moved faster, that she could be carried forwards into tomorrow in the blink of an eye.

42

All lights were off in the house when Sara approached. She walked cautiously once around the perimeter, looking through the windows for any sign of movement, before crouching down in front of the lockbox.

The home rental service app on her smartphone showed there were no tenants booked for this week.

Voices had been rattling around in her mind all afternoon during the orientation. They were quiet, like whispers in a church, and just beyond her perception. She took a deep breath, battling them away in her mind.

Her friend and companion, *The Handbook of Clinical Psychopharmacology*, could not pinpoint definite aetiology, nor conclusively name her condition. The most it could do was suggest a range of possible treatments. Sedatives reduced anxiety, but Sara knew from experience they took too much edge off. Antidepressants adjusted serotonin levels, but loosened her connection with reality. Beta-blockers shut down the effects of adrenaline, but could limit awareness of the environment.

She mixed and matched ingredients to suit the needs of the day, sometimes combining what she took with caffeine tablets to add a spike of energy, which countered any soporific side effects from the drugs.

This was the war she fought. Every hour. Every day.

She preferred not to remember what things had been like before pharmacological forces arrived to break her siege. There were only vague memories, of schizoid worlds into which she retreated, dimensions where people and things were bound together with strange acausal connections.

Drugs had redrawn the battle lines, hemming in the madness and allowing her to reconnect with the world.

She concentrated on the job at hand. She needed to open the lockbox.

It was a simple device, and she inserted the tension wrench she carried with her into the bottom of the keyhole while with her other hand she placed a needle at the top of the lock. She torqued the wrench slightly while pushing the needle. The lock pins fell into place, and the box opened.

She unlocked the front door and stared down the dark corridor.

The drugs were doing their work, shaving layers of anxiety away.

The shadowy interior of the house, which would have been menacing to her at any other time, looked simply unlit, inanimate and lifeless.

She stepped inside, keeping the lights off, and guided herself by touch to the living room, which was the largest of the downstairs rooms. She drew the curtains and took one of the desk lamps and laid it on the floor. It cast a low, diffuse glow along the expanse of the grey carpet, keeping the top of the room still cloaked in shadow.

She dropped her carry-on bag to the floor, unzipped

it and rooted around, removing the iPad inside and taking it to the couch furthest away from the window.

The data files were arranged under two headings: the locket and the Polaroid picture. Like an archaeologist, Sara clung to these relics, working tirelessly to find some clue that would connect her to her past. Each file had thousands of entries. She had stared at each of the clues for so long that she sometimes felt she was like psych patients who look for faces in cloud formations. The locket's number string was, at times, a direct message from her mother and at other times a meaningless sequence of digits.

Sara flipped to the last data file, the front cover of which was the scan of a dog-eared photo, fading to sepia, of a man in his mid-twenties, in a suit and tie, with a short, military haircut. Its image had been pored over so many times by her it now seemed bleached of any significance. She flipped the image to the left, revealing a more recent picture of the man, now in his fifties.

Charles Salt.

The message had been clear.

DO NOT TRUST THIS MAN.

Too many questions had accreted over the years. Who had written the message? Was it even addressed to Sara? Could the message be trusted? In the absence of any answers, she had set this man as her north star, the only link she had to the mystery of her identity.

But who was he to her?

Ally. Friend. Enemy.

She had no idea, although at various times over the

years she had created elaborate fantasies, painting Salt as each. And in each daydream she was different too, moulding herself to the contours of the persona. Without memory, her identity was plastic, a narrative easily reshaped.

Her eyes continued to flit rapidly back and forth between the current and older photo, her mind flipping between the connections and assumptions in her head.

Before falling asleep, she carefully peeled off the thin film covering her fingertips, placing each in a row on the coffee table next to her.

The fake fingerprints resembled a series of tiny pink upturned seashells.

43

The website peered down on Waterman from the main cinema screen, like an animated Orwellian billposter, ticking down each second, keeping them all in a constant state of tension.

132:12:05.

132:12:04.

132:12:03.

It made Waterman's gut twist every time he looked at it.

'There was a bully in my school. Jenks . . .'

Waterman turned to see Hunter was standing next to him, also staring at the screen.

'. . . he told me once he would, at some point over the following week, punch me hard enough to burst my nose. Like a tomato.'

Hunter's shoulders twitched, as if the memory still caused shivers to run up his spine.

'Kept repeating his threat,' continued Hunter, still staring ahead, as if he was in a confessional, 'reduced me to a state of terror.'

Hunter finally looked at Waterman.

'It took me many years to realize that was the point.'

Waterman nodded and they both looked back at the screen.

132:01:17.
132:01:16.
132:01:15.

'We need each other at times like this,' said Hunter. 'Congratulations on the promotion.'

Waterman looked down and saw Hunter's hand extended towards him.

'Do you believe in ghosts?' he asked Hunter, taking his hand.

Hunter looked back in confusion.

'I don't,' continued Waterman, looking back at the screen. His expression remained inscrutable. 'But sometimes you get a sense of things. Your reptilian brain begins working. And you feel this can only be the work of one person. But it can't be, because . . .'

'. . . Orpheus is dead,' finished Hunter. He shook his head. 'Hellfire missiles flattened the building.'

'Let's hope to God you are right.'

44

At the best of times, John Harker's job required late hours.

A typical review of a GCHQ personnel file involved deep-dig background checks. By the time he had finished with each of them, he would know not only their Internet search history, but the reading material on their nightstand for the past five years.

His mind was foggy with sleep. But he couldn't quit for the day yet, as one more search needed to be complete for him to have his daily quota. He called up the employee report from today's staff intake on to his system and scrutinized it with a professional eye, taking a sip from a second cup of coffee.

The standard criminal and general history checks had been complete when the employee had first enrolled. These were keyed off fingerprint and other biometric scans and had revealed nothing of significance.

But since Waterman had increased the internal security controls, an additional layer of screening had been added. It was a highly secret and controversial one, borrowed from the surveillance techniques used on suspected homegrown jihadists returning from training camps in Syria or Afghanistan. To apprehend them,

RAF aircraft with sensitive listening equipment circled the skies above English cities, seeking voiceprints captured by spy planes flying sorties overseas. GCHQ employed a similar method, monitoring each new employee's phone calls and seeking voiceprint matches from existing terror and criminal databases.

Harker needed to use the bathroom, so initiated the voiceprint search, pushed his seat back and was about to head to the toilet when he heard a ping.

His computer function was set to let out an audible alert when there was a discrepancy on a name under review.

Harker leaned forward to get a better look at his screen.

The voiceprint had failed. The voice was of someone else.

He put his coffee down and began typing, programming a wider search based on the voiceprint.

Two more pings came back in quick succession.

He pulled them up: two other false identities now matched to the same voiceprint.

He stood, confused for a second. He had sat through procedures for how to deal with this event. But it had never happened before.

GCHQ's biggest fear, that a mole could get access, had remained only theoretical to date.

He hesitated, then forced himself to start moving, walking quickly along the row of cubicles towards the centre of the hall and his supervisor's desk.

Before Harker left his station, he switched on the mute function on his computer.

The pings from his loudspeaker had become so frequent that they had become one long continuous siren.

45

Sara looked around her.

All the other secretarial staff were focused on their terminals, their features studies in concentration.

She had been assigned to update a map of a certain section of the wilderness of Afghanistan. From the satellite view she had been given, it resembled a lunar surface, but on the ground, reconnaissance reports indicated there were camouflaged encampments dotted around the countryside. She was tasked with updating the map with the new intel.

All around her, programmers followed similar tasks, updating intelligence reports with new data that required human sensitivities. Each of them wore Plantronics phone headsets, through which they communicated with a central bank of analysts in a room on the other side of the facility.

Her plan was to spend a few days learning about the sprawling facility, testing its defences and finalizing her plan, not least exploring the viability of her escape route. There was a limit to what could be learned over the web, the missing pieces required on-site reconnaissance. But first, she needed to blend in; her anonymity was essential to her ability to gather the rest of what she needed.

Sally Shaw, the supervisor of her pod, sat at a desk on a raised dais, keeping a watch over the floor. The subject of much talk during coffee breaks, her short bob hairstyle and brusque manner placed her in the indeterminate space between a masculine woman and an effeminate man.

As Sara was typing, a tingling ran up and down her spine, faint and indeterminate, like the deadened alert a spider receives when a fly lands on a frozen web. The drugs flowing through her system dulled her senses, creating ice floes in her bloodstream, slowing down the rhythms of life around her. But whatever had just happened was enough of a threat to send a jolt of electricity through her system. Some part of her, buried deep in the frost, shook itself awake.

Sara responded immediately, peeling off her headset and walking quickly past the rows of terminals to the side door, even as the front doors of the main entrance pushed open and a man strode quickly to Shaw's desk, his eyes searching the rows of heads at monitors. He lowered his head and whispered something in Shaw's ear. By the time Shaw pointed to Sara's empty chair, Sara had already swiped the side door with her key card and was stepping out of the room.

She looked quickly around her, trying to keep her breathing regular. They had discovered her. She must have been caught by some invisible tripwire.

Whatever protocols existed at GCHQ for containing a threat through infiltration were underway now. The facility would go into lockdown. They may not have her true identity, but they had her face, and the black orbs that studded the ceiling throughout the building would sweep the floor space for her.

There was no longer any choice. She had to move now or be caught.

That morning she had checked the large framed map of the facility that hung on the wall in the reception area for non analyst staff. The room she was looking for was on the analyst side of the facility. She needed to get to the other side.

The challenge was that the entire building was quarantined into separate areas, with each district divided by plate-glass electronic turnstiles that responded to colour-coded swipe cards. Sara's card – with a green vertical swipe – provided access to her non-analyst section only. The other part of GCHQ was as good as hermetically sealed from her. This was the access issue she expected she would solve over the first few days, but it now came crashing forwards, a problem that needed to be solved immediately or she would be lost.

Outside in the corridor, staff mixed with uniformed security, who patrolled the corridors, their Glock pistols strapped to their belts. She noticed that the badges that hung from the belts of the security officers were the only ones without a colour. Each of the badges dangling around the necks or from the belts of the other employees had different-colour stripes on them: some green, some red, others purple, beige or black.

It was impossible to know how many different checkpoints there were between her and her destination, and which badges would provide access to them. All she could be sure of was that using her own badge, assuming it was still active, would announce her whereabouts as effectively as a flare shot into a cloudless night sky.

It took her less than a few seconds to formulate a plan. She needed to follow the group of people flowing forwards towards the first set of gates. Once there, she could get a sense of whether there could be a way to bypass the system. She was so fixed on the other people that she didn't notice the tall, bearded security officer until she had crashed right into the back of him.

'Sorry, my fault,' said Sara, her hands held up in apology, 'I wasn't looking where I was going.'

Without taking his eyes off her, the officer felt for his gun, an instinctive reflex, before softening his features and nodding.

'No problem, ma'am.'

After he turned and continued walking, Sara looked down into the palm of her hand, where the pure white security clearance card nestled.

She swiped the card and walked along the curved walkway, past recessed rooms where analysts sat facing monitors that flashed in the dark like fluorescent aquaria.

Sara was within one hundred feet of her destination. She could see its green door ahead of her.

Frank Levy's job was to guard the guardians. While GCHQ's powerful gaze was directed outwards, a small team within the facility looked inwards, painstakingly checking security and vetting each employee and visitor.

Levy, an affable father of four, led the team. His pride in his job was equalled only by his record; there had been no major security breaches in the five years he had been there. Sleep-deprived at home and at work, he existed on a diet of sugar and caffeine. Right now, his knee bounced frenetically under the table as he opened a can of diet Coke, his second of the hour. A suspected mole was MIA from her desk and the entire facility was sealing itself off in sections, damming employees into districts while guards sifted through them and Levy's eyes-in-the-sky scanned each face.

As he coordinated the actions of his staff, he noticed a light flashing on a security console. A data anomaly had appeared. He touched the screen in front of him and called up the details.

GCHQ monitored its own physical security in a similar manner to the way it gathered information on outside threats: through human and computer intelligence. The human kind patrolled the corridors and monitored the CCTV cameras embedded in the ceilings. The computer intelligence had many facets, from the employee reviews his number two, John Harker, undertook to the mapping of anomalies in security card use across the facility.

Levy twisted in his chair and looked over to Dan Rush, a young trainee in his first month on the job.

'Security guard just gained access to Section 3. First time he's ever been there. What do we do?'

Every opportunity was a teaching moment. Rush paused for a second before reciting the answer from memory.

'If he's been here one month, then the deviation from the norm isn't much, but if it's one year, then it's unusual.'

Levy gave him a nod.

'Good. Look him up.'

Rush rattled on the keyboard, then cast his eye across the security file of the guard which had appeared.

'He's been here three years.'

'And that's the first sweep he's done of Section 3? Pull up the ceiling cameras for that section right after access.'

Levy pushed his rolling Aeron chair to Rush's console, where a pop-up window appeared in the monitor, showing an aerial view of the main circular corridor.

'Access the personnel file of the guard. His name is Bob Cape,' said Levy.

Rush nodded, directed his cursor over a file with employee data and found the sub-file on the security guards. He pulled up a photograph of a heavy-set man with a large bushy red beard.

Levy turned from the picture of Cape back to the aerial view, and looked closer at the figure who had just used Cape's card. They couldn't see the face, but the rest was clearly visible.

'That doesn't look like Bob Cape,' said Levy drily, reaching for the phone.

*

Sara approached the final set of glass turnstiles. Small lines of people snaked back from the three glass partitions, and she joined the nearest line. When her turn came, she swiped the card.

Nothing.

She wiped the card on her sleeve and tried again.

The gates remained closed.

She tried it once more, this time triggering a red light on the machine.

The card had been deactivated.

She stepped out of the line. In front of her, across the other side of the turnstile, she could see four security men coming around the corner. And at the end of the corridor behind her, a door opened, and two security men exited and began walking towards her. They were thirty yards behind her, closing in.

Sara let instinct drive her and pushed her body against the person in front, a tall woman with bright-red lipstick and heavy-frame glasses, driving them both through the turnstile at the same time. The woman twisted around in protest, yelping in dismay as she was carried through to the other side.

'Sorry, in a rush,' said Sara, passing her and making for the green door.

The security guards were ten yards away and stopping all women walking in their direction, checking ID cards.

Sara pushed through the green door and stepped inside.

46

The room was barely larger than a janitor's closet. Other than a metal storage cupboard that took up half of the opposing wall, it was empty.

A metal fire escape door on the other side of the room was the only other exit.

Sara locked the door behind her and pulled at the metal closet doors. They rattled but stayed closed.

She pulled out her tension wrench, her hands shaking, and dropped it on the ground. In a tranquil setting, where guards weren't closing in, seconds away from her capture, picking the lock of an office supply locker would be a walk in the park.

She picked it up and gritted her teeth.

Come on, Sara. You can do this. Breathe.

She knelt down and inserted the wrench, twisting it until the catch gave and the door pulled open.

Inside, a wall of wires, pulsing with colour, snaked from the floor to the ceiling. This was the information highway flowing down from the dish satellites on the roof to the neural computers housed in the basement.

Sara pulled out a transparent plastic box the same size as a portable sewing kit from her pocket. Fibre optic taps – thin blue jacks attached to orange wiring that connected to her phone – nestled inside. Her assumption — that this access point would be within the formidable firewalls that ringed the perimeter of the facility's IT systems — was about to be tested.

She ran her fingers down the wires until she found the lettering she was seeking.

NEURAL NET.

She spliced the fibre taps into the wire and tapped an app on her phone. Instantly, geometric shapes bubbled and popped on screen, dissolving and reappearing into schematics of a database system.

She could hear voices approaching, and doors swinging open and slamming shut in a progression that suggested every room was being checked.

They were close. Her door would be next.

Steady. Keep steady.

She tapped her finger lightly on her iPhone screen, over and over, qualifying each choice she made, zeroing in on the exact location she was seeking.

Suddenly, the handle of her door twisted down, once, then twice.

'It's locked. Over here!' came a voice from outside.

There was a moment's silence and then the entire door thudded up against its frame as a heavy foot kicked at it.

'Get the keys!' a voice shouted from outside.

Sara kept tapping the screen until the file she was seeking dropped down like a blind. She saved it to her hard file and pocketed her phone just as she heard a key scrape into the lock behind her.

47

Sara pushed open the emergency exit door and stepped inside. She was at the top of a flight of concrete steps that headed down one floor.

She was at the physical limits of her plan. From this point, she was flying blind.

The stairs might lead to an exterior door, or they could lead deeper into the facility, cornering her, ending her search and depositing her in a military prison cell for probably the next twenty years.

The thought of being cooped up in a low-ceilinged cement box sent a jolt of panic through her, robbing her of purpose. She stood for a second, teetering on the hang of the step, as if invisible wires tethered her to the exit door behind her. The image had a particular terror for her, like being buried alive. She wasn't sure why.

Don't think. Move.

Before any other thoughts could come, she thundered down the stairs, her arm gripping the iron balustrade for support.

Behind her, a crash signalled the entry of the guards into the storage closet. They would swarm through the room and be at the top of the stairs in seconds.

Sara leaped down the last few stairs and landed on

both feet. She was on the second level, a short passage-way dead-ending in metal doors in both directions.

She quickly took her bearings. One of these doors would be closer to the outside shell of the building and one would be an interior door.

Behind her, she could hear the heavy boots of the guards on the stairwell.

If she chose the wrong direction, she would be sunk.

She hesitated, retracing her steps, conjuring up in her mind a three-dimensional model of her route in the past few minutes. She had turned a one-eighty from her entry through the green door one floor above her. The courtyard had been on her left-hand side as she had entered. That meant whatever was behind the door to her left was closer to the outside of the facility.

She ran down the corridor and pulled open the door.

It was a utility closet.

Empty, other than a sink fixed into the far wall and a dirty mop lying on the floor.

A dead end.

The guards had reached the lower ground floor. Their voices were amplified as they bounced against the walls of the stairwell, creating the impression that she was being pursued by an army. It was too late to try the other door.

She had no option now. There was only one way to go, and that was forwards.

She slammed the door shut behind her and locked it. *Think. Every problem has a solution. Think.*

She had come too far in her search for it to end here.

This was not going to be the end of her story. Not after everything she had been through. Why did she choose this direction?

Heavy fists began pounding on the outside of the door, creating a cacophony that crowded the thoughts from her head.

Sara willed her synapses to keep firing, guiding her.

If her instinct had been right, then on the other side of the far wall of the utility room was the north end of the car park. The wall to which the sink was fixed must be an exterior wall of the building.

Her thoughts had not yet taken the shape of words when she kicked the sink as hard as she could: a shotgun blast that shifted the sink, causing it to dip significantly on the side.

Sara kicked it again, harder this time.

Spider web cracks appeared in the wall, running outwards in seams from the point of connection of the sink.

She put her head closer to the taps. She could just about make out the thinnest line of clear sky through the hairline fracture running through the concrete.

Sara stood up and took a step back, breathing hard to build up her strength for a final kick. A jangling sound could be heard on the other side of the door. A wheel of keys was being turned, someone sifting for the right one.

Her next move would decide her future.

She took two strides at speed and scissored her heel at the sink. It split cleanly in two, falling with a loud cracking sound on to the floor, and immediately released a fountain of water that drenched Sara to the skin. The main water pipe had been damaged, and the size of the aperture and the quantity of water combined to give the fountain the power of a high-velocity fire hose. The entire cell was caught in the spray, coating the surface of the gunmetal-grey walls immediately.

The destruction of the sink had created a porthole-sized breach in the wall.

Sara willed her feet to move and cross the length of the room.

But she was staring down at the floor. In only a few seconds, the water had collected in a thin film that covered the entire surface. It was halfway up her heel now.

Wham! An image of a young girl hit her. She was sitting in a bath, water rising and covering her knees and chest, until she had to tilt her head at an angle and raise her nose to breathe.

The image robbed Sara of breath, leaving her gasping. It dropped out of nowhere and yet had the emotional force of a memory.

The spray of water from the ruptured pipe pummelled the far wall.

Wham! Another image hit her. Hours bleeding into each other as the girl sat shivering in the dark.

The force of it transported her back, immobilizing her. She was not just seeing these images. She *was* that little girl.

Move, Sara. Move.

The door handle was pumping down, keys rattling in the lock.

She took a final look behind her and ran for the far wall, throwing her arms in front of her and diving through the gaping hole.

48

Two security guards flanked Salt as he walked quickly from his office to a private lift that led down to a basement garage.

Less than three minutes after getting the alarm, he was sitting in the back seat of his armour-plated government car, staring through bullet-proof glass as it surged up a ramp and into the halogen glow of street-lamps framed against night sky. The car was still accelerating, pressing the back of Salt's head to the leather head rest. He knew the driver wouldn't stop until they were on the motorway, a mile away, an asphalt escape route that would take them straight to London. The car phone built into the seat rang once, and Salt swiped it up.

'We're pretty sure it was a solitary intruder,' said Waterman, without preamble. 'We're searching the car park for her. We believe you were the target.'

'Who is she?'

'We don't know yet. Fake ID. One of the best we've seen. An entire alternative history.'

'How do you know she was after me?'

'She hacked into the neural net. Accessed only one thing: your employee file.'

Salt looked out of the window, thinking through the

repercussions of what Waterman had told him. He was silent long enough that Waterman cleared his throat.

'What about the other hack?' said Salt.

'Caleb Goodspeed?' Salt could almost hear Waterman shake his head. 'It was self-serving. He was trying to access data for his . . .'

Salt interrupted him.

'There's no coincidence in our world. Find Goodspeed. Bring him in. And send me her fake ID.'

Salt hung up and pulled an iPad from his briefcase. The car was equipped with an encrypted Wi-Fi network. He found the drive to and from home each night was his most productive time of the day. Insulated from all but the most urgent calls, he could review the crises of the day and give his mind essential time to make connections.

An email dropped into his folder from Waterman. Salt opened the attachment and looked at the copy of the plastic ID card.

Gazing at the camera was a face that stirred a memory for him. Where had he seen it before? Somewhere.

Black eyes stared at him, as if she knew, at the time the orientation picture was taken, at some point Salt would be staring back.

No earnest smile – the ubiquitous feature of their ID cards, employees projecting as much trust as they could – instead, a wary look, assessing. Like a predator watching from the safety of a thicket. Or was Salt imagining it all?

She was attractive. Enough so that she could probably

make her living from her looks. But instead she devoted her life to learning about detection modalities, spyware and hacking. The skills needed to break into one of the most secure military facilities in the world.

Salt turned over the thoughts in his head. Right now, Waterman would be running her image through their databases, looking for hits. The software had been upgraded recently to run permutations on prospective physical identity changes. The system not only recognized faces from known criminal registers, but also could recognize attempts to change them from over one hundred and twenty plastic surgery, make-up and other alteration procedures. Skills as good as their mystery woman possessed would still leave footprints. Within a few hours, they would find out her identity.

Salt looked out of the window, seeing that they were entering central London, the car hovering above the west of the city, speeding along the overpass. Below, the city lights winked, spreading out into the distance like a bed of pearls on a black satin sheet.

He had vowed to never leave London, so when he agreed to take the job at GCHQ he had insisted on a car and driver so he could commute. The journey was tiring at times, but it worked in his favour to separate his private life from work. The length of the drive gave Salt the excuse he needed to avoid socializing with his work colleagues. He continued to occupy the four-storey townhouse off the King's Road he had lived in for twenty years, the one thing he chose to keep after the divorce.

'Do you need anything else tonight, sir?' asked the driver, interrupting Salt's reverie.

They were one street away from his home. There were no lights on inside any of the houses. It was as if the street itself was sleeping. In contrast with the eternal nature of operations at GCHQ, this sense of normality was precious to him.

'No,' he replied.

The car slid into place in front of his home.

The driver waited while Salt walked to the front door. He doubled as a wheel and body man while on Salt's detail, charged with ensuring the head of GCHQ made it inside his front door safely each night.

Once inside, the threat of harm to Salt became so remote as to be negligible. MI5 had supplied the contractor who had reinforced the security of the house. Windows were replaced with durable, abrasion-resistant polycarbonate sheets five hundred times stronger than glass and sufficient to thwart an RPG attack. Bombproof iron doors sealed the house at the front and rear exits, and outward-facing locks were Israeli-made: floating, with magnetic and perpendicular tumblers and undrillable carbide plates, virtually impossible to pick.

He unlocked the front door and stepped into the hall. The maid had left dinner in the oven, and the roasty aroma clung to the air, making the house feel inhabited, which was the secondary intention. He dropped his keys into the silver tray by the door. A wedge of mail sat unopened next to the tray. Letters were addressed to a

Mr Henry, who was registered on the electoral roll as a retired schoolteacher.

Susan had decorated the house, and the hallway was an especial focus for her. It was the birth canal to their home, the first experience a visitor would have of their domestic life. Elegant picture frames crowded the walls on both sides, chronicling the life they had built together. Their engagement and their wedding, the birth and growth of their two children, family holidays and family events, formal dress and vacation attire, joyful faces smiling at the camera, innocent of the rupture that was to come. Salt was the curator of this gallery, of this family that existed only in the past. Losing it was the price he had paid for his career, something he was going to make sure he never forgot.

He stopped halfway down the hallway, in front of the locked door that led to his study. Salt wanted to check to see if Waterman had uncovered any further information on today's trespasser.

Before he opened the door, he found himself staring at a small frame, the size of a hardback book, on the wall in front of him. This was his one concession from the family wall. It was his first MI5 identity card, ornamentally placed on a black background. Salt often contemplated that card, and the Polaroid picture of his twenty-five-year-old face staring from it. At times, he felt a will to connect with his younger self that was so powerful it kept him rooted to the spot for what seemed like hours. He wanted to reach into the picture, reach back through time, and speak directly to the man he used to be, ask him whether he was disappointed with the man Salt had become.

His career had begun in a blaze of glory. Anything seemed possible. At the time the ID card picture was taken, an asset had walked into Salt's life who promised to reshape the entire face of British intelligence. Salt's career trajectory had no limits. The restart of Operation Orpheus was the most dramatic development in British military intelligence in the last seventy years.

Salt kept the identity card because he wanted a reminder of the look on his face. The look of a young Caesar, his rule about to begin, looking down on a world to be reshaped.

Within a few years, the asset would have disappeared and the operation abandoned. Salt's career would continue down a more traditional path, not an everyday life by any means, but not one that redefined his world. The look on his face came to be replaced by the look of a man who must play a part, even if unremarkable. Salt touched the picture, as if it was a holy relic, and unlocked the door.

The stairs led down to a set of rooms he had converted into an office. The floors were new, a redesign prompted by the installation of secure communication cables running under the floor.

He sat down in his chair, wincing slightly from the back pain. Too much time spent sitting was wreaking havoc on his lumbar region. He switched on his desk lamp, not bothering to turn on the overhead lights when he went in, and powered up his laptop.

He had just signed into his email account when he realized he was not alone.

His fingers froze, suspended over the keyboard, senses becoming suddenly keen, every hair standing on end, adrenaline coursing through his system, a rolling wave of fear surging up his neck and scalp.

He looked up as his hand slipped below the desk. The rest of the room was deep in shadow, he could not see the back walls, but he could just about see the outline of the person sitting in the armchair in the corner of the room.

'How did you get in?'

Salt's voice was calm, curious, like he was addressing a friend.

On the underside of the desk, his finger rested on the ornamental pearl button. He pressed it once, sending a bolt of data at light speed through cables. The warning LED would light up almost immediately in the main communications room at MI5 HQ at Thames House. In the drills conducted a year ago, the police and armed services vehicles arrived nine minutes later. They were waiting for the signal to be given that time, so Salt factored an extra minute for additional preparation. Ten minutes. He had to survive for ten minutes before unmarked vans arrived and stormed the house with lethal force.

'Do you remember me?'

It was a woman's voice. Equally neutral, devoid of any agitation. This was not a break-in by a fanatic or madman.

The outline stood up and walked out of the shadows. She moved slowly, and Salt found that his heart was jack-hammering before she stepped into the light.

She sat down in the chair in front of his desk.

The same face as on the ID card.

And it was then that he placed it.

A faint resemblance of the girl, like the first sketch from which an oil painting is created.

'The prodigal returns,' he said at last, almost to himself. 'Of course I remember you.'

Something flew up from where she sat. It landed on his desk, lying sideways across his blotter.

It was an old Polaroid photograph. Salt's face looked out at him.

He recognized the picture immediately. Knew where and when it was taken. It was the moment it all began to slip away for him. Phoebe had just run away with Orpheus. He was personally leading the search, combing the streets near the safe house, a sense of growing desperation in his chest. He was the man who had captured a unicorn only to lose it.

Phoebe must have been less than fifty feet from him when she took the picture. He was so close.

He turned the picture over and read the warning on the back. It was ironic: the mother's picture had unwittingly led to a quest that had brought Sara back to him a quarter of a century later.

'Why do I have this picture?' asked the woman.

Salt's eyes flicked at the clock on the wall.

Eight and a half minutes to go.

Right now, boots were running into covered garages, unlocking ammunition cases, pulling sub-machine guns from the armoury wall, checking siege armaments – stun and flash grenades, repelling equipment – slamming doors. Corrugated metal garage screens were *clack-clacking* as invisible hands in dark interiors propelled them upwards. The firing sounds of ignitions were coming from within, followed by the throttled sounds of engines. Headlights were flipping on, like the eyes of malevolent monsters opening in dark caves.

He had to keep her talking.

There was only one way to keep her attention: tell her the truth.

'We first made the connection in the Second World War. Intelligence won that war. In both senses of the word. Turing, Welchman, Alexander and Milner-Barry: the finest minds of their generation. Chess champions, mathematicians, scientists. Their IQs were off the charts.'

He shifted in his seat. Seven minutes.

'And that's what got military intelligence thinking. Because humans have two very different operating systems. The left side is the newer part of our brain, developed after prehistoric times. It's analytical and conscious. Perfect for solving puzzles. Quantified by IQ. When you compared Turing and the others with regular people, they were like gods. So, we thought, what about the other side of the brain? The limbic system, our subconscious. It's the oldest part of our brain. Instinctual. Among other things, it houses intuition. The question we asked ourselves was: could we find the gods of this side of the mind?'

He paused, waiting for her to respond, but she stared at him, drinking him in. It was then that he realized he was being assessed. Her eyes scanned his, flicked down to his mouth, then his neck, then dropped to his chest to gauge his breathing.

She was seeing if he was lying.

He'd forgotten what it was like communicating with Orpheus. Was she doing it intentionally, or was it second nature? It was impossible to tell. If she didn't like an answer he knew she was capable of leaping across the desk and snapping his neck in one fluid movement, before his nervous response system would even have a chance to send a signal to his body to react.

The great white whale of British intelligence was sitting in front of him. If his strategy in the next hour was sound, if he played things perfectly, he could achieve his most profound wish – to recapture the past, to step back in time a quarter of a century and bring Orpheus back into the fold.

'We were interested in a specific part of the limbic system,' he continued, trying not to let his voice betray his excitement. 'A tiny area of the hypothalamic region called the parahippocampal gyrus. The seat of intuition. People with ability like yours have high levels of brainwave activity in this area. Unlike analytical intelligence, it seems to be genetic.'

'You don't need to keep looking at the clock,' she said. 'I'll tell you when they get here.'

Salt's entire body stiffened, like the predator hunting his prey who realizes he is himself being stalked. Never underestimate your own creation.

'Why are you here?' he asked, his curiosity cutting through the artifice. 'What do you want?'

'I want you to keep talking.'

Salt kept his eyes away from the clock, keeping them on hers. It must be five minutes now.

'The Naval Intelligence Department, the precursor to MI6, led the search. They met with stage performers, gypsies, mystics, anyone they thought might have that alternative power. The majority were frauds. As is often the case, it was difficult to gauge that at the time. The one exception was a Scot called Helen Duncan. Your great-grandmother. The reality of her powers took the entire British military establishment by surprise. Unfortunately, the story does not end well for her. She made enemies in powerful places. They soon realized they could not control her, and ordered her arrest in 1941. Helen became the last person to be tried in Great Britain under the Witchcraft Act 1735, and was convicted and imprisoned in Holloway Prison. The government then began a secret campaign to smear her reputation. After that war, and as the Cold War was beginning, we realized our mistake and reapproached her, but she refused to have anything to do with us. We reached out to her children, but none of them had the same abilities . . .'

The convoy of trucks would be flying through Victoria now, their sirens screaming as they ploughed a furrow through the traffic. When they arrived, he would need to use them as leverage, to bargain with Orpheus and show her there was no way out, other than agreeing to come back into his protection.

'It took us a year to find out about Aileen, your grandmother. Helen had her when she was sixteen, illegitimately. Aileen refused us as well. Aileen then had Phoebe, your mother. She was the first to make a deal with us. We would pay for your education, and in return, we would train you and her . . .'

'Train us as what?' she interrupted. She was sitting forwards in her seat, fully engaged.

'As spies, of course,' replied Salt. 'That was the agenda. To weaponize intuition.'

He let the words hang in the air. This was his phrase, one that laced each of the confidential memos he wrote about Orpheus at the time.

'What happened to my mother?'

'After hiding you, she came right back to us. The programme continued,' said Salt. 'We never understood how you disappeared for so long. Someone with your abilities we were sure would surface sooner rather than later. But Phoebe told us she had made sure you would never be found.'

He watched her as she processed this, the grotesque irony of her lifelong search settling on her. Phoebe's brainwashing was likely intended not only to make Orpheus forget but also to damage her hypothalamic region, stunting her supersensory abilities. A clean start. But Phoebe couldn't reboot Orpheus' nature. That persisted, tugging its subject remorselessly back. Orpheus was Orpheus, and a thousand lifetimes would bring her back here, to him.

Two minutes or less, by his count. When they arrived, sniper units would take positions behind the bonnets of the cars, combing the rooftops, while tactical teams would pull battering rams from the backs of vehicles and prepare stun grenades. Even if she thought she knew what was coming, there was little she could do about it.

They would be near Sloane Square now, driving at high speed, weaving through cars, racing through traffic lights, flashing across intersections.

'How did the programme continue without me?'

Salt looked at her, in confusion for the first time.

'You don't remember anything?'

She shook her head.

Salt sat back in his chair, a realization dawning over him.

'When you escaped, we found a new recruit. He became Orpheus . . .'

He lifted his arms in a dramatic flourish.

'The king is dead. Long live the king.'

'Who was it?' she asked.

'Your brother. Christian,' said Salt.

That's when he heard it. The faintest sound, like a sigh coming from outside, brake pads compressing in a sudden, controlled stop. He looked at her. She had heard it too. Before she could say anything, he pulled open the drawer of his desk, grabbing for the Taser.

Even as he gripped it, she was kicking the desk from

the other side, lifting it up and tipping it over him. He stood up as quickly as he could, scrambling backwards, avoiding the heavy oak bureau as it crashed towards him, stepping back over the chair as it tipped to one side.

By the time he regained his balance and lifted the Taser up, she was gone.

49

Sara ran up the stairs to the ground floor, along the corridor and then up the stairs to the next floor.

What Salt had told her created an overpowering urge to vomit. This anonymity which she had felt so suffocated by her whole life was in fact a gift from her mother, an act of maternal protection to keep Sara safe, from a predatory military machine, and from herself. She had tugged on an errant thread with such persistence that everything had come undone. She finally knew who Salt was, the puller of puppet strings that her mother had sacrificed everything to protect her from. And here Sara was, in his house, running for safety. She damped down her spinning mind. She had to run, her priority now was to not get caught.

Sara could hear the sounds of more vehicles arriving, thudding into place, at the front and back of the house.

They would storm the street-level doors first. There was only one option, which was up. If there was a way out it would be up through the roof.

She had reached the top floor, her lungs screaming for air.

Doors slammed open on the ground floor, and she

could hear shouting and the sound of bodies filling the entrance.

She was on a short landing, a black metal door with a fire escape bar facing her. She launched herself at it, smashing into it at full speed, the momentum carrying her off-balance on to a tiny, tarred roof terrace wrapped in a black metal railing.

She channelled all the emotions that threatened to overwhelm her into her escape. All her anger – at herself, at Salt – all her grief – for the life she could have had, for growing up alone.

A high-decibel alert shrieked into the night, jarring her back to the present. The opening of the door had tripped an alarm.

'She's on the roof!'

The shout came from the street, followed by a voice she recognized. Salt.

'I want her alive!'

The sounds of heavy boots came pounding up the stairs.

The roofs of the terrace of houses extended in either direction, a series of bare aerial plots each encircled by a metal railing. She was in an arid landscape of chimneys and satellite dishes, in the middle of a block that ended on either side with a last roof that formed a cliff edge into the night.

'No live fire!'

The boots were almost upon her, and she began running, leaping over the balustrade nearest to her and landing in a light crouch on the next property. Sara ran across to the other side and vaulted over the fence.

She ran across the length of the roof and leaped over the railing, landing on the roof of the next house. The last roof of the terraced row was several houses away, and she ran across each roof, leaping over each balustrade, approaching the cliff-edge into darkness. Only two roofs away.

She was about to leap over the final barrier when a deafening noise erupted behind her, a series of firecracker explosions. At the same instant, a wave of projectiles flew through the air around her. The effect was startling, like being caught inside a flock of crows taking flight. They smacked into the fence and chimneys with loud cracks and flew over the edge of the roof, disappearing into the sickly yellow light cast by the streetlamps.

A white-heat pain stabbed her leg, like a horse had kicked her from behind. She screamed in agony and lost her balance, flop-rolling on to the last roof on the terrace, her arms loose and her body bumping over the shells of rubber bullets strewn on the floor.

Shouts came from behind her.

'She's hit!'

Boots were running.

'Hold your fire!'

Sara stood up and tried to put weight on her leg but immediately cried out. She looked quickly behind her.

There were at least twenty of them, approaching

in a slow sideways march: black fatigues and bala-clavas, the zebra stripe line of the police combat colours across their chests, rifles raised and pressed into shoulders.

She hobbled to the edge of the roof and looked over. There was an alleyway forty feet below, cobblestoned, and on the other side, a row of garages. A quick calcu-lation: the roof of the garage was twenty feet below the roof on which she was standing and about fifteen feet away.

There was no way she could make it.

She took four large strides backwards, her leg explod-ing with pain each time she put pressure on it.

'Don't do it. I can protect you!'

She didn't need to turn around to know who was calling to her.

Sara began running, each other step like a dagger plunged into her thigh. The edge of the roof was approaching, only feet away now, the momentum of her run carrying her past the point of no return, speed-ing up for a leap into the abyss.

She blocked out every rational voice in her mind, a primeval chorus of screams to stop running, to live for another day. She ignored them and listened instead to the whisper, the barely heard murmur deep inside her head, telling her something quite different.

She leaped over the edge of the building, her back foot planting itself on the gutter and propelling her into space, her arms reaching out, her legs bicycling furiously as she step-stoned on air, bootstrapping her body into a parabola, willing herself to reach the other side.

But gravity tugged at her insidiously and even before she reached halfway she was falling, falling, the garage roof still too far and the cobblestones coming at her at the speed of an express train.

50

The impact was violent, the air smashing from her lungs and whipping her head forwards, a concussion wave that ripped at her body, driving her into the pavement, crushing her frame into the bricks. She struggled to retain consciousness as long as she could, gripping the last precious second of life with her fingernails.

A fine rain was falling, barely more than a mist, haloing the streetlights above her, which leaned over, like skeletal passers-by stopping to stare.

This was it. The moment of her death. The sights around her, the last thing she would ever see. The infinitesimal beat bridging life and death, beyond bodily pain but before surrender.

Her search for meaning had brought an answer, and it was the wrong one. Like a monk, after a lifetime of devotion, dying only to find an angry god screaming at him in a language he cannot understand.

Her only choice now was acceptance of the tragedy of her life.

Her breath came out slowly. She pursed her lips to slow it down, savour it.

And then she inhaled abruptly, a sudden involuntary gasp, and the agony returned, driving a bed of nails into every part of her back and legs, pulling her back down into the ground with heavy weights. The pain was excruciating, but it brought with it hope, that life was returning.

A groan escaped, and she rolled over to the side, looking down in confusion at the glossy black shell that cradled her. She was lying in a metal crater she'd created by the impact of her fall.

'We need to go. Now!'

She looked up at the speaker, her eyes woozy, light and shadow tracing in her vision. Someone was standing over her, only the top half of his body visible. She put her hand down and pushed herself upwards, wincing as needle-stabs punched at her ribs.

She was lying on the destroyed bonnet of a car, the four corners twisted upwards like the petals of a flower from the force of her landing.

Hands were reaching over for her.

'They're coming!'

Sara twisted away from the hands and rolled off the bonnet, collapsing on to the cobblestones on all fours.

Shouts rang out, near and far, rolling around her head like a carousel. With all her effort, she put a hand out and pulled herself up.

She was standing by a black Range Rover, the front of which looked like it had been struck by a single blow from an industrial hammer. A man was opening the driver's side door and stepping behind the wheel. Tall, thirties, tailored jacket and t-shirt, handsome were it not for the sadness that seemed to have taken up residence in his eyes.

At the end of the street, black blobs ran around the corner, coalescing into a group, rifle barrels sticking out like antennae.

'Got her!'

Sara pushed herself off from the car and took an exploratory step. Blinding pain radiated through her entire body.

She began to move in the opposite direction, pushing past the open passenger door of the Range Rover, pulling her body with awkward steps towards the other end of the alleyway.

'Get in!' said the driver.

Sara hesitated, looking inside the car. Her vision was clearing, the blurred shapes coming into crisp focus. A few of the armed police stopped and knelt in the road to take aim.

'I know where your mother is!' shouted the man, his voice increasingly desperate.

Sara stared at him for a second, her mind still sluggish, groping its way back to life. And then she was climbing inside the car, the wheels of which were spinning even before she closed her door, slipping on the wet stones as the man pressed the pedal to the floor and the car zig-zagged in reverse before he regained control and spun them into a turn. The rear window exploded as a hail of rubber bullets pelted the car. The man shifted gears and threw the car into drive, pressing Sara into her seat with such force that she felt like she was landing on concrete for the second time.

The car tore down the road, the driver sitting up in

his seat to see over the damaged bonnet, which rattled precariously as they tore around corners.

Sara kept her eyes on the rear-view mirror, waiting for company.

'Bailing out at this moment would be risky,' said the man, smiling and looking across her. Sara followed his eyes and saw her fingers were gripping the door handle, ready to tear it open at any moment.

'I'm Caleb Goodspeed,' he said, holding out his hand.

51

Salt flashed his security badge at the grilled entrance to Downing Street.

He nodded at the policeman guarding the large black door and stepped into the lobby. The size of the building never ceased to surprise him. You never forgot you were in a converted residential house, no matter what room you were in, even though it was stripped of bedrooms. The remaining spaces had been converted into reception areas, with every effort having been made to ensure it did not resemble an office building.

A slim, red-haired man with a brisk, efficient manner marched up to him holding an appointment book in his hand.

'Sir Charles, you could at least have called.'

'He'll want to see me,' said Salt.

'You are lucky. He's still awake.'

Tim Sergeant, the Prime Minister's Permanent Private Secretary, was already walking away by the time he finished the sentence, and Salt followed him through the lobby and up what was called the Grand Staircase.

'Can I ask what this is about?' asked Sergeant.

Salt didn't reply. Sergeant should have known better than to ask.

'Follow me,' said the PPS curtly.

Salt followed him into the study at the back of the house.

Sergeant knocked once with the knuckle of an index finger, an announcement more than a request, and opened the door.

It was a fitting statement for 10 Downing Street that even the room called the study did not have a desk in it. It was a sitting room with a fireplace at one end, next to which sat four chairs arranged around a mahogany coffee table, and at the other end was a round table large enough to sit eight chairs. Bookshelves with lattice doors covered two of the walls, and framed portraits of previous prime ministers hung from chains affixed to the ceiling above the fireplace.

The Prime Minister sat at the dining table, a large red box open at his elbow. Salt could see reports, spread out across the desk, covered with bright-yellow sections that had been marked with a highlighter. The PM looked up distractedly as Salt entered.

'Charles, now's not a good time.'

'I just had a nice chat with Orpheus.'

The PM looked in alarm over the top of his half-moon spectacles.

'You caught her?'

'No. But we will.'

The PM stood up, leaving his papers, and walked over to where Salt was sitting, taking a chair opposite.

'Make sure you don't lose her again,' said the PM. 'This is our last chance at the Orpheus programme.'

Salt shook his head.

'Actually, the sister didn't attack Ultra. She's only just realized what she is. And that leaves only one other person who could be behind the attacks. Christian. So, both assets are in play.'

The PM said nothing for some time, the flames in the fireplace casting dancing reflections on his spectacles.

'If he really did survive the drone strike, then he's more powerful than we thought. What's your advice?'

Salt smiled. The night had left him invigorated; he felt like he was in his twenties again. There was no more doubt in his mind. He knew the way forwards.

'We're going to kill two birds with one stone.'

52

'Stop the car. Now.'

They were speeding down the Embankment, the river opening up like a black chasm on their right.

Caleb checked his rear-view mirror, then twisted the steering wheel and pulled the car into a side street, decelerating rapidly, bringing the car to a sudden stop.

Sara held up her hands.

'OK, who are you?'

'No friend of MI5, that's for sure,' said Caleb. 'I know they've been chasing you. Since you were a child. My wife . . .' A flicker of emotion overtook him, an infinitesimal hesitation, like a moment of vertigo, and he changed direction. 'They think you attacked a military base. Killed everyone in it. They showed me a video of you as a child. I saw you weren't capable of that. I wanted to get to you before they did.'

Sara held him in her gaze. Memories of her childhood were bleeding back, the blackouts, the school fights and the part of her that seemed to lurk in the shadows. His faith in her outweighed her own. Did she know what she was capable of? Attacking an army base sounded alien to her, as if Caleb was describing her sprouting wings and taking flight. But how much did she really know about herself?

'And how do you know where my mother is?'

'Your locket,' said Caleb.

He switched on the overhead light, dousing the front seats with a faint glow.

Sara's hand went instinctively to her necklace and gripped it protectively.

'What about it?' she said.

'Can I see it? I will give it back. I promise.'

Sara weighed his words and then pulled the locket over her head and handed it to him.

Caleb took it, holding it with infinite care.

'We need more light for this,' he said, reaching into his pocket and pulling out a thin matchbook. He pulled out a match, striking it and holding the bottom of the locket up to the flame.

'I saw the locket in the video. Look at this number.'

He tipped the side of the locket towards Sara.

515195140126923.

He handed the locket and the matchbook to Sara and pulled out his phone, opening an app and typing in the number.

'I ran it through some software I designed. It hacks codes. Look.'

515195 14 01269 23.

515195 N 01269 W.

$51.5195°$ N $0.1269°$ W.

'A longitude and latitude, run together as one number,' said Caleb. 'Your mother used a key, replacing N with its numerical position in the alphabet, and did the same with W. The locket code was a set of coordinates.'

She reached out for the phone and took it from Caleb. Her chest was so tight she could hardly inhale. She typed the coordinates into the Google Map function.

The map plunged from its default aerial view of Europe across towards England, and then tilted down into London, causing districts to expand and separate again until the Bloomsbury area of the city filled the screen.

A red flag planted itself in a spot a hundred yards from the British Museum.

Sara pressed the Street View option. A photograph appeared of a three-storey Victorian building covered in dishevelled building works. It looked abandoned.

She stared at it, mesmerized.

What she had been carrying around with her all this time was a coded message from her mother.

The locket was a fail-safe: a map to somewhere with answers. Her mother had not abandoned her. She had left her a compass to find her way.

53

'This is it,' said Caleb.

He pointed to the GPS on the dashboard of the car. 51.5195° N 0.1269° W.

He parked on the pavement, the looming silhouette of the British Museum dominating their peripheral vision.

In front of them was a three-storey, nineteenth-century terraced house, the only one in a line of white houses in which lights were not blazing. It stood out, like a rotten tooth in the white enamel line of the street.

This was the end of her quest. Some mysterious hand had pointed her here, from behind the fog of her forgetting. She looked over at Caleb. It was unsettling for her to be sharing this intimate moment with a stranger.

She opened the car door and stepped out, looking up at the house in front of her.

Some part of her was disappointed. Deep down she had hoped the locket would turn out to be a calling card left by her mother for Sara to find her way back into her arms. But there was no chance of that. The house looked like it had been abandoned decades earlier. Scaffolding covered the entire structure like an exoskeleton. If there were answers waiting for Sara inside the house, they were going to be dusty and inanimate.

In front of her, two sides of aluminium siding were tied together with string, marking the makeshift entrance to the building.

'Shall I come in with you?' asked Caleb.

Sara shook her head.

'Thanks. But . . .'

'Of course.' Caleb nodded. 'I'll go and park the car, it's too conspicuous here.'

Sara watched him drive off and then lifted the corrugated metal flap at the front of the building and ducked inside.

The building was little more than an empty husk.

She could see all the way through to the back. It was a large space, covered with discarded debris from building operations. An overnight light lit the space in dim fluorescent white, giving it a clinical air. Debris lay everywhere in the form of loose fittings, wiring and aluminium sidings.

She could see the building work was being done on the remains of an older house, as original brick and ironwork peeped through in several parts of the floor and wall sections. The effect was unsettling, as the house seemed neither one thing nor another, and had been stuck in this state for so long that even the renovations that had been attempted now seemed dated.

Whatever she had been expecting, this was not it. The place was lifeless. There had been no one here for years, possibly decades. Her mother was clearly not here. What Sara was looking at seemed to be the very definition of a dead end. But whatever doubts she had, she still had the bone-hard conviction that the locket held answers.

But what answers could there be here, in this abandoned site? Why would a woman brainwash a young girl, then abandon her, only to give her clues to this empty space?

Unless this wasn't the space to which her mother was directing her.

Maybe there was somewhere else her mother wanted her to see?

About ten feet away, two desks were pushed against one wall. A layer of dust, over an inch thick, covered them both. On top of one of the desks, a heavy industrial flashlight the size of a car battery lay face down next to a schematic.

Sara picked it up and turned it over.

It was a design plan of the property as purchased.

She could see the plans for the commercial building, drawn up in the 1950s, built over the top of the Victorian house. As she lifted up the blueprint, another one slipped off the table on to the floor. She reached down and picked it up. It was an identical drawing, but in it there was an outline of another structure inside the Victorian house. It was an ornate construction, an elaborate room with a domed roof.

In a tiny gothic font above it was written a date: 1685.

There was a building-within-a-building that predated the Victorian structure; something else on which the Victorian house itself was built. Sara pulled the outline she had seen of the current building and laid it on top of the new one. The plans were on vellum, and she lined up the two plans neatly on top of each other.

The effect was eerie; three successive structures built on each other, each separated from the other by hundreds of years, none cognisant of the other, yet adapting their contours to them, like the generations of a family.

This must be the reason why the property was derelict. The developers must have discovered the ruins of the seventeenth-century building and had to abandon their development plans.

She ran her finger along the pages, looking for some connection between the buildings, some common structure they might share. If something existed, it could be the way to pass between them. Her finger stopped as she traced a line.

It was some sort of flue that connected all three.

She grabbed the larger flashlight from the desk and headed deeper into the building. Her heart was beating faster now, not with panic but with anticipation.

She noticed that the centre of the structure had no Victorian elements at all; it was all sanded-down concrete and wiring.

At the rear was a wall section of rust-coloured brick, and the recessed square of what must be the old fireplace.

A few feet away there was a lead pipe.

The third strike with the makeshift battering ram

loosened the brickwork. She pushed a few bricks, and they began to work loose. A few more strikes and she was able to remove several more. A cool wind blew between them, and sooty darkness peeped through the gap.

She shone the flashlight in, and hunched close to the brickwork on her haunches to peer through. She could just about make out the flue of the chimney, the gate to a dense blackness the flashlight could not penetrate. She leaned in further and angled the flashlight to illuminate the other walls and corners, but the angle was too constrictive. She stood up and hacked at a few more bricks. Another loosened and came free in her hands.

She shone the light into the chimney and then what she saw caused her to stumble back, arms flailing, losing her centre of gravity, tipping back into a heap on the floor, her breathing ragged.

Her flashlight dropped a few feet away, and, as it rocked back and forth on the floor, the beam picked up the object of her panic.

54

The rat was the size of a house cat and sat on the brick-work, staring back at Sara, its red eyes flashing in the darkness.

She threw a brick at it, and it disappeared.

Steeling herself, she stuck her head back through the opening in the chimney, angling her light down into the dark. The shaft was square and two feet in each direction. The brickwork was soot-covered, causing the light to bounce off it. Sara tipped the angle of the light vertically. The vent plunged down, deeper than the reach of the beam.

She took a coin out of her pocket, held it over the opening of the abyss and then let it go. In her mind, she counted slowly:

'One. Two. Three . . .'

No sound.

'Four. Five. Six . . .'

An aching stillness.

'Seven . . . eight . . .'

Nothing.

She considered for a moment. It was possible that the coin had landed on something soft and she hadn't heard it. But she knew that wasn't likely. It was so quiet around her that her ears were actually ringing. She would have heard it land, whatever the surface, especially given the echoes that would likely come from the enclosed space. Which left one solution, which was that the flue went straight down over a hundred feet and possibly more.

She stared down into the darkness. The duct was the width of a coffin. And she had no idea if it tapered as it descended. If she were to lower herself into it, she could become trapped, her body wedged in tight, unable to descend or move her arms to ascend. She could become entombed there, most likely to lose her sanity before she starved to death.

An image flashed in her mind – a young girl buried alive in a porcelain box, slowly losing her mind, abandoned and alone.

The epiphany landed like a blow to her solar plexus. For the first time since her teenage years, she realized all those images, those sights triggered by her claustrophobia, were of her. She was that young girl. She had been witnessing the moment of her transformation.

As terrifying as it was to consider heading into the chimney, she knew that she would never have peace until she had followed the path she was on to its end. She ignored the palpitations in her chest and the sweat that pricked her palms and reached back into the chimney.

An examination of the sides with her light showed the brickwork was uneven, with some bricks jutting out further than the others: some by centimetres, others by inches.

She took off her belt and created a makeshift noose around her neck from which she hung the flashlight.

She hoisted herself up and then braced as she dropped feet first into the shaft. The width of the space was just wide enough for her shoulders to pass through, and the tips of her shoes felt for irregularities in the brickwork on which she could find a purchase. The beam of light shone down her torso and straight into the blackness below her feet.

She descended slowly, her feet feeling for holds while her arms were pinned to her sides, holding her weight against the bricks. After a few minutes, her limbs were shaking with fatigue and a sheen of sweat covered her body.

She had gone about thirty feet down when the first wave of panic hit her. She could not see the gap in the chimney above her any more, and the walls suddenly felt tight around her body. There was nowhere to go, and even if she did start to ascend, she had no idea if she could find the same footholds. Before she could think, the scream rose up from her sternum and then her throat, and then finally out through her mouth as she howled in the dark. Her arms began to shake, and her elbows pummelled the walls around her, causing shooting pains up her arms.

A snapping sound, like branches splintering, stopped her cry short.

To her right, her elbow had smashed the side of the wall with such force that the wall had ruptured. She looked closer to see that it was actually composed of wooden slats, which ran the length of the side wall. Sara slammed her elbow into the slats repeatedly, until she could discern a space on the other side. The hole she had created was large enough to crawl through.

As she lifted her arm back to shove the wooden slats a final time, the belt came undone, and the flashlight slipped from her neck. She made a grab for it, but it was too late. The light made a banging sound as it disappeared down the shaft, its beam piercing the dark like an erratic Klieg light as it caromed against the walls. After what seemed like an eternity, it became a speck below her and then disappeared.

Sara threw one arm and then another into the hole she had created, and lifted herself in.

55

She sensed she was in a vaulted space, although it was impossible to know how large it was. The air was stale, tasting like burned ash on her tongue. She was the first person to enter here in decades, she was sure of it. The floor was hard and polished. Marble from the texture of the surface.

She needed some form of illumination.

Then she remembered.

The matchbook Caleb had given her.

She fumbled for it in the inside of her jacket pocket, her breath becoming more frantic as she pushed past notebook, pen, notes, keys and pocket-knife.

There it was.

She felt inside the cover and peeled off a single strip of match.

When she struck it, the flame illuminated a huge space, the size of a barn.

As she looked up, she immediately cried out. A reflex shout of surprise.

A hundred eyes were watching her from above.

Her gasp blew the flame out, plunging her back into darkness. She stood there now, her senses on the edge of panic, feeling backwards for the far wall. She could still sense them, staring at her, in the darkness. She was utterly exposed, without any defence or place to hide. Her hands patted around until they felt a small heavy structure at waist height behind her.

She crouched behind it, fumbling in her jacket for the matchbook again. Breathing through her nose to calm herself, she ripped another match from the book.

She could tell that after this one, there was only one left.

The match burst into flame, illuminating the whole room for a second, then contracting to cast a glow that lit her hand like a bubble.

In the second that the room was lit, she saw them.

The eyes were static, painted. Covering the whole of the ceiling, hundreds of them, staring down at her. Each eye was identical; five concentric rings around each other, the outside, deep blue, then the next black, then a white one, followed by an azure ring, then finally a black dot.

It was the symbol of the all-seeing eye: the identical one to her necklace.

She had found it. This was what her mother had wanted her to see. For the first time in her conscious life, she felt her mother communicating with her. For the first time, she didn't feel alone.

56

Sara stood up slowly, holding the match high, and looked around. A long desk ran down the shorter side of the oblong-shaped room. The wallpaper seemed to be flaking above it, so seriously that it gave the appearance of feathers pasted to the wall. The desk was covered with papers too, and in the fraction of time before the match went out, Sara saw an old gas lamp sitting at the edge of the table.

She took out the final match, desperately hoping that it would light.

She struck it and felt euphoria flow through her when the flame flared up. She gently lit the wick, then closed the glass hatch to the lamp. A rosy glow flooded the room, causing the darkness to retreat to the four outermost corners.

She looked at the eyes. They were remarkable: an entire gallery watching her every move. Each of them a ring-within-a-ring-within-a-ring. Sara knew the same symbol was also a protection against harm. Perhaps whoever painted these eyes felt they were creating a sanctuary here.

Suddenly, a force began shaking the room, like an earthquake. Dust fell from the ceiling, and a high-pitched whine pierced the air. Sara grabbed the desk, which had begun shaking. The noise changed into something thunderous.

Sara braced herself for what was coming.

Something huge and moving fast slammed against the side of the wall and flew past.

The noise mutated again into a clatter-clatter of a train flying past at close range. The tube tracks must be close. A minute later, the end of the train whizzed by, and the sound began to recede.

A final scattering of dust fell from the ceiling as the train's clattering died away. She lifted up the lamp and shone it in the direction of the dust fall.

In the corner of the room near the hole she had created. She could see it now. A steel ladder fixed to the wall. Heading up through a hole in the ceiling. At least she knew what might be her exit route.

Sara pulled her attention away and looked again at the desk. The closest thing to her was a framed, sepia-stained photograph of a statuesque woman in her fifties staring off camera.

Sara looked closer at the photograph. It was not an unkindly face. Black-and-white photography always lent images an innocence.

On the base of the frame, inscribed in the wood, were the words HELEN DUNCAN.

There was something in that face that mesmerized her. It lacked the element of presentation that other portraits have: there was no effusion or bravado. There was only one emotion that flickered across Helen Duncan's face: apprehension.

Sara turned her attention to the materials on the desk. Pushed up against the wall were ten stacks of identical moleskin notebooks, five books in each stack. From the side, she could see the journals were padded, so they looked like they were stuffed with something.

Old newspaper cuttings were strewn across the surface of the desk, around a blotting pad and a nib-and-wick fountain pen.

Sara picked up a press cutting from the desk. On it, there was a photograph of Winston Churchill. Underneath, a bold headline stated:

Mr Churchill visits convicted witch Helen Duncan in prison.

Sara stared closer at the photograph of Duncan. There was something around her neck. She peered closer until she could get a better view, although up close the definition was lost as the image dissolved into a pixelated blur.

It looked like Sara's locket.

Sara picked up the closest of the moleskin notebooks and opened it. On the inside front cover, the owner had written her name.

Helen Duncan

1944

She flipped open the book to a random page. A date,

28 August 1939, was carefully inscribed in the corner, and underneath, in a spidery hand, was written:

The Beast will move, first to the East then to the West.

Slipped into the space between the pages was a clipping from a newspaper, the *Daily Mail*, dated 3 September 1939. The headline screamed: 'WAR!'

Great Britain and France are now at war with Germany. We now fight against the blackest tyranny that has ever held men in bondage.

She picked up the moleskin books one by one. Each was stuffed with clippings, filleted from newspapers and placed alongside an accompanying entry. The notepads were chronologically laid out, from left to right. She reached for the pad furthest away and opened up the first page.

1 January 1908

It will rain 128 days this year.

Based on the date, and the photograph in the initial clipping, the entry must have been written when Duncan was a child. The notepads seemed to be the journals of Helen Duncan, from her earliest childhood. They ended only when she was imprisoned for witchcraft during the Second World War. Sara lifted her finger and touched the locket around her neck.

This room, with its talismans and protections, was her great-grandmother's way of making sense of her power. A pre-modern context for what now came up in MRIs and mind-mapping techniques. Salt said military intelligence had wanted to find the gods of the other side of the mind, but in Helen's time the world wasn't ready, so they called what they found a witch instead.

It was as she began to search the desk again that she saw something below it on the table. It was propped up against an ancient letter stamp.

It was an envelope.

She reached over until she could read the word clearly written on its front.

SARA.

57

Sara picked up the brittle letter paper from the desk.

Decades of condensation had made the paper mushy to the touch, and the corner came off in her hands.

As she began reading the letter, a voice came back to her, one that had laced itself into her dreams and nightmares, a woman's voice, soft yet firm, flat but with a trace of accent.

8 August 2005

Dear Sara,

I will call you by the second name I gave you.

It was a new name for a new start. I hope that proved to be the case.

You are standing in our family home. The entire house was ours. We were wealthy once. And happy I am told (although I can't remember that).

You are reading this in your great-grandmother Helen Duncan's study. A secret place. I discovered it only by accident. Ten years after we were evicted.

I know the spies will have tried to find you. They will never stop. That is why I did what I did – that terrible thing I did to you. I wanted to hide you from them. And hide your true nature from yourself.

*They offered me security, a powerful thing for a single
mother of two. They said they just wanted to study us in return.
I was naive. What they really want, have always wanted, is to
control us.*

*I knew I could not change what was coming. I believed that
if I could not change the future, I could change the past. By
making you forget.*

*I left you your great grandmother's locket, knowing that you
would find your way back here if you needed to.*

*I have come here each week, looking for you. But I am
getting old, and this will be my last visit. Come and find me.
I am at the retirement home in Bromley. Part of me hopes I
won't see you. It is better you start fresh. But the selfish part of
me hopes to see you again. There are things to be said.*

Your mother,
Phoebe Duncan

The paper seemed like branded stationery of some
sort. At the footer, in letters almost too small for reading, was the address of the home.

Sara shook the envelope to see if there was anything
else inside. Something shifted. She delicately opened
the flap. Inside was a Polaroid picture.

The black backside was dimpled and swollen, warped
through years of condensation. One corner of the
photo was missing, peeled off, while a heavy furrow
ran along the border of the Polaroid, as if it had sat
under the weight of a hollow object for some time.

The photograph was of an attractive woman in her

mid-forties, standing in a field. She was bending to the side, accommodating the weight of a baby girl slung on to her waist. Sara. She must have been only one or two years old. Tiny flowers stuck out from the woman's long brown hair, and her dark eyes were staring at the camera, seemingly oblivious of the child clinging to her.

Sara knew the picture was intended as a gift to her from her mother, a keepsake of happier times. But, for her, the picture was unsettling. Her mother only had eyes for the person taking the picture. The baby seemed like a distraction from whatever connection was happening between the photographer and his or her subject.

The dappled sunlight fell through the trees, warming Sara's tiny hands. Nearby, Christian played with a plastic spade and bucket, sitting on the same blanket as her. He could see them close by, but was ignoring them. Sara watched transfixed as the two naked bodies moved in syncopation against each other.

58

00:45:01.

00:45:00.

00:44:59.

The truck downshifted gears as it slowed its approach to the guard post.

The outline of GCHQ loomed on the horizon, sleek and futuristic, like a mothership from another galaxy had landed in the middle of the tiny Cotswold town.

A one-armed guard came out to meet the vehicle, one empty sleeve folded across his chest and carefully pinned to the opposing breast pocket. Another guard walked out behind him, straining against the weight of an Alsatian that lurched forwards.

The driver lowered the electric window and held out his identification, which the one-armed guard took, checking the name and photo, and then pocketing the driver's licence and pulling out an iPad wedged under his arm. Having one hand made the process awkward, but he handled it dexterously, reading the electronic itinerary.

He walked to the front of the vehicle and tapped the licence plate gently with his foot and then walked to the side of the vehicle and took a close look at the name of the haulage firm painted on the side.

Finally, he walked back to the driver's side door and took a final look at the licence before handing it back.

Jeremy Johns' father was a civilian policeman, and Jeremy grew up listening to his dinnertime stories of foiled bank robberies and frantic street chases. As exciting as these seemed to the young boy, growing up in the turbulent 1970s stimulated a yearning for adventure, and the military police seemed the perfect fusion of foreign travel and the protection profession.

His first station was Beirut. It was there one sunny morning in June that a Tata Mercedes lorry pulled to a stop in front of the fortified British Embassy compound. The rear was crammed with fruit crates, the vehicle bound for the kitchens.

The smiling driver handed his papers to Jeremy, who did a walk around the vehicle. It was an old truck, its engine rattling away like a lawnmower. The protocols for checking vehicles seeking entry were threefold: match the vehicle to the roster, then match the driver, and then . . . use your best judgement. Licence plates could be screwed on, and a simple paint job could replicate the name of approved suppliers. Which meant, to Jeremy, that judgement was what saved lives.

He walked back along the side of the lorry towards the driver's side. And that's when he saw it. The driver's face in the side mirror. He wasn't smiling any more.

Alert, Jeremy walked to the driver's door and handed back the papers, keeping his eyes on the driver's face.

He had always been able to read people. Few people could disguise what was on their mind. Even at peace, the face betrayed inner thought, like the swish of a fish's tail sends ripples to the surface of a pond.

The driver looked back at Jeremy, the smile reappearing as if it was switched on. And that's when Jeremy turned and began running, his torso dipping, inclining down to the ground, a sprinter coming out of the gate, leaping the last few feet to slam his fist on the button to raise the bomb gates.

The truck was packed with enough explosives that it destroyed the outside wall. Staff found one of the wheels on the roof of the Embassy. Jeremy survived that day, although it cost him an arm.

Since then, he had turned down numerous promotions. That sunny day in Lebanon had taught him something invaluable: his vocation in life, the best place he could be of service.

He knew where he was needed now.

He was placed on this earth to stand sentry, to keep those inside from harm.

Jeremy looked at the truck driver's face, looking for any sign, any ripples to indicate what was going on below the surface.

Satisfied, he nodded to the K-9 handler to raise the barrier and stood back to allow the vehicle to pass.

The driver put the truck into gear and drove through the gate.

The side entrance of GCHQ led to the underground access road, for deliveries of heavy equipment.

As the vehicle approached the tunnel opening, the driver tossed the ID in his hand into the rear of the cabin, where it landed on the man who had been driving the truck this morning, his hands and legs tightly bound, tape strapped to his mouth.

The tunnel blanketed the truck in darkness and a second later the headlights flicked on. A few hundred yards inside, a controller in a reflective jacket motioned the truck into a parking bay the size of a playing field.

Orpheus parked and dropped down out of the truck's cabin, landing lightly on the asphalt road. He walked to the back of the truck and lowered the tailgate, hopping on and pulling thick tarpaulins off the containers stacked high within. He lifted the top off each of the lead pigs, revealing the rods held in place by semicircular cradles.

When they were all exposed, Orpheus knelt down and opened a briefcase containing an electronic timer. The timer countdown was perfectly in sync with the website timer.

00:39:23.

00:39:22.

00:39:21.

'Driver, are you there?'

The voice came from outside.

He could hear steps approach the front of the vehicle and a clanging sound as a body stepped up to the driver-side door and peered into the cabin.

'Driver? You can't stay with the vehicle.'

The truck shifted back as the man dropped back

down to the ground. Footsteps walked down the length of the vehicle, approaching the rear of the truck.

A radio crackled with indeterminate voices.

Orpheus didn't move, even though the guard would see him in less than a few seconds. As soon as he turned the corner, Orpheus would be in plain view, kneeling in a vehicle filled with an enormous device rigged to a timer.

Orpheus' heartbeat remained slow and steady, as he calmly looked out through the back of the gate.

He knew there was no cause for alarm. All he had to do was wait. In two steps, the guard's radio would squawk an order telling him to return to the main tunnel to regulate traffic flow. The guard would stop and hesitate, considering whether to continue his investigation. He would then turn around and march away, his footsteps dying out after a few seconds, leaving Orpheus in silence.

This was Orpheus' world. A perpetual data stream from the future. There were never surprises. His field of vision was four-dimensional. People were no longer agents in their own right, capable of free will. Instead, they were disassembled into actions, their existences just a series of events flowing through his data stream. Pre-programmed players moving through time, labouring under the illusion of choice but, in reality, playing out a plan that he had already seen, had already studied. He lived in a deterministic universe.

Over the years, what had initially given him a sense of power now gave him nausea. Without agency, people were cardboard cutouts, automatons shuttling back and forth, mechanized toys on tracks. It disconnected him from them, enforcing his isolation.

After the man had left, Orpheus hopped down off the tailgate and closed it behind him, arranging the end of the tarpaulin so it covered the contents. In a few hours, the device would wreak its reaction. He knew this would happen because it had already happened in his mind, the event was simply in escrow, waiting for the buffer of time to catch up with it.

59

Everything was coming back to Sara now.

Raindrops pebble the windows as Sara stares through them to the front path, where her mother stands with two men holding umbrellas. They have come before but are never let in. The last time was months ago. A lot has changed since then. It's just their mother and them now, and life feels precarious, a train coming off its tracks. Sara cannot see what they are saying as the umbrellas cover their heads.

The children flank their mother, as she carries a suitcase in each hand and steps off the bus. Phoebe is reading from directions written on the back of an envelope. The instructions guide them to a field outside of the town. Just when they are about to ask for directions, they see it. An abandoned air-force base. Two buildings either side of a runway, through which weeds sprout.

The two men give them a tour. Dobbs and Salt are their names, although Salt gets into a car and leaves within an hour. It's the last time they will see him. Dobbs makes them food and shows them to their quarters. Their new home feels more comfortable than the house they've left, with its dirty, unmade beds, broken crockery on the floor and the perpetual sound of sobbing coming from behind the closed door.

Dobbs is not like any adult the children have ever met. He is kind and attentive. He cooks each meal for them and lays out their clothes on the bed each morning. The games they play with him are strange and alien, obstacle courses and fighting with long sticks. Every day is an adventure.

The arguments start after two years. They can hear their mother's voice, shaky and wet with rage, the words indistinct, and Dobbs' low murmured response, a Zen master facing down a lunatic.

A noise above surprised her, shaking her out of her reverie.

Caleb appeared half in half out of the opening in the ceiling, standing on the metal stairs.

'Did you find what you were looking for?'

'No, not yet,' she replied. 'But I know where my mother is.'

She walked to the stairs and began climbing up. Caleb climbed too, and was waiting for her when she appeared through the hole in the ground. Before leaving the stairs, she took a final look down at her great-grandmother's study. Her mother had returned here, to reconnect with the past, as had her great-grandmother, the first of the family line who had suffered as a result of the British secret service. It was a refuge, a place where the family's abilities could exist on their own terms. Although ultimately hidden. Would there ever be another option for her, between hiding and confrontation?

She suddenly felt woozy and she realized she had not eaten in almost twenty-four hours. She lost her balance and made a grab for the rail of the ladder. Caleb's hand darted out and grabbed hers, his fist enclosing her bare wrist.

The moment their skin made contact, the colours

of the world around her seemed to wash away until her surroundings resembled nothing more than a three-dimensional sketch space. A new world was superimposed on it, a virtual reality displacing her own.

She was on a metal platform looking at Caleb, who was standing on tiptoes, teetering on the edge. For a moment, he hung there, his windmilling arms keeping his centre of gravity sufficiently forwards, and then his body weight carried him over and he was in free fall. She ran to the edge to see him plummeting, hundreds of feet below her, finally being swallowed by huge, skyscraper-sized icebergs that violently clashed and scissored against each other in an ice-ocean. It was an impossible setting, like a dream. She watched as Caleb disappeared beneath the surface of the frozen water, knowing with certainty she had just witnessed the moment of his death.

She pulled her hand away from his as if she had just been burned and looked at him in shock.

'What?' asks Caleb.

Sara stares back, unsure of what to say.

'Nothing,' she says.

60

Bromley Retirement Home

The lobby was a low-ceilinged, dreary room with bristle carpet, empty reception desk and three corridors that extended from it. The early light of dawn lit up the back of the room, turning the faded yellow covering into a wall of grey.

The smell of disinfectant permeated the building. To most of the visitors, that was all they could smell. But what lay beneath lingered in Sara's nostrils, an aroma of decay. It soaked into the faded wallpaper and cheap floor.

Caleb and Sara stood in front of the desk, unsure of how to proceed.

'Hello?' shouted Sara into the nearest corridor.

Caleb moved behind the desk and began opening the drawers.

'There's got to be a list of occupants here,' he said.

'Sorry, who are you?'

A female nurse in her sixties with thick-lens glasses was approaching them from the nearest corridor, her brow furrowed and her lips compressed into a line.

'We're here to see Phoebe Duncan,' said Sara.

When she caught up to them, Sara could just about

smell a residual aroma of alcohol lingering below the coffee breath.

'It's too early for visitors,' she said, folding her arms.

'We have some urgent news for her,' said Caleb, taking a step forwards. 'It can't wait.' He spoke with natural gravitas, and Sara saw a shift take place in the nurse. Caleb had read her perfectly.

'If she's a resident, then you could try the main room.'

The nurse led them through bland corridors with anodyne prints on the walls until they reached a dining hall walled by sliding glass doors. Elderly residents sat in clusters at tables spread out across the room, eating in silence while a television blared out a rerun of a game show.

'They're up at dawn here. She'll be at one of the tables,' the nurse said.

Sara searched those sitting at the tables, looking for some glimmer of the woman she saw in the photograph. But they all looked like desiccated versions of people, shrunken in on themselves. The nurse left them without another word.

'Phoebe Duncan?' Sara said out loud.

A few faces looked back blankly.

'Can I help you?'

A rail-thin nurse sat behind a station on a raised platform set against the back wall of the room.

'We're here to see Phoebe Duncan.'

The nurse gave them an encouraging smile. Clearly visitors here were rare.

'Let me see. She's not a current resident, or I would know. But let's take a look. When was she admitted?'

She bent down and pulled out a thick lever-arch file. Sara consulted her mother's letter.

'Around 2005.'

The nurse slapped shut the huge file she had opened.

'OK, well, not that one then. It only goes back to 2008.'

She put her hands on her hips, looking around the disarray of the nurses' station, which was stacked high with yellowing papers and files.

'We're still working on putting this all on computer, but let's see, there might be something . . .'

She bent down again, patting the out-of-sight shelves, feeling for other records.

'Here.'

She pulled out another thick stack, its cover worn and frayed at the edges. She let it fall open in the middle and then began flicking through the pages.

'Duncan . . . Duncan . . . No, sorry. That year we only had Davies, Deacon, Dickenson, Dunbar and Dunleavy. No other Ds.'

'Can I see that?' asked Caleb. He gave her an affable smile.

The nurse nodded and turned the file around to face them. Names were marked down, one on each page, with dates of admission handwritten and doctors' visits underneath.

Caleb pushed the file closer to Sara and held a finger over the centre, where the serrated stub of a page could barely be seen jutting out of the spine.

'There seems to be a page missing,' said Caleb to the nurse, holding the file up to her.

The nurse frowned, shaking her head, looking genuinely confused. 'It might be a spoiled page. Or sometimes a resident is admitted and then the family changes their mind.'

Caleb looked at her sceptically. 'Maybe, but why tear the page out?'

The nurse shrugged, not sure what else to say.

'I'll be right back,' she said, 'I just need to check on them.'

'Salt and his crew were here,' whispered Caleb, after she had gone. 'They found her.'

Sara looked in despair across the dining room. Reading her mother's words had worked some alchemy on her, like the mystery resurrection of a dead plant when it is watered. A sense of self was seeping back into her. She no longer felt blank, an outline etched in space, undetermined and open for interpretation. But she needed more. She trusted her mother, who had guided her this far. If she had been taken, if there were circumstances beyond her control, then the trail would now be cold. Sara's only option would be to confront Salt and likely walk into a trap. There was no point staying here. Military intelligence had won this round, but she would not give up. She was going to find her mother.

'Let's go,' she said to Caleb.

'You could ask Stanley,' shouted the nurse after them, just before they reached the door. 'He's been here since the nineties.'

Sara followed her pointed finger over to a man of about ninety sitting in a chair near the window. The overall sense of him was dishevelment. Tufts of thin grey hair stuck out in all directions, as if he had recently received an electric shock. Black frame glasses with one lens missing sat on his hawkish nose. Unlike the other residents, who sat facing their tables, he had turned his chair to the window, although his eyes were fixed to the ground. The nurse walked up to him and crouched close to his face.

'Stanley.'

If he heard the nurse call his name, he didn't show it. His gaze remained down, vacant eyes holding the middle distance.

'He would have been here when your mother was here,' said the nurse, breaking away. 'But I've only heard him say a handful of actual words, and that was when I started.'

Sara approached Stanley and pulled up a chair to sit next to him. The odour of mothballs clung to the air in his immediate vicinity, mingled with a smell like dead leaves. Dandruff coated the shoulders of his cardigan, like a dusting from a walk in the snow.

'Stanley, do you remember Phoebe Duncan?' said Sara. 'She was here. I'm her daughter. I'm looking for her, Stanley.'

She waited. There was no movement in his eyes. Shallow breath inhaled and exhaled, as if powered by a tiny bellows, pulling and pushing air over thin wet lips. It was as if the final sign-off from the mind had failed to reach the body, which continued stubbornly, dragging forward, following blind duty until it powered down itself.

Unwilling to give up, she moved in front of him and crouched down, her face breaking his line of vision. His eyes held her in his gaze now, empty brown puddles reflecting nothing back.

'Stanley,' Sara said, softer this time, with an urgency that propelled the word across the space between them.

Nothing.

She stood up, looking at the nurse, who raised her arms apologetically.

Sara was about to leave when she looked at Stanley one final time.

He was no longer staring at the ground.

His eyes were now fixed on her. Staring with intensity at a point just below her neck.

Sara took a step to the side and watched Stanley's eyes track her movements. They were glued to her. Or, more specifically, to her locket.

'Stanley?' Sara said again. 'Can you hear me?'

Her necklace was stirring something in him, but there was no way to find out what it was. Whatever was left of Stanley was entombed deep within him, impossible to reach.

Sara looked at him for a long moment and then realized what she needed to do.

She reached out and grasped Stanley's frail fingers.

61

At first there was nothing, just Sara and the old man holding hands in the day room.

And then something flashed in front of her eyes, like a subliminal image embedded in a film. And then another image, too quick to perceive. And then another, until it was like watching photographs flipped in fast motion in front of her eyes.

The same room. Tables. Chairs. Residents sitting facing each other. Their faces keep changing, though. Like the letters on an old-fashioned electric noticeboard clacking over. Stanley watches it all, stock still, a man in a time-lapse video.

Stanley gets up, and the perspective shifts to his own. A point-of-view camera that floats six feet above the ground, weaving through the chairs and tables of the room, towards the exit. It stops at the first resident's room and pushes open the door.

'Show me, Stanley,' whispered Sara.

The room is small and, impossibly, filled with sand. At the other end, waves lap hypnotically, the ocean's edge coinciding with the far wall, the water the colour of jade. Rocks refract through the endless ripples undulating across the surface. The camera looks up at a tent of brilliant blue sky. Nearby, a family sits on folding chairs. Stanley lifts his hand experimentally in front of the camera. It is that of a little boy.

'These are old memories, Stanley,' coaxed Sara, gently.

The camera retreats from the room, closing the door behind it. It approaches the next and pushes the door open. It is now looking down at a child's shoes as they climb up wooden steps and walk on to the stage. Teachers sit on plastic chairs, backs to the wall, looking out over an auditorium, clapping. A trophy is handed directly to the camera, and a teenage hand accepts it. Proud parents look back from the audience.

'Still too old,' breathed Sara. 'Concentrate. Where did you see the necklace?'

The perspective drifts out of the room again, moving down the corridor, doubling back on itself, a bewildered person lost in a maze.

'You can do it,' said Sara. 'Let me see.'

The camera bobs for a second, unsure, and then floats towards another room and opens the door. The ceiling of the room is filled with eyes staring down, wide open, all-seeing. The rest of the room is covered with framed photographs, every surface square inch is taken. The same boy and girl stare out of each picture. The camera floats through and bobs near the window, partially hiding behind the curtain. Outside, a woman in a wheelchair is being pushed up a ramp leading into the rear of an expensive-looking people carrier. There is writing on the side of the vehicle, but the perspective is rack-focus, everything blurred, as if the image has been smudged. The only clear point is the woman, who stands out in startling definition, the centre of Stanley's world. The ramp is removed, and the doors close, the driver moving back to the front of the vehicle, passing the indistinct blobs of writing on the side of the van.

'Please remember, Stanley,' urged Sara.

The camera breaks its tracking of the man and bobs back to

333

the writing, which remains indistinct. The engines start, and it begins to move, cruising forward, about to leave Stanley's world for ever. And then, for a split second, almost as if the camera has squeezed tight and wrung the words from the image, the lettering becomes clear.

Sara stood up, breaking contact with Stanley.

'Thank you, Stanley,' she said.

But his eyes were staring at the floor again.

62

Five Seasons Assisted Living Centre

Large, ornate gate posts rose in front of them, well over twenty feet high. Beyond them, the road, flanked by lush flower beds, snaked to a huge house that must at one time have been a stately home.

The gates were open, and Sara and Caleb approached the house, their feet crunching on the gravel, the fragrance of roses perfuming the air around them.

The Centre could not have been more different from the public home in Bromley. Everything about it was elite. Three large people carriers were in the car park, identical to the one Stanley had shown Sara.

Sara tried to open the front door. It shook in its frame but remained closed. She was about to pull her tools out of her bag when Caleb stepped forward.

'Can I try?' he asked.

'Help yourself,' replied Sara, standing back to give him room.

She watched him as he pulled out his wallet and crouched next to the lock. The apparition of him falling to his death had alarmed her. They had only met the previous night, but there was some easy connection between them that she had not experienced before.

There was no one in her world she could trust, but she immediately felt at ease with Caleb. However, the sight of the impossible surroundings – ice-oceans and ice-mountains – felt so tenuously connected with their world that it lessened the threat. She resolved to tell Caleb about it once their search was over.

He pulled the handle, and it popped open.

'Do you make a habit of breaking into old people's homes?' said Sara, pushing through the door into the lobby, a gleaming cave of ivory and marble.

'One day I'll need to learn to break out of one,' replied Caleb, looking around in awe. 'Though maybe not this one.'

It looked more like the lobby of a five-star hotel than a retirement home. Unseen air-conditioning units controlled the room temperature, bringing it to the perfect level, and soft classical music played just on the verge of perception.

A plate of frosted glass was mounted on one of the walls, on which was etched a list of residents with their room numbers.

Sara saw her mother's name immediately.

Monaco wing, room 5.

A map on the opposing side of the glass indicated its location.

No one challenged them as they wandered through the dim corridors, lit through recessed lighting. The Monaco wing was adjacent to the lobby and the rooms were sequentially numbered.

1. 2. 3. 4.

Sara stopped in front of the room, struggling for breath. This was the end of her journey.

She knocked once and stepped in.

But the room was empty.

There was also little or no furniture in it. No pictures, no framed photos, no keepsakes or mementoes. Just a bed, a side table and some medicine bottles.

'This can't be her room,' said Sara in confusion. 'It looks like it's unoccupied.'

Caleb walked over to the medicine bottles and checked the labels. He looked back at her and nodded. They were in the right room.

It seemed like her mother had forgotten her as cleanly as Sara had forgotten Phoebe. Although in Phoebe's case, it didn't require any brainwashing.

Sara didn't know what she was expecting to find, but it wasn't this. She was no longer wanted or needed. An orphan in an adult's body. First, her mother had disappeared from the location she had given Sara and now it looked as if she had expunged her daughter from her mind.

A thought occurred to Sara, and she walked to the side table and placed her palm flat on it, waiting for a connection.

But when her hand made contact with the table, the only thing she experienced was a static hiss, like the sound a free diver hears underwater. Sara walked to the bed and sat on it, letting her palms rest on the bedspread, simulating the same experience, pressing her fingertips in, inhaling the trace aroma released by the bedding.

Again, nothing other than an atmospheric hiss.

'It's strange,' said Sara. 'I can't get any sense of her here.'

'Let's try the common areas,' said Caleb, walking to the door.

They followed the corridor to the back veranda of the house, which looked out on to a huge landscaped garden. Along one side of the manicured lawn, two box hedgerows ran in a line to a gap in the garden wall, over which hung a bowery laced with bougainvillea.

Sara and Caleb found a fire exit and walked down the gravel path through the gap. They were in a tiny garden from which headstones jutted out from the carefully trimmed grass, like empty seat backs in an auditorium.

Standing by one particular grave was a tall man in an elegant suit.

It was Charles Salt.

63

Salt looked over at Caleb.

'Can you give us a few minutes?'

Caleb looked at Sara for approval, and she nodded.

She walked up and stood facing him, on the other side of the grave.

'She died a week ago,' he said, his eyes on Phoebe's grave. 'You just missed her. I'm sorry.'

He looked up at Sara. There seemed to be compassion in his eyes.

'I tried to hide Phoebe here from the rest of the world,' said Salt. 'She's still an asset of ours, after all. Even after all these years. Couldn't have the Russians or Chinese getting their hands on her. When you came to my house, I knew it wouldn't be long before you found her.'

Sara looked back at the home behind her. Its rear façade looked like an Italian palazzo.

'How could she afford this?' she asked.

'I arranged payment. Whatever you may think of me, I always tried to do my best for your family.'

Sara looked down at her mother's grave. It was the least gaudy of the headstones around her. It wasn't tall, or cast from marble, and the calligraphy was simple, a plain font, slightly old-fashioned. Garlands of flowers were etched into the border of the grey stone, splashes of vibrant red and yellow. She wasn't sure how she knew, but some instinct told her it was something of which her mother would approve.

'You chose the gravestone,' she said, a statement more than a question.

Salt nodded. 'There was no one else.'

Sara let her eyes run along the tops of the walls of the garden in which they stood. There were no visible signs of anyone keeping watch on them: no marksmen, no armed units, no other support.

'I came here alone,' said Salt, as if it was his turn to read her thoughts. 'My relationship with your family was more complex than you think. It may surprise you to learn, I was the one who axed Operation Orpheus.'

Sara looked at him closely, gauging his veracity. In the distance, she could hear something approaching, like a distant drumbeat at a frenetic pace.

'It was the toughest decision I ever made. But I could see the stress it was causing your mother.' He stopped and looked at her. 'I see your scepticism. I wasn't motivated by charity. Young children need parents, and your mother was losing her mind. Dobbs thought he could be a father figure, but he was wrong. Your family unit was straining against itself, a centre that couldn't hold. Ready to implode. Dobbs made a video for me, to show your powers, a last appeal to keep the operation going. After seeing it, I gave the order to close down the operation. The plan was going to be to give Phoebe time to convalesce, and to adjust the programme so she would be cooperative. But she beat us to it and escaped that night with you.'

'But why did she come back to you afterwards?' asked Sara.

'You don't remember your brother, Christian,' replied Salt. He pulled out a packet of cigarettes from his jacket pocket and placed one in his mouth but made no move to light it. 'Although only a few years older, we could already tell he was different. And not in a good way. He exhibited early symptoms of psychopathic behaviour. Your mother was afraid that training you as a spy would ruin you. Ironically, she hoped doing so for Christian would make him less of a savage. It didn't work. She returned, but two years later, I closed the operation for good. Christian was simply too sadistic to be of use as an asset. He left your mother to go on his own barbarous odyssey.'

'What was my mother like, at the end?' asked Sara, thinking of her mother's spartan room, empty of memory and love.

The sound was getting louder now, mutating from a frenzied beat to a chattering sound.

Salt was silent for a long time before replying.

'Your mother wasn't well. She suffered from a number of nervous conditions. At the end of her life, she wanted to put the past behind her. Maybe she wanted for herself what she had done for you. A fresh start. For the last ten years of her life, she lived in peace here, alone. Purged of the past. It was too painful for her, so she put it behind her. Don't begrudge her that.'

Sara looked at the grave. There was still one question that was nagging at her.

'What about my father? Who was he?'

Salt shrugged his shoulders.

'We never knew. Some wanderer. He didn't hang around . . .'

Suddenly, a helicopter flew over the walls of the garden and climbed up into the sky, banking higher and then hovering above them.

Salt pulled the cigarette out of his mouth and took a step closer to Sara, shouting to be heard above the din.

'. . . we need your help, Sara. Christian has targeted us. He is going to hit us at home, at GCHQ. There's only one person who can stop him, and that's you.'

'Why should I trust you?' asked Sara.

'Because I'm all you have, like I was all Phoebe had,' said Salt. 'I'm the only person living who understands your power. What it can do, its limits. You chose to remember, and now the genie won't go back in the bottle. You need someone to help guide you, Sara.'

'You mean control me?' said Sara.

'Have it your way,' said Salt. 'Then just help us with Christian.'

'I'm not going to hurt my brother,' said Sara.

'I'm not asking you to,' said Salt.

The helicopter landed fifty yards away. Its huge bulk, like an enormous metallic insect, lowered itself on to its undercarriage, the wheels straining under the weight, the downwash of air from the blades pummelling everything within the garden walls.

'I just want you to talk to him. You're the only one he'll listen to. This can still be resolved peacefully.'

64

Salt watched as the helicopter rose vertically into the air, blasting the tree branches on either side.

He walked back to the front of the Centre, where his car was parked. The driver stepped out from behind the wheel and opened Salt's door.

Salt settled himself into the back seat, which was empty apart from a large battered suitcase.

He flipped open the lid of the case and looked inside.

'You're sure this was everything?' asked Salt.

The back of the driver's head nodded.

'Yes, she had them resting on the surfaces. None of them were hanging. So, no holes in the wall. I wiped down the furniture afterwards. That's all of them.'

'Good,' said Salt.

His fingers searched the contents of the case. There must have been sixty framed photos inside, of the girl and boy. The mother appeared sporadically across them. The room must have looked like an antique frame shop before the driver swept it. It was a comprehensive chronicling of a family until the girl was six years old. A family frozen in time. Similar to his own hallway gallery. Two families remembered, pickled and preserved, to remind the curator of what their interaction with military intelligence had cost them.

Salt did not feel guilty about hiding the pictures from Sara. It was Phoebe who had taken her daughter's memory. She had given her a blank screen, something to be repopulated and reshaped, a new identity. He was finishing what she had started.

65

The interior of the helicopter resembled the insides of a stainless-steel animal, large metal ribs running from floor to ceiling. The sliding side door was open, and Sara leaned forwards, elbows on her knees, looking out on to the bumpy landscape of clouds below her.

She and Caleb were strapped into a bench, opposite a line of soldiers on a facing seat, their weapons lying on their laps.

She could see two other helicopters flying in formation behind them, matching their speed as they flew towards GCHQ.

She wasn't sure what she was feeling. Could you feel grief for someone who didn't exist in your conscious memory? If it wasn't grief then it was empathy, for Phoebe and her broken life, another casualty of the mysterious strands that wrapped themselves around her family's DNA, blighting each generation. Strands that allowed the family to peep over the hedges of time and yet blinded them to the outcomes of their own fate.

Caleb said something to one of the soldiers, who handed him a canteen and an oatmeal bar. Caleb passed them to Sara.

'You should eat,' he said.

The cool water flowed down her throat, its reviving power channelling through her body.

Caleb nodded to the canteen.

'Have some more.'

She took a second revitalizing swig and, with a jarring feeling, the emergency of the situation hit her. Her brother was deemed a sufficient threat that an aerial armed fleet was being sent to confront him. Christian, who had remained in the programme to hone and perfect his powers, now needed an army to take him down. What did that mean for her? Was she on the same road now, one that would inevitably bring a monster out of her shadows?

66

Bob Swift looked at the countdown as it slipped below the thirty-minute mark. Waterman had told them to keep an eye on anything unusual, a second line of defence to the AI and algorithms that churned permanently in the neural network computers, seeking threats and anomalies from the galaxies of data that flowed through them.

A flicker passed through the screen in front of him. Like something had swum close to the surface. Swift blinked, clearing his vision. He must have imagined it, his mind foggy with exhaustion.

Then it happened again.

It was as if the screen had transformed into a flat pool of water and a submerged body was probing from within, its mass displacing the area around it.

Swift was running a diagnostic check when he heard Hunter shouting out at Waterman.

'Something's happening to our central control functions.'

'What areas are affected?' said Waterman, looking at his own screen for verification.

'GCHQ defences,' said Swift in disbelief. 'Communications with the guard posts are going offline. The armament room has sealed itself. Lifts are offline. Oh shit.'

'What?' asked Waterman.

'Surface-to-air missiles have just come online. Auto targeting procedures just engaged,' said Swift.

Waterman snatched up the nearest phone.

'It's beginning. Clear the airspace above us.'

67

Sara could see GCHQ below them.

'We're going to put down near the entrance to the underground access road,' said the soldier in front of her.

A sudden wave of fear rolled through Sara as she stared through the open door at the ground thousands of feet below.

'We're not safe here,' she said to the soldier. 'We need to leave. Now!'

She began to take off her harness, her fingers trembling.

The soldier shook his head.

'Don't. We can't be a target . . .'

A high-pitched electronic scream boomed through the interior of the helicopter.

'Incoming!' shouted the soldier, his face rigid with fear and confusion. He twisted around to the pilots. 'How can that be?'

Through the window, Sara saw two puffs of smoke rise from the roof of the facility, and from within them plumes streaking towards the helicopters.

'We've been targeted by GCHQ's own surface-to-air missiles!' shouted one of the pilots.

And then the world turned upside down.

It seemed to happen in slow motion.

She could feel the energy of the machine, sense its immense power and forward thrust.

And then, in a second, an explosion rocked the back of the aircraft, and the energy was snuffed out. They were flying in a metal corpse, high in the sky, with all the ability to remain airborne of a car driven off a cliff.

The rotor blades swiped two or three times, slowly, lazily, natural momentum propelling them forwards, before stopping completely.

Shouts rang out on the edges of her perception. It was impossible to tell if they were instructions or panicked screams.

The helicopter tipped sideways first, morphing from a forward momentum to a downward one, dropping like a rock. Seated bodies lurched forwards, thrown against their restraining harnesses with such force that the occupants cried out, and Caleb staggered, his hands grabbing at the air, at the very edge of the open cargo side door. His body was in silhouette against the bright sky. Towering white cumulus clouds reared up behind him, like angry giants reaching for him.

Sara watched in shock.

This was it.

This was the moment she had seen before.

The crashing mountainous glaciers, the frozen waves, Caleb being swallowed into the depths. Her vision.

They had been clouds, not an ice-ocean.

'No!'

Her arms were outstretched even as his centre of gravity carried him over, outside the helicopter, backwards and falling, beyond her reach.

68

The helicopter dropped with the swiftness of a bird killed in mid-flight. They held on, straining against the seat belts that crisscrossed their torsos.

Without her harness, Sara tumbled over and over around the interior until she held on to a safety harness that was attached to the floor.

'Crash positions!!' screamed a voice from the cockpit.

She looked up from the gridded metal floor to see the two facing rows of men grab the back of their heads and pull them into their laps.

Then there was quiet. An eerie silence, on to which was layered a faint whistling sound.

She twisted her head and looked out through the front cockpit window.

An urban landscape of greys and blacks was hurtling towards them, indistinct, shuddering. Dark-grey lines juddered across the canvas created by the front window. She realized they were office buildings. They were close enough to the ground that she could see the vague shapes of the people in the windows watching.

Tiny details embedded themselves in her mind.

Spinning dials on the dashboard . . .

Blood-bleached knuckles gripping steering paddles . . .

The faintest whispers above her of what sounded like prayers . . .

The green of a playing field lurching and bouncing towards them . . . the sunlight refracting off the surface of a canal, sparkling like a line of crushed diamonds . . . less than a hundred feet away now . . .

The helmets of the two pilots pressing themselves right back against their seat, feet jamming on the floor . . .

A muffled cry, 'NOW!!'

Hands pulling back on control sticks with every ounce of force they had . . .

Her legs sliding across the floor as the helicopter tail tipped back . . .

And then there was an almighty crash, as her body was shaken with world-ending violence.

69

The helicopter crashed into the canal, creating a towering plume of water that detonated above it like a mushroom cloud.

On impact, her body was thrown out of the side sliding door.

Her trajectory was an inclined cannonball into the canal, her body shot into the deep, cocooned in bubbles.

She came to rest a hundred yards from the helicopter, which floated for a few seconds on the top of the water. It then twisted to one side and sank down, its bulk making an agonized scream as it plunged into the depths. Inside, there was no movement. No sound.

Sara hung, face down, suspended in the water, far below the surface. Lifeless. Her hair floating around her head like seaweed drifting with the tide. A head wound stained the water crimson around her hair like a halo.

Her half-open eyes were glazed, inert: her mouth still open from her last silent scream.

Beneath her semi-closed eyelids, a sense of submission washed over her. Ice-cold water was seeping into her extremities, her fingers and toes becoming numb. The sensation spread through her body, up her legs and down her arms towards her torso.

A gentle resistance came over her, as she found herself drifting down on to the sandy bed of the canal floor. The dust shifted to accommodate her, and she sank into it, sliding down as the canal claimed her.

It covered her like a soft lid.

And in that second, a memory hit her.

The *thump* of the corkboard as it covered the bath, entombing her child-self in darkness. The dirty, lukewarm water puddling around her. The sense of panic that gripped her chest. Her child sense that she should do what the adults told her. And deep down, another feeling, a certainty that what was happening to her was wrong.

That feeling spread within her now, and a series of sparks ignited in her brain, and for one brilliant second, they illuminated everything, like lightning flashing a landscape seen from a hilltop, every memory, every thought and feeling came back to her. Phoebe, Christian, the dim figures of men next to her mother, the chaos and the joy, and then the tailspin of her escape. Baz returned, as did Lionel Dobbs. And then Phoebe was sitting by the bathtub again, doing her best to protect Sara in the only way she knew. Sara saw this all as she was suspended in that moment, teetering on the edge of permanent sleep. For that second of bliss, she felt whole, reunited with the scattered parts of her self.

A sharp intake of breath sluiced water into her lungs, and her entire body shook. Her eyes opened wide, and she kicked hard, shaking her body, and then twisted around, locating the surface. Now she was fighting, her muscles pushed back, her lungs screamed for air. She kicked her legs with her last remaining energy and clawed her way to the light above her.

She broke the surface with a loud gasp. As she coughed and spluttered, her body violently trying to expel the water from her, her feet wildly kicked out to remain above water.

She remembered everything.

70

She looked at both sides of the bank, feeling for her location. GCHQ was on the north side, the top of the facility peeking out above the grassy bank.

Around her, heads were surfacing, bursting out with the energy of newborns, shaking their heads and then launching themselves towards the banks.

The soldiers in the helicopter appeared to have survived, and then she saw one body hunched over in the water, not moving. It was not dressed in military fatigues, and by the time she reached it, she recognized the jacket.

She twisted Caleb around so he was floating on his back and dragged him with her to the north bank, struggling against the weight of his waterlogged clothes and his unmoving body.

It took her three attempts to pull the main part of his body out of the river and on to the bank. When his torso was lying on the grass, she dropped down on to her knees and tipped his head back, pinched his nostrils and blew into his mouth. She counted down and then repeated the action.

'C'mon, c'mon, Caleb. Don't give up.'

She was on the fifth repeat when Caleb's head and legs tipped upwards and he retched violently. Sara rolled him over on to his side, patting his back.

Caleb moved on to all fours, his back humping with each cough, until no more water was expelled and he was breathing in deep, whooping intakes.

Finally, he lifted himself up on one knee.

'Thank you,' he said at last.

'It's good to have you back,' said Sara. 'Wait here. Medics will be here soon.'

Caleb took another breath and stood up.

'I'm coming with you.'

Sara shook her head.

'It's a miracle you're alive. You're in no condition . . .'

Caleb shook his head, resolute. He removed his jacket and rolled up his sleeves.

'You're not going in alone. End of discussion.'

Sara regarded him, sensing something in him she hadn't seen before, but dismissed it. Now was not the time to go down that road.

Sara looked around. Bedraggled soldiers were beaching themselves on both sides of the canal, gasping for breath and then looking around, waiting for their orders. She instinctively knew they were no match for Christian. There was only one way for her to connect with him, and that was on his terms, matching his power with her own.

Something was about to happen, she could feel it, a sense of expectancy hung in the air like a storm cloud pregnant with rain sitting low on the horizon. Whatever Christian was planning was imminent, and the sensation made her heart begin to hammer, tightening her chest and throttling her breath.

And then time seemed to divide itself, like an amoeba

splitting in two. She saw herself in both realities at once: in one she was standing next to Caleb, looking at GCHQ, and in the second they were hundreds of yards ahead, moving towards a gaping underground access road. And then her perspective split again, with more realities layering in, populating her vision with multiple worlds like a kaleidoscope: they were in a subterranean parking bay for trucks, peering into the backs of vans; Sara was hopping on to a flatbed, looking in alarm at large rods linked to a timer; Sara was moving through the tunnels.

She could feel the textures, sounds and smells of each moment, like a memory lived forwards. They were so real each second felt as if she had already inhabited it, turning it into the past through occupation. Without warning, her hands stung with pain and she clenched them, pressing them under her arms for protection. The soles of her feet burned as well, and she cried out, causing Caleb to look at her in alarm. She waved him off and was silent for a long time before turning to look at him, her eyes refocusing as she returned from the trance.

She looked at the palms of her hands, twisting them over in surprise. They were undamaged, free of blemish.

'What happened?' asked Caleb.

'I have a plan,' said Sara, looking resolutely at GCHQ.

71

Caleb checked his watch.

'There's less than five minutes left on the count-down.'

They were far along the tunnel, the entrance just a glimmer of light behind them, the size of a coin. On their left was an opening to a bay filled with trucks parked in long lines.

'This way,' said Sara, weaving through the gaps between the vehicles until she stood at the rear of a particular truck in the middle of the space.

She pulled down the tailgate and leaped up on to it, pulling the tarpaulin aside to expose the contents of the flatbed.

'Holy shit,' breathed Caleb. 'Is that a bomb?'

Sara walked down the length of the truck to a brief-case lying next to the rods, on which a timer counted down.

'Can you defuse it?' asked Caleb.

Sara shook her head. 'No, this thing is going to blow. There's no way to stop it.'

Caleb looked at her uncertainly, waiting for her to complete the sentence, to add the caveat that she knew what to do. But she didn't respond, instead kneeling down and picking up a crowbar lying next to the briefcase. She walked back towards him and jumped off the end of the truck.

'Why did we come here?' asked Caleb.

'For this,' said Sara, waving the crowbar and setting off back towards the main tunnel. 'Now we need to get to the computer room. It's one floor above us.'

72

Caleb pressed the lift's up button. It didn't light up. He pressed it again, then looked at the other lifts in the bank where they were standing.

'Looks like these aren't working.'

'The whole lift system is offline,' said Sara, as she jammed the crowbar into the break in the doors and threw her weight against it.

'Little help?' she said, turning to Caleb.

They both pushed, levering the maw of the lift open, creating a gap large enough to squeeze into. Sara wedged the crowbar into the gap, which shook precariously as the automatic doors fought against the foreign object blocking their path.

Sara stuck her head through the opening.

It was a three-lift shaft with pulley and wires strung across the space like tendons. The lift on her left was tugging wildly at the suspending cable, straining against the brakes that were mooring it in place, the pressure raining sparks down into the shaft. These must have ignited something on the ground, as flames leaped up from below, ten feet and higher, like angry snakes trying to escape from a pit. A sudden high-thermal blast of air roasted her face, and she pulled back.

'There's got to be another way up,' said Caleb.

'There is,' said Sara. 'An emergency exit door leads to stairs. It's a short walk from here. That way.'

She pointed down the corridor, and Caleb nodded, walking quickly towards it.

'I'm sorry, Caleb,' she said, stepping through the gap in the lift doors. 'I have to get there before the clock runs out.'

'No!' shouted Caleb, reaching for her.

She pushed the crowbar with both hands from inside the shaft, and the doors slammed shut.

Sara looked at the closed interior of the door. There was no option but to proceed.

A metal ladder ran up the inside of the shaft. She was about to grab hold of the rung at her eye level when she stopped herself, her fingers hovering inches from it. Intense heat pulsed from the metal. Her fingers were still inches away from the ladder now, but the heat was so strong she could feel her outer layer of skin begin to singe.

She pulled her gloves out of her pocket and looked at them. A version of them had been her constant companion since childhood, thick, triple-enforced leather that blocked out everything. They would hold off the heat long enough that the damage would not be permanent.

She pulled on the gloves and gripped the rung, immediately feeling the searing heat channelling through the material to her fingers. When she lifted her hands to grab hold of the rung above, the fingers of the gloves fused themselves to the metal and she had to peel them off.

The acrid smell of burning leather filled the air, and

she increased the speed of her ascent as the soles of her shoes began sticking to the rungs.

Sweat pricked her skin, sticking her shirt to her back and dripping into her eyes.

When she was halfway up the ladder she could begin to feel the heat mounting, her palms pricking with the intense burning sensation.

She wasn't going to make it.

There were four rungs left to go, but the burning was so intense that she had to control her reflex to let go of the ladder.

She stifled a scream and kept clambering up, the smell in her nostrils mutating from burning leather to burning flesh.

She was at the level of the lift door one floor above.

Next to the sealed doors was an emergency switch, and she reached out to it. The extra pressure on the one hand that now held her caused her to cry out in agony.

She reached the switch and flipped it upwards.

She launched herself through the open lift door, falling on to the ground and throwing off the tattered remnants of her gloves and destroyed shoes.

Ahead of her was the door to the computer room.

She tried to stand, but screamed immediately as the soles of her feet sent shooting pains up her legs.

There wasn't time to recover.

She steeled herself and limped towards the door.

73

As she stepped through the threshold, all she could see were rows and rows of white servers.

The chill in the room froze the sweat to her skin and provided a blessed relief to the burns on her hands. The cool stone floor was like a cold compress on her feet.

She walked on tiptoe down the central aisle, peeping into each server row.

Sara running through a wood, peeking behind trees, searching, feeling frustrated, knowing Lionel was waiting for them. Christian once again taking a game too far.

A static sound was filtering into her hearing, becoming louder the deeper she went into the room, like a white-noise machine was washing the audio in the room. It was identical to the sound she had heard in her mother's room at the Five Seasons Assisted Living Centre. As before, the noise was a herald, her perceptions were becoming stunted, her senses muffled, as if the world around her was muting out.

She turned into one of the rows, approached the break in the servers.

He was kneeling on the ground, next to a case filled with wires. As she approached, she could see his back stiffen and his hands freeze.

'Christian?' said Sara.

He turned around to face her. The likeness was immediately apparent. He was the man the boy had become. The facial characteristics, the mischief dancing in his eyes, the cheekbones and the fine brown hair.

Christian and Sara spar with long sticks. She pulls each blow, sparing him the sting, while he whacks her, giggling at her cries.

That sense of amputation that she had felt all her life, she had always thought it was her memory she was missing, but now she realized it was Christian.

He smiled at her in response.

'Hey, sis. That was smart of them to send you.'

He turned back to what he was doing, pulling wires out of the case and attaching them to the server. He connected the wires to his smartphone, then pressed the screen several times.

'. . . being around each other, always interfered with our senses,' said Sara, realizing.

'Yup. Like having an acoustic feedback loop. Can you pass me that wire?'

Sara found herself talking to him as if she had seen him that morning.

'. . . I heard it today, in Mum's room.'

She knelt down next to him and handed him the wire. She could see inside his case now, and saw the timer.

00:00:45.

00:00:44.

00:00:43.

'We just get a lot of noise when we're too close to each other,' said Christian, staring at the screen. He was engrossed in what he was doing. A child with a toy. 'If I'd known you were coming, I'd have changed the software commands to the missile controls. Sorry . . .'

'Christian . . .' interrupted Sara, her voice urgent, bringing him into the present. She needed to understand things. Before the time ran out. 'They said you killed soldiers. Is that true? Is that who you've become?'

She was once again the admonishing big sister.

He looked at her, his shaggy-dog hair falling over one eye, as if he'd just noticed her.

'They've been trying to take me out for years!' he said indignantly. 'Those weren't soldiers, sis. That was a hit squad. Look, forget them. I want you to see him.'

Sara took a breath, exasperated.

'Who?'

'Our father.'

'Salt said he was a drifter,' said Sara.

'Charles Salt? The puppet master extraordinaire? Don't trust him. He's made it his life's work to stop me finding out about our father. I thought I had it a week ago. I tracked down the hospital form from when mother went into labour with you. There was a next of kin listed. I have a name. And now I've matched it with an address.'

He twisted his phone so it faced her. She read a name and an address. They meant nothing to her.

Christian looked around quickly. There was a movement in the corner, a blur of black.

'Shit,' said Christian, 'keep your eyes open. Having you and me close together makes us sitting ducks.'

367

'I know,' said Sara, 'it's a trap. Salt is using me to interfere with our perceptions.'

Christian looked at her, his expression hovering between shock and surprise and doubt.

'What?'

'There are sniper teams in the room already,' said Sara, nodding to the far side of the room. 'They'd never be able to get close to you if I wasn't here.'

00:00:20.

00:00:19.

00:00:18.

'What's the plan?' asked Christian.

'It won't hurt too much,' said Sara.

Christian looked at her in confusion and then was scrambling to turn around.

Blam! Blam!

The shots rang out, reverberating in the space.

Both bullets thumped into their target, spinning him around in a circle, sending his phone sliding into one of the servers.

'Hold your fire!' shouted Sara, standing up, her arms raised. 'He's down.'

Two snipers with balaclavas crept towards her down the row. Behind them walked Salt and Waterman. At the rear was Caleb, looking in shock at Christian on the floor.

Christian was on his back, patting his hand to his chest, where red bloodstains were blooming.

Sara knelt over him, lifting up his head.

Christian's face was pale, and his breath came in short gasps.

'Find him, sis,' he said. 'Find him.'

Salt shouldered past the snipers and picked up the countdown.

00:00:07.

00:00:06.

00:00:05.

'What's this, Sara?'

Sara's voice was calm.

'There's a device. Underground. It's about to blow.'

Salt went white and then was moving quickly, shouting to those in the room.

'Take cover!'

And then they were running for the far side of the room.

00:00:01.

00:00:00.

The explosion was heard as a distant rumble in the server room.

And then the lights in every corridor and room, on every computer screen and every control panel in the facility, flickered and then shut down, entombing everything and everyone in darkness.

74

'The back-up generators should have come on,' whispered Waterman to Salt.

The darkness was thick and utterly impermeable, coating everything in tar. No one moved, for fear of walking into something or giving away their location.

'There's only one thing that could have taken out all our systems,' said Waterman. 'That's an EMP . . .'

Waterman could hear Salt move in the darkness, shifting his body.

'The disruption should last only a few minutes.'

They waited in the darkness, their hearing hyper-keen, every sound slicing through the silence.

A light pinged on in the corner of the server room. Then another, until the overhead ceiling lights were all on, then a humming started as the computers joined them, rainbow controls sparking into life.

Salt scrambled up and ran back to where Christian, Sara and Caleb had been gathered.

But they were gone.

75

Sara knelt by her mother's graveside, tending the fresh flowers she had brought.

She listened, her ears keen.

In a few seconds, the latch on the metal gate would lift, and the gate would open. Charles Salt would enter the garden and walk along the borders of the grave-stones until he was standing next to her.

He would ask her again about Christian's where-abouts, and she would once again maintain her silence. Christian was safe, recovering in a place they will never find. Deep underground, in a room watched over by a thousand protective eyes. He and Sara had spent much time together, and there was still so much to be said. Sara was no longer alone. There was another like her, although he was also unlike her in many ways.

Salt would again ask her whether she would work with the Secret Service, partner with him to explore her powers, learn to unlock them to their full potential. He would tell her that, with her, the Orpheus project could work as he had never dared to imagine. She could have a purpose in life. She could save the innocent, fight the enemies of the state.

Even as he said this, she would know that Salt would not change and that she would always be just an asset to him.

Her mind kept returning to Helen and Phoebe and the decision each of the generations of her family had had to make. Hide away in a basement, or risk coming to the light. Helen and Phoebe took the risk. One was imprisoned and the other lost her children and her sanity.

But Sara also knew she wasn't either her great-grandmother or her mother. She had been trained by the very men who sought to control her. She had absorbed everything they had to teach and then kept learning. She could protect herself in ways no women in her family had ever been able to do.

She had the potential to create a third choice: to step into her power and use it, on her own terms, to protect those in need and the ones she loved.

This idea was taking hold of her when she heard the garden gate latch open.

Before Salt had even reached her, Sara stood up and turned to face him.

'I accept, but my name's not Orpheus. It's Sara Eden.'

Acknowledgements

I hope you enjoyed the book. Its creation was only possible thanks to the mentoring and unflagging support of my incredible agent and friend Luigi Bonomi. I give thanks for him every day. I have also been blessed with a brilliant editor in Jillian Taylor. The words 'agent' and 'editor' don't do justice to the contributions of both of these exceptionally creative and talented people. 'Partner' would be closer to the truth. I also owe a debt of thanks to the wider team at Michael Joseph – thanks to them you are reading this – and to the wonderful Sylvie Rabineau for her encouragement and support. I would also like to thank my family – my parents, Ali and May; my son, Ethan; my brother, Andrew; my sister, Ellie; my sister-in-law, Neecy; and my nephew and nieces, Max, Evie and Maya – for their love and support. Finally, to my wife Shannon, who coaxed this story out of me on our first holiday together, road-tripping on the glorious A8. It all began with you.

He just wanted a decent book to read ...

Not too much to ask, is it? It was in 1935 when Allen Lane, Managing
Director of Bodley Head Publishers, stood on a platform at Exeter railway
station looking for something good to read on his journey back to London.
His choice was limited to popular magazines and poor-quality paperbacks –
the same choice faced every day by the vast majority of readers, few of
whom could afford hardbacks. Lane's disappointment and subsequent anger
at the range of books generally available led him to found a company – and
change the world.

*'We believed in the existence in this country of a vast reading public for intelligent
books at a low price, and staked everything on it'*
Sir Allen Lane, 1902–1970, founder of Penguin Books

The quality paperback had arrived – and not just in bookshops. Lane was
adamant that his Penguins should appear in chain stores and tobacconists,
and should cost no more than a packet of cigarettes.

Reading habits (and cigarette prices) have changed since 1935, but
Penguin still believes in publishing the best books for everybody to
enjoy. We still believe that good design costs no more than bad design,
and we still believe that quality books published passionately and responsibly
make the world a better place.

So wherever you see the little bird – whether it's on a piece of
prize-winning literary fiction or a celebrity autobiography, political tour
de force or historical masterpiece, a serial-killer thriller, reference book,
world classic or a piece of pure escapism – you can bet that it represents
the very best that the genre has to offer.

Whatever you like to read – trust Penguin.